MW01222805

SLOG

Richard Bellush, Jr.

Robert D. Reed Publishers • San Francisco, CA

Robert D. Reed Publishers
750 La Playa Street, Suite 647
San Francisco, CA 94121
Phone: 650/994-6570 • Fax: -6579
E-mail: 4bobreed@msn.com
www.rdrpublishers.com

Editor: Jessica Bryan
Book Designer: Marilyn Yasmine Nadel
Cover Designer: Julia Gaskill

ISBN: 1-931741-09-3
Library of Congress Card Number: 2001098155

Printed in Canada

This book is dedicated to

Sharon Bellush

CHAPTER 1

SWEAT

History is a pack of lies. "Bunk" was Henry Ford's famous monosyllable. The official version flatters the powerful. The revisionist version flatters those striving for power. Politics. I should know. I made up most of the lies myself for both camps here in what is now called Morrisbourg. It would be fun for once to tell the truth, at least the parts that don't embarrass me too much. My name is George Custer. No, not that one. Another one. One of the advantages to these times is that only a few people know enough really old bunk to make jokes about my name.

It is odd how the years of my youth feel more recent than what happened last week. It seems only yesterday that I sat by the edge of the swamp and skipped a stone across the black water. Ripples on the surface reflected flashes of red from the rising sun. The temperature had cooled to 90 degrees overnight. A 15-foot long alligator lay motionless in the early morning shade on a narrow strip of beach.

The air was full of flying insects, which grew to enormous size by the old standards. Dragonflies with one-foot wingspans hovered in the morning light over an algae mat. It is surprising how quickly after the climate change the insects reverted to ancient forms. They must have had dormant genes that were triggered by climate cues. The insects were lucky. Our human genes simply told us that the world had grown too hot.

The humidity, as all too usual, was over 80%. The temperature could be expected to climb to over 120 degrees by midday. At noon the air grows still and the normal jungle cacophony reverts to an eerie quiet. At that time even the dragonflies seek shade.

By 2:00 in the afternoon breezes typically pick up and insect wings sputter and roar like car engines just before the race. Once again they would take to the sky.

Humans were totally unprepared for either the speed or the scale of the change. We knew, of course, about the past major swings in global climate that had left clear marks in the geological record; but these had not occurred within written human history, and so they seemed a matter of academic interest only. They seemed to have as little to do with real present day life as evidence of ancient oceans on Mars.

Climatologists once enjoyed debating the cause of the shifts between ice ages and interglacial warming on our own planet. The effects of volcanic outgassing, changing heat transfer patterns of ocean currents as a result of sea floor spreading, periodic changes in the earth's orbit and orientation, and even meteor showers that affect atmospheric reflectivity were incorporated into conflicting climate models and theories. Considered by itself, each theory was persuasive. Considered together, all were unconvincing. The idea that the sun's output simply was variable was suggested occasionally. The notion, however, generally was dismissed. The sun disregarded the disregard. It was going through a hot spell. The world's surviving physicists continue to argue over the stellar mechanism responsible.

Those same climatologists had once debated even more fiercely the effects of humans on climate. Mainstream opinion was that the use of fossil fuels was slowly raising global temperatures. The projections varied enormously as to numbers of degree and the amount of time it would take. Most models predicted a change over the next few centuries of between one-half degree and three degrees Celsius. At least that argument for the moment is mute. Nature totally overwhelmed the activity of humans and did it in less than a decade. Many of the most severe effects were felt in thc first year of the sun's burst of hyperactivity. Now there are too few of us humans left to affect the climate.

In the wake of the climate change came waves of unspeakably horrid tropical diseases. Some were known, such as Marburg and Ebola, but they were none the less frightening for having names. Others had never been seen before outside, perhaps, some remote central African villages.

It is not known for certain why they struck with such virulence. Some disease breakouts were to be expected. As the organisms followed the spread of their natural habitats outward from their equatorial lairs, they encountered new populations of animals and people that were inexperienced and therefore without resistance. It is darkly suspected that the worst outbreaks, however, were brought upon us by ourselves.

There is reason to believe that in the social breakdown that was occurring, biological warfare weapons were loosed. One hopes this was accidental, but it is not beyond human psychology or capacity to have set them free on purpose. One must search hard in the universe to find something deadlier than a human with a perceived just cause. Distraught workers, doomsday cultists, nationalists, idealists of various kinds, and just plain evil-minded pranksters are all capable of such a thing. The comeback of smallpox, supposedly eradicated in the twentieth century, looked especially suspicious. So also did the fierce varieties of anthrax that spread everywhere. Anthrax, of course, was a favorite of bio-weaponeers because of its rapid and easy transmission; also, one's own troops can be inoculated against the specific strains of it that one is dropping on the enemy.

Nearly seven billion people died in only a handful of years. There is no way to convey what this really means to anyone who did not experience it. On most of the world's surface civilization ended. A tiny few of us, including myself, were lucky. Very, very lucky. We were immune to the infections we encountered – or at least resistant enough to survive them – and we somehow avoided contact with the ones that would have killed us. Other folks, especially up north, managed to isolate themselves until the worst of it was over. A few northern governments were successful enough in their bio-defenses to preserve a modest fraction of their people. After a decade or so, the global population grew too sparse to maintain the epidemics. An infected person was likely to die before passing the disease on to anyone else. The diseases burned themselves out after that.

Twenty years after the onset of the disaster it was no longer a death sentence to meet a stranger. It was simply unusual.

I turned away from the languid bayou waters and walked up

the narrow path formerly known as Pine Street in what once was called Morristown. The wooden homes of suburbia already had subsumed to the riotous growth of foliage. New Jersey. The Garden State.

Unrelieved heat and daily deluges of rain had transformed the whole Northeast into swamps, sand bars, and islands of thick jungle less equatorial in appearance than Mesozoic. The concrete, steel, and masonry of the urban centers resisted the onslaught, but greenery was winning out even there. For two years I had enjoyed solitude in the remains of this moderate size town center. The handful of other local survivors literally had run for the hills, which were drier and a few degrees cooler. That wasn't my style. Just before the big change, when I was seven, I was in the Poconos with my family and didn't like them. There was snow on the ground and I was cold! Snow wasn't much of a risk now anywhere much south of the Arctic Circle, but Morristown still was my hometown and I was staying. I had abandoned my childhood house only after it was engulfed by vines and became a home to far too many snakes, but I had moved scarcely more than a mile away. I took pride in being an obstinate lone local resident. In the previous two months, however, the population had risen again by three. I was feeling crowded.

I turned left on South Street and withdrew my machete in order to hack my way through newly grown tendrils. Less than 50 feet from the corner was the old Community Theater where I made my home. Nearby crepitations in the underbrush hastened my step. The day before I had spotted something tawny and big with stripes. A tiger was not an unlikely sight. As the Eastern seaboard depopulated, softhearted keepers opened zoo gates before punching their time cards for the last time. Present day wildlife is both rich and scary.

The Community Theater was a large red brick building with classic white columns and solid steel doors. A relic of the grand old movie house era, it was strong and defensible with a cavernous interior. The theater had closed for business well before the movie-going public vanished from the region. Modern multiscreen cinemas had stolen away its customers by offering choice and shopping mall conveniences. For a time the theater was used for live performances, but major acts generally bypassed Morristown for nearby New York City or the casinos of Atlantic City. Oddly, stacks of old movie reels were still stored in the projection room. As I entered the building, Gene Kelly was singing in the rain. The screen was dim and the colors were awful, but the sound was surprisingly clear. I trudged up the stairs for my daily scraping chore on the roof. The solar cells were adequate for the air-conditioner and a few other circuits, but they required constant maintenance. Fungi and green plants spread rapidly over the panels. The air-conditioner kept the temperature within the theater under 100 degrees on all but the most extreme days. With the fans it was bearable.

As I emerged onto the roof, I noticed Joelle standing by the edge. She peered through the jungle canopy. The first of the new arrivals to Morristown, and by far the most welcome, Joelle was an attractive young woman whose pale features seemed out of place in the swelter. I loved her accent. She said her family was Belgian. Her father had some sort of consulting job with IBM in Connecticut when everything fell apart. Her native country, except perhaps for the Ardennes, probably was even more swampy and submerged than New Jersey. Beyond this brief biography, Joelle was a mystery. She refused to explain where or how she had survived in the intervening years or how she had acquired an obvious education – the decaying shelves of the Morristown Public Library were responsible for my own. "That's all in the past," she would say dismissively and then she would change the subject.

One day she simply had arrived all alone in a little motor dinghy with a collapsible canvas roof. I remember hearing the putter while fishing off the New Jersey Transit bridge by the train station. I was astonished to see a petite woman at the helm dressed in immaculately clean khaki pants and shirt, polished black riding boots, and pith helmet. She spotted me at once and steered toward the stairway to Morris Avenue, a road now under several feet of water. My surprise did not have a wholesome effect on my gallantry. I made no effort to help tie up her boat or even to say hello. I simply stared and continued to fish. After tying up her own boat and climbing the stairs, she smiled at me winsomely and said, "Hi, handsome. Know any local hot spots?"

My response was socially inept. "Miss, what are you doing here?"

"It's a new world...what's your name?"

"George."

"I'm Joelle. Joelle Perrault. It's a new world, George, and this is the frontier. This is where it's at."

"This is where what's at?"

"The future."

"I see." I didn't see at all.

Even by my criteria, her response to the global disaster was quirky. She went beyond fatalistic acceptance of the sort that made me proud of myself. Her approach to life, and to our local mire, was more like a joyful embrace. She acted as thoroughly at home in the new world as she looked alien to it. I did not understand. When I pressed her more about why she found a deep swamp so cheerful a place she just gave her shoulders a dismissive shrug. It was to be a favorite gesture of hers. It grew to be a favorite of mine too. Those shoulders were cute, and they were able to carry or deflect many an argument.

It was no easy task carrying and dragging the contents of her dinghy to my home. It took four trips. She had brought a sizable cache of arms and trunks full of more clothes and perfume scented bottled stuff than seemed altogether necessary.

Joelle was suitably impressed by my mechanical expertise in having adapted the Community Theater to living space. Most of the appliances and plumbing worked. She commented that she probably would have chosen to occupy the

federal style brick and marble post office building by the Green, but she added that the Theater suited me somehow. Occasionally thereafter it would occur to me that it was odd she preferred the post office when she had just arrived. How could she have known about it? It was not visible from the bridge where she had tied up or from the path to the theater. We had not yet visited the Green, the central town park, now all too aptly named. Had she seen an old photograph of the town somewhere? I never asked. It didn't seem important.

I faced the awkwardness of negotiating sleeping arrangements the first night by not facing it. The only actual bed and mattress were mine, but there were plenty of sofas and pillowed surfaces from which Joelle could choose. I told her to make herself at home wherever and however she chose. Clad in shorts and tee shirt, I slid into my bed. Joelle chose to slide in next to me. We unclad. She made love to me that night as though it were the most natural thing in the world for two strangers to do. I hadn't expected it. I didn't object either.

I never would have admitted it at the time, but despite the fact I was approaching the age of 30, Joelle was my first woman. This should cause no astonishment. First of all, there hadn't been a lot of opportunity. The closest I had come to female flesh in the past seven years were photos in the magazines on the back rack of the newspaper shop on South Street.

Prior to seven years ago, there were two or three young ladies living within a 10-mile radius. Pursuing them, however, would have been evidence of a desire to commit. I don't know which was more dangerous, the still present chance of contagion or the sure wrath of their male protectors. The girls disappeared shortly thereafter along with all of my other neighbors. Presumably they are dead or in the Poconos. She said nothing, but I think Joelle knew my level of experience.

Thoughts of that first night together occupied my mind very much as I watched her delicate form lean out over the rail on the rooftop. As usual, Joelle wore more protective clothing as a barrier to insects and vermin than I found bearable for myself. Despite that, her long-sleeved shirt was dry. I was chronically drenched in sweat. Joelle heard my approaching footsteps, but didn't turn her gaze away from a nearby tree. Instead she waved in back of herself with her right hand.

"Banana trees should grow well here," she spoke as I neared.

"They probably would."

"Iguanas," she said.

"What?"

"Iguanas are in that tree, George. I wondered when they would get here. They belong here."

"They do?"

"Yes."

Fauna and flora were a favorite topic for her. She once carried on for most of an evening about how well the catfish were doing. I hate catfish.

That morning my mind was focused not on iguanas or on catfish but on a human denizen of Morristown who had arrived shortly after Joelle. This coincidence should have alerted me more than it did.

"Does Ulysses belong here too?"

"For now," she answered with amusement. Her smile was irksome since it implied jealousy on my part. More irksome still, it implied correctly.

To this day I am deeply suspicious of the name "Ulysses S. Johnston" even though the man stuck to its use tenaciously. Ulysses was a barrel-chested man in robust health. Although he perspired as much as I did, his energy was undiminished by the sun. His booming voice was suitable for an actor in an outdoor theater with poor acoustics. I first heard it while examining the post office building that Joelle liked so much. "Hello, sir! Yes, you!" he shouted behind me. I turned and watched in wonder as the second person I had seen in less than a week strode confidently toward me. He wore mud-stained cotton that once had been bright white. A rather large automatic handgun was in a holster on his belt. When I reached out my hand and announced my own name he paused with the hint of a smile on his face.

"Pleased to meet you, General!" he exclaimed at last.

Then he introduced himself by his unlikely moniker, gripped my hand, and shook it vigorously. The man had a strange and unsubtle sense of humor. It would be just like him to want to outrank my namesake in two armies. A thick black beard actually gave the man a Grantean aspect; so too, I later learned, did his fondness for alcohol.

Ulysses had not arrived in a dinghy. His 24-foot motor launch was equipped with twin sixty horsepower outboard engines. This was far more power than the craft required for navigating New Jersey's rivers and bayous. Speed in these waters was likely to cave in a hull from a submerged log or sunken car. From a distance the boat's deck looked disheveled, but a closer look showed that it was simply crowded. The boat was heavily outfitted with ropes, winches, pulleys, tools, and supplies. One .30 caliber machine gun was mounted to port and one to starboard. From flagpole on the stern Ulysses playfully flew the Jolly Roger. Perhaps he was not altogether playful.

The man claimed to be a salvager. His putative trade was indeed lucrative for someone with the means to carry goods back to the handful of civilized areas that had reorganized in the northern latitudes. The major cities of the Eastern Seaboard had been ransacked and ravaged quite thoroughly in the social breakdown that occurred as thermometers rose, rivers swelled, and survivors preyed on each other. Suburbs and smaller centers such as Morristown were abandoned with more speed and less violence. Much was left behind. These places offered tempting prizes to ambitious salvagers. Ulysses had ambition.

The mother ship for Ulysses' launch was a 120-foot yacht originally built for some Middle Eastern prince. The yacht was tied up near the old Short Hills Mall at the Route 24 overpass. Route 24 now lay beneath the swollen Passaic River. The overpass was as far upriver as the yacht's draft and length safely would allow. Ulysses explained that after "shopping" freely with three crewmen at the Mall he had taken the launch up the tributary Whippany River to Morristown.

Ulysses had left two of his crew with the yacht. One had come upriver with him. I rarely saw this companion. He never introduced himself to me or, more surprisingly, to Joelle. The fellow was notable chiefly for his silence and for obedience to his boss. I encountered him once outside a Jewelry Store on Park Place. His pockets were bulging. I told him my name and held out my hand. He looked at my hand silently for a moment before walking away. I believe this was an attempt to appear menacing. If so, he achieved some success. It was partly offset, however, by the effect of the dozen or so pearl necklaces on his neck and the three sets of clip-on sapphire earrings attached to his ears.

On our theater rooftop I pulled my eyes away from Joelle's shapely form, which somehow had seized their attention. To the northwest of our building, I could see the upper floors of Headquarters Plaza where the salvager and his lackey had chosen to stay. The Headquarters Plaza was a glass, steel, and concrete high rise complex with a shopping mall on the ground level including restaurants, shops, and a 10-screen cinema. Above ground level were offices and hotel rooms. The name was a reference to George Washington's military headquarters, which during the Revolution were located someplace else.

In many ways it was an advantageous site. The upper floors were comfortably furnished and they were well above the danger and stench of the jungle. The abandoned shops on the mall level were stocked with valuables and with enough canned goods to last two men for years. Some satellite communications equipment in the building was still functional when hooked to a generator. The drawback was that the structure was built on a steeply sloping lot with a multi-level parking garage open to the lower elevation at Spring Street in the back. Spring Street and the lower garage levels were flooded by swamp water. They were home to alligators and poisonous snakes. These creatures had deterred me from choosing the building for myself. I had no wish to encounter some reptile with a bent for exploration in the hallway. If the presence of these animals disturbed the building's new residents, they did not show it.

Ulysses doggedly persisted in calling me General long after the joke had worn thin. I tried not to let him see how much it annoyed me, but the very fact he persisted indicates I failed. The prankish irony in his tone toward me sharpened to genuine sarcasm after he met Joelle.

I thought it best to introduce the two myself. We sought him out in Epstein's department store by the Green and invited him to a fried catfish brunch. He stared at Joelle rather rudely, I thought, and then accepted with an "At your service!" We picnicked on the marble steps of the post office where we had a clear view of any approaching crawling thing.

During and after that first meeting he was expansive with Joelle. He told her of his trips to Lisbon and Cherbourg. He told of plans to visit Paris and her hometown of Brussels. He regaled her with hunting tales and vividly portrayed varied slaughters of birds, alligators, and wild pigs all along the American coastline. He told of a sea battle with pirates whose ship went down with everyone aboard thanks to his machine guns.

She listened with polite attention, even though she had never hesitated to interrupt me when my speeches grew pompous or boring. Ulysses spoke to Joelle even when answering one of my questions, a pattern that continued after this first brunch. This would have been less annoying if Joelle had found it less amusing. Then there was the offer made right in front of me to take Joelle away from all this.

"You can have your own stateroom on the yacht, Joelle.

It is a fabulous ship outfitted with every luxury."

"Isn't a yacht technically a boat rather than a ship regardless of the size?" I interposed.

Ulysses ignored me and continued speaking directly to Joelle, "We'll be heading north out of this steambath soon. You are a beautiful young woman. This backwater is no place for you. Surely you would rather be back in civilization in Quebec or Canada. Have I told you about my ranch in Greenland? It is pleasant and dry. You can see the sky, the air is fresh, and we actually have cold days when you need a coat."

I was feeling seriously outmatched, and it was with pleasant astonishment that I heard Joelle's response.

"I'm staying."

"Why? The General?" He stifled a burst of laughter at the idea.

It would have been nice at this point if Joelle had said something about me as a reason for staying, but instead she gave one of her shrugs.

"The earth belongs to those who adapt themselves to the world or the world to themselves," I offered pedantically and with only marginal relevance. Paying this interjection the same heed as the last, Ulysses awaited a verbal response from Joelle.

"I'm staying," she repeated quietly but definitely. He looked thoughtful and shifted his gaze to me. I noticed he fingered his weapon as he did this. Then, without a word he tossed the remains of the fish he had been eating into a nearby shallow pool. A secondary splash indicated the remains had attracted attention. Ulysses rose from his bench.

"It has been a pleasure, miss. Thank you for the morning victuals. We shall meet again soon." He nodded his head, turned on his heel, and returned to his treasure hunting.

Joelle tittered.

"What is funny?" I asked.

"Both of you."

At least Ulysses had announced his plan to leave soon. It was the one element in his remarks that pleased me. It was weeks, however, before his silent companion delivered written invitations to a farewell party at the Headquarters Plaza. The cards, fancy with embossed RSVPs on the covers, looked as though they came from a bridal shop. I tried not to attach significance to this.

Standing on the rooftop with Joelle, I shifted my gaze away from the Headquarters Plaza and squinted in order to see the iguanas at which she had pointed. I saw trees, vines, and leaves. The natural camouflage of the lizards was too good for me. I saw iguanas on later days so I'm sure Joelle was right about them then.

"The farewell party starts just after the afternoon rains today," I reminded her. "I guess he is going home tomorrow. Are we going?"

"To the party or Greenland?" she teased.

"The party."

"We don't get invited to many parties. It may be some time before we attend another one. He is serving alligator. I saw them getting butchered yesterday. The tails are excellent if they're done right."

"Did I do them right last week?"

She shrugged. "You had better attend to the photoelectric panels."

I wasn't ready to be diverted. "I will. We need to be careful. He is a dangerous man. I don't trust him."

"I know."

"We should go armed."

She looked at me while assessing my meaning. "We always should go out armed, but only because of the wildlife. You're not planning something stupid, are you?"

"No." Lunatic maybe, I thought to myself, but not stupid. My sense of foreboding was deep. Joelle's equanimity was disturbing. The sky grew hazier and distant thunder rumbled.

My namesake is best remembered for a spectacular loss.

Most of the time, though, he won. He succeeded by the simple technique of moving fast and hitting first. He knew that much larger enemy forces could be beaten easily if they were caught off guard. He apparently failed to consider that one day an opponent might be very much on guard. He should have prepared for retreat in case the occasion arose. He didn't. The occasion arose. His military record both of victory and defeat is instructive.

Ulysses had not threatened me overtly. Yet, I felt sure my life was at risk that night. Saving it required taking the initiative. I needed to prepare for a rapid attack and for an even more rapid retreat. He was too experienced and cunning to be surprised by a simple frontal assault. My only hope was something cockeyed and unexpected.

"I'll be back before the rain starts," I told Joelle.

She nodded acknowledgment. She didn't question where I was going. This was odd, since she liked to keep track of me. Her mind must have been on something else. A more reflective person than myself might have worried about what else. I simply was relieved. Female beauty often makes a man willfully thickheaded.

Most of what I needed was at the old construction supply yard on Ridgedale Avenue. I commandeered Joelle's dinghy to cross the intervening bayou. The lumberyard was high enough to be relatively dry. The site was protected by a chain link fence. A padlocked gate guarded the driveway entrance. For some reason the owner had locked the place up tight at the end of what he surely knew to be his last day at work. Perhaps he acted out of habit. A fallen tree had crushed a section of the fence to the left of the gate. I balanced myself on the trunk and walked onto the property.

The outdoor piles of lumber were overgrown or rotted, but the warehouse roof was intact enough to have preserved the building's contents. These included tools, door locks, plywood panels, PVC pipes, nails, paints, electrical wires, and other home improvement supplies. I found most of the items on my list quickly enough but feared that the explosives would be absent or hidden. After much searching around the yard, I pried open a steel shed in back of the warehouse. There were the dynamite, blasting caps, detonator boxes and fuses for which I was looking.

I had one more piece of luck before I left the yard. An opossum peeked around the corner of the warehouse. He stood still in the crosshairs of my Remington 700. A Vietnam era sniper rifle, this is a marvelously accurate and well-made weapon. The military had reservations about the rifle because it required a modicum of care, which it didn't always receive under combat conditions. The Marine Corps was quick to order modifications after the war; the wooden stock, for example, was replaced by a more stable fiberglass one and the rifle generally was made more resistant to water, dirt and grime. The later rifles may well have been preferable in war, but I still liked the wood finish and the feel of the original. It was rugged enough to serve my purposes, and I had the time to keep it clean. It was my usual choice for hunting.

I do not hunt for sport, but I am no vegetarian either. Neither chops nor leather bother my conscience. Fresh meat no longer comes from supermarket shelves. On this day I needed bait and the marsupial fit the bill perfectly.

Having fully equipped myself, I motored the dinghy to Spring Street. Ulysses' launch was gone from its usual mooring by the Headquarters Plaza. This was an unexpected break but his boat surely would return before the rains came. This gave me an opportunity for something less crude than attempting to blow up the building. Besides, it was a large building and I wasn't entirely sure what part of it Ulysses occupied. I suspected he lived on the top floor since, he had told us, he had gone to the trouble of getting an elevator operational. Today, however, he might have planned to ready his party in one of the lower floor banquet rooms or in one of the old restaurants. The odds favored him surviving such a blunt attack, and it would not be wise to attempt to kill Ulysses and miss.

At this late date I like to think that I would have balked at assassination even if I did know exactly where to plant a bomb. It is more comfortable to believe I had rejected any such idea out of hand and that any violence by me was meant to be purely defensive. In that case, simple Boy Scout type preparedness is the explanation for my having packed quite so much dynamite as I did along with a variety of detonators and fuses and timer switches. Some well-placed, timed explosions would be useful diversions if the party turned out as nasty as I expected.

Whatever surprises I could arrange, speed was essential. I grounded the dinghy and trudged carefully up the slime-covered concrete sidewalk toward the front entrance of the Headquarters Plaza. The heavy pack and long coil of rope on my back sapped my energy in the relentless heat.

The glass doors resisted most of my full weight before opening. They stayed open when I entered. An oppressive aroma of decay in the building made me gag. The shopping mall on this level was a wreck. Broken glass littered the hallway. Yet many store shelves were untouched. A row of pink and white teddy bears stared at me as I passed a gift shop. I passed through the mall and entered the lobby of the hotel area.

Ulysses had told me, or rather had told Joelle, that he had started an emergency generator he found on the top floor of the building, and used it to power an elevator. Sure enough, when I arrived at a bank of elevators and pushed the "up" button, a door slid open. I entered and the door shut behind me. The elevator knocked, jerked, and mechanically groaned, but it climbed subsultively to the top floor. I exited and took the stairway to the roof.

I set explosives by each satellite and microwave dish and wired them to a timed detonator. For the moment I did not set the timer. On an earlier day, from the top of the Community Theater, I had noticed Ulysses and his henchman fussing with the dishes. If matters became messy there was no sense letting Ulysses call to the crew on his yacht for help.

My long rope, securely tied at the edge of the roof, provided me with a possible escape route to the ground. Returning through the rooftop door, I left my Remington and more explosives on the top step.

I next searched the top floor for the building generator. A distinctive hum led me to it. I planted my remaining dynamite under the machine. This time I did set the timer. The lights would go out at midnight.

The elevators were my next targets of opportunity. The opossum back at the lumberyard had given me the idea of loading an elevator with an unwelcome surprise. It was important for the surprise to show up at the right moment. Timing, as they say, is everything. As I had guessed, the building generator actually supplied power to the entire bank of four elevators. All but one of them was simply turned off. I experimented with powering up the others. One did nothing, no matter what switches I flicked. Another accepted power but proved totally jammed. The third lift, however, was still operable. With the power switch on the control panel activated, it creaked and rattled but it moved.

Rigging the elevator that Ulysses had activated so it could be disabled was simple enough. It is always easier to destroy something than it is to fix it. I removed the control panel cover and adjusted the wiring so that punching the B parking level button would short out the entire panel. I thought it unlikely anyone other than myself would touch that button.

Readying the other functional elevator for my purposes was the next chore. I found a push broom in a nearby utility closet and removed the handle. After climbing up through the ceiling hatch of the elevator carriage, I reached down from the ceiling and pressed the button for parking level C. I tossed the rapidly ripening opossum in the back of the elevator. The carriage creaked and shook its way down the shaft. Level C was awash in several inches of water. Water sloshed in as the door opened. I held the end of the broom against the "open door" button and waited.

After a wearisome wait in this awkward position, the head of a monitor lizard nosed hesitantly into the elevator. I had hoped for an alligator, but this animal was nearly twelve feet long and would serve my purpose. Komodo monitors are more deadly than they appear — and their appearance is far from reassuring. They have strong claws and long serrated teeth. The teeth are so infested with bacteria that the bite of the creature is effectively poisonous; prey not killed outright almost surely will die of infection and gangrene. Over short distances the lizards can run 20 miles per hour. It is advisable to keep one's distances long.

After testing the air with a darting tongue for what seemed an interminable time, the monitor entered and snapped up the opossum. I released the button. Twice the doors closed, caught the lizard's tail and reopened. I tapped on the wall with the handle tip. The creature looked up, hissed, and spun around. A swipe of the front claws knocked the broom handle out of my grasp. The tail slid inside. The doors closed. I had my surprise package wrapped and ready.

My joy was short-lived. In one of those unlikely accidents that so often plague complex schemes, the reptile spun a second time and flicked off the power switch with his claw. This was a problem. The power needed to be turned on again but the switch was uncomfortably close to the lizard. Hanging upside down from the ceiling and reaching over those jaws with bare hands was not a welcome prospect.

I climbed up the cable to Level B and pulled open the doors. I quickly darted about looking for an appropriate tool. A long stick would have sufficed but any such object stays remarkably well hidden when one needs it in a hurry. Level B was empty except for a few parked automobiles. At last, in the back seat of a Cadillac Eldorado I spotted an umbrella.

The Caddy was locked. A Ford Explorer, however, was open. From the back of the Ford I retrieved the jack and its handle. The handle was too short for my needs, but the jack could be used as a universal car door key. I threw the jack with all my force through the side window of the Eldorado. The glass shattered gratifyingly. I unlocked the door, snatched the umbrella from the Cadillac, and ran back to the shaft.

Having dropped back down to the top of the carriage, I reached down with the umbrella and turned on the power. The umbrella was seized from my hand. I nearly fell through the ceiling hole onto my head. The lizard shook the umbrella viciously in its jaws.

Having gone to all this trouble I added one more refinement to my surprise package. I had one timer switch left over so I spliced it into the elevator's power circuit. I found the grounded wire in the power cable feed and spliced in the timer. The hot wire probably would have electrocuted me. I set the timer to activate at 7:30 that night. Until then the elevator would be dead. I figured the party would be in progress by 7:30. I was proud of my work. My self-satisfaction was only slightly muted by the sudden realization that I could have avoided the acrobatics with the handle and probably the umbrella by splicing in the timer before I even started. I could have turned the power on and off from the elevator roof. I shimmied up the cable to the next floor, took the stairs up to the entry level and left the building.

I now had several distractions in place which I hoped would give me a momentary advantage in case I needed to attack or flee. Later tonight, if I needed to escape

Ulysses' party, I could run up the stairs to the roof where my Remington awaited. Pursuers would likely run down the stairs — or take the elevator. Of course, if Ulysses simply planned to shoot me on arrival there was little I could do except avoid going to the party at all. I didn't think this was the case since he had had many opportunities to do away with me already. Anyway, I wanted to go to the party. I must admit I was curious as to what he had in mind. It is remarkable how often people risk their lives for the sake of curiosity. This too, along with the aforementioned lust induced stupidity, must be a trait selected by evolution.

The thick hazy air reverberated from the outboard engines of the approaching launch. I made tracks for the Community Theater as the first drops of late afternoon rain fell. It had become a torrent before I reached the door of the building.

Joelle had started to get ready a full hour before I did. Yet she continued to add finishing touches to her makeup, hair, and clothes as I waited restlessly on the bed. I didn't see why it was necessary to look so pretty for Ulysses. She never wore makeup for me. I didn't even know she had any. We were going to be late. This was not just a concern of courtesy: the timer on the lizard's elevator was ticking inexorably.

At long last she turned around and faced me. The results of her endeavors were spectacular. By this time I was ready to chuck the party, and would have done so, had Joelle been willing. I didn't manage to get the first word of a proposal to stay at home out of my mouth before Joelle cut me off with a pointed finger and a shake of her head. She looked devastating in her light summer frock, white boots, artistically painted eyes, perfect hair, cherry lipstick, and AR15 automatic rifle.

Despite her admonition that arms were only for protection against wildlife, she had chosen a military weapon. When I commented on it she responded with Emerson's dictum, "Consistency is the hobgoblin of little minds." I think Emerson was wrong about that one, but I chose not to argue. It gave me an opportunity. Having equipped herself thus, I reasoned, she hardly could object to my choice of similar armament — unless, it occurred to me, she was broadminded enough to be inconsistent again. I snapped a clip into a Kalshnikov. Joelle took a deep breath and was about to speak when she saw this, but she changed her mind, exhaled and shrugged instead.

The AK47 is less wieldy than its American competitor, but it is notoriously reliable and its 7.63 ammunition packs a heavier punch than the 5.56 AR15 round. It can stop a bear. The AR15 is, of course, entirely effective against people. I had discovered this particular AK47 in the abandoned house of a private collector. As the gun was fully automatic and of Bulgarian manufacture, the collector was in violation of New Jersey law.

Joelle chose to comment on my attire rather than on my firepower. "Khaki? How daring," she antiphasized.

We left the Community Theater as my watch read 7:16. In my haste I kept walking ahead of Joelle on the trek to the Headquarters Plaza. This annoyed her.

"Slow down!" she ordered. "Are you afraid Ulysses will start the party without us? If I mess up my appearance I'm going back to fix it."

I slowed down.

We reached the main entrance as the day faded into twilight. The door pushed open easier this time and ever so slowly closed itself. The mall's main hallway had been swept clean. On the floor several large red-painted arrows pointed us toward the hotel lobby. Crepe with balloons festooned the walls along the way. The fountain in the hotel lobby was working. It gurgled and spat. By my watch it was 7:28 by the time we reached the elevators. I wondered how accurately I had set the timer switch on the elevator with the monitor lizard.

I pushed the "up" button and held my breath. The safe elevator door slid open. I exhaled. Joelle eyed me curiously and stood her ground for a few seconds before entering.

Red tape in the shape of an arrow pointed at the button for

the tenth floor. Joelle pushed it. She smiled at me on the way up. "This should be fun," she predicted. Despite her lighthearted air she thumbed the safety on her weapon repeatedly as we rattled and shook our way up. While exiting on the tenth floor, I punched the "B" button. This knocked out the elevator on which we had arrived. If the timer switch down below worked properly, the elevator with the reptile was now activated.

Only a few of the overhead florescent lights in the hallway worked and these hummed angrily. They created a disturbing pattern of brightness and shadow. No further directions were painted on the floors or walls, but a Rolling Stones album from one of their many Final Tours was playing somewhere down the hall. The air smelled distinctly of incense, cigar smoke, and roasted meat. We walked in the direction of the aroma. From a side door thirty feet ahead Ulysses emerged wearing a paisley tuxedo and a white top hat. Joelle laughed.

"Welcome, Mademoiselle! You too, Colonel." I had been demoted. It did not escape my attention that "Colonel" was my namesake's final rank.

Ulysses bowed deeply and kissed Joelle's hand. She curtsied theatrically and then brushed past him into the suite. I acknowledged our host with a hand twitch and followed close behind her. Despite my possessing a larger bulk than Joelle, I managed the entry without brushing our host.

The party was larger than expected. All three of the crew from Ulysses' yacht were waiting inside the suite. They wore blue denim, sidearms, and solemn arrogance. They had all the charm of militiamen in some Balkan civil war. They stood in front of a large table covered with food and alcoholic beverages. Over the banquet table was a hand made banner with the red-lettered legend "Crazy Horse Saloon." Ulysses slapped me on the back as I read it. The suite was elaborate and large. The banquet room had double doors that opened into a bedroom with a king-size bed. The bathroom had a marble floor and a whirlpool tub. It must have been the hotel's most expensive quarters.

Ulysses started to speak, but then stood back and folded his arms. He assessed all five of us quietly, and sighed. Every one of us carried a gun.

"Only the old US government thought Alcohol, Tobacco and

Firearms belonged together," he remarked. "This is a social event. I must insist that we put the guns away. It will be safer and more pleasant all around if we aren't watching each other's muzzles all evening. Please. Just for the duration."

"What do you suggest we do with them?" I asked. "Give them to you for safekeeping?"

"Why Colonel, if I didn't know better I would think you don't trust me. No, don't give them to me. Just put them away. The closet to the right of the table will do. It has a lock. You, General, may even hold the key." Somehow the inflection he gave the word "General" took the promotion out of it.

He walked to the closet, held open the door and nodded to the sailors who, without a trace of hesitation, unhooked their gunbelts and tossed them inside. For the record, a gun never should be handled that cavalierly. Ulysses withdrew a Colt .45 automatic from his shoulder holster and added it carefully to the pile. He opened his tuxedo jacket and spun with a flourish to show he carried no backup. "You may search the premises for anything hidden," he added expansively.

He had just bet his life on civilized standards of behavior from us. The man sometimes was almost likable. Joelle shrugged and stashed her AR15. I briefly considered delivering a lesson on the evils of gambling, but after some hesitation I placed the AK47 in the closet, shut the door, turned the lock, and pocketed the key. After all, murder might annoy Joelle. I did not suppose I held the only key or that the closet held the only weapons in the building. I knew of at least one more on the top step of the stairwell. However, the elevator began to concern me. There appeared to be at least a chance that the evening would go more serenely than expected. If this was just a party, and not an ambush, my lizard would need explaining.

I hated to admit it, but the party was fun. It was the first such event I had attended since I was a child. The music was loud, the jokes were raw, and the laughter was genuine. A fine selection of wines and liquors flowed freely, although I practiced moderation in order to keep my wits and reflexes sharp. The crew served marinated alligator with onions from several overflowing turkey pans.

Ulysses was his boisterous self. He bragged again about his

ranch in Greenland, which by his description was indeed a fine place. He related more of his various adventures including how once he barely had outrun a Russian coast guard boat that had chased him all the way from Murmansk to Spitzbergen. He neglected to mention the cause of the Russians' ire. Joelle sang along to Under My Thumb in French. She and Ulysses actually listened as I explained the ideal mix of AC and DC circuits when using photoelectric power sources. The sailors took turns dancing with Joelle in the foot stomping style formerly common in biker bars.

The atmosphere grew ever more surreal as the hours passed, the general level of intoxication increased, and the view outside the windows faded to black. When the night was deep, Ulysses reset the light switches with startling effect. Somewhere he had found black light florescent bulbs. They lit up Ulysses' paisley and Joelle's white in an otherworldly glow. From the far side of the room her dress seemed to hover in the air without an occupant, like a scene out of the movie Topper. Oversize insects drawn by light fluttered against the fixed windows.

There comes a point in every party when one too many drinks has been poured, one too many songs sung, and one too many jokes told. Good parties end quickly after this point. Bad ones wind down slowly and often end in drunken arguments and brutal hangovers. This one ended quickly. Shortly after midnight a very drunk but remarkably composed Ulysses suddenly ejected the CD in the middle of *Some Girls.* All amusement was gone from his demeanor. The party was over. The crewmen resumed their default setting of quiet attention, although one wavered on his feet and repeatedly steadied himself by placing a hand on the wall. Ulysses turned on the white florescent lights, switched off the black lights, and marched to the other end of the room. Joelle and I watched with interest as he tipped the dining table and spilled the remaining food onto thc floor. I had a slight headache that the change in lighting made worse. From a corner umbrella stand Ulysses retrieved two large rolled maps. He opened one and spread it on the table.

"General, come look at this." My promotion sounded more secure. I was surprised Ulysses had addressed me at all instead of Joelle. I walked over. The soles of my shoes squished in the spilled alligator marinate. The map was actually an enhanced Landsat photograph. Despite the massive flooding, the area depicted clearly was the Lower Hudson Valley. Skyscrapers rising out of the water preserved the shape of Manhattan, although many of the streets were now canals.

"New York City," he stated.

"So I see.

"So what do you think about it?" He pounded Times

Square with his right index finger.

"Not much. Too crowded. A few hundred crazies are still fighting over the scraps. The steel frames of the flooded buildings are probably rusting. Some of the skyscrapers may start crashing soon. It's a giant junkyard. Why? What do you think about it?"

"You see the whole picture, but you don't see the whole picture," he uttered gruffly.

"Show it to me... and explain why you are showing it to me rather than to Joelle."

"Parlez-vous Francais?"

"No. What are you talking about now?"

"Quebec is stealing a march. They're claiming everything from Maine to the old Mexican border if anyone can figure out where that is anymore. There'll be screams at the UN in Reykjavik because of the precedent, but the other powers are in no position to interfere. They're more worried about the Swiss rampaging through what's left of

Europe anyway. A couple hundred Quebecois troops landed in the city earlier today if they kept their schedule."

"How did you learn their schedule?"

"The foreign minister likes Monet. I stumbled across a few on my expeditions."

"Very lucky stumbling."

"It helps if you pick your place to trip carefully."

I was about to ask if he had landed on anyone, such as the rightful owner, as he fell. The wisecrack was halted by an unrelated suspicion that fluttered across my mind. I realized that Ulysses shared it. "Did you know anything about this, Joelle?"

"About Monet?"

"No, about Quebec."

She shrugged. The gesture was losing its cuteness.

"Can anyone here tell if that French accent is Walloons or North American?" I asked the room at large. There was an observant silence from Ulysses and a stony one from his crew.

"Well?" I asked Joelle.

"Would you accept my word either way?" she asked lightly.

I turned back to Ulysses. "Okay. That is all very interesting. It is nice to keep up with current events, but the question remains, 'So what?' New York is still a junkyard regardless of who claims it."

He picked up the other map and unrolled it on top of the first. This map was an old topographic survey of the same region. Flooded areas were stenciled in. "The waters are not really all that deep. A sea wall along a few bits of the old shoreline will allow engineers to drain the flooded parts of Manhattan. Most of it is high and dry anyway. The whole city could be ready for reoccupation in a year. It is doable. The Dutch might still be holding out in Europe if the Swiss hadn't blown the dikes. Public services can be restored quicker than you might think. We don't have to worry about freezes anymore, so new temporary water lines can be run above ground where the old ones are broken. The demand for power and sewerage will never be as big as in the old days, so it can be met easily. Ten thousand people could be living in New York by the end of the decade. I mean productive citizens, not those scavenging swamp rats living there now. Then the city can then be a springboard for the South and the interior section of the country."

I began to grasp the possibilities, but I needed time to think out my position. Joelle's Earth Mother routine regarding bananas and catfish took on new meaning. "Go on," I urged him.

Ulysses sighed in disappointment with my apparent slowness. "Real estate, General. We are on the verge of a boom. All cities teeter on the edge of starvation. They need constant supplies from the surrounding countryside of food, fuel, and resources. Just look outside here. Literally tons of fish, alligators and lizards can be plucked almost by hand. They could feed thousands. The wood can't be cut fast enough to hold back growth. Even the water is valuable. Everything closer to the harbor is brackish or polluted. The Quebecois need all this if they plan to hold New

York. We are partying in a treasure chest!"

"Whose treasure chest? Isn't Quebec claiming New Jersey too?"

"Yes, of course. But that is just sovereignty. As property it can be ours! We can make it ours!"

"Okay, suppose for the moment we can. I'm still a little surprised at you. You already have that wonderful estate in Greenland you told us so much about. Why live in this swamp? Even if Quebec recognizes your title here — or our title since for some reason you are including me in this - somehow I don't picture you as the proud proprietor of an alligator farm."

"How about proprietor of a colony?"

"Come again?"

"The government is bringing back proprietary colonies in order to spur resettlement — a sort of supersized Homestead Act. You must understand how overextended they are. The New York project will nearly bankrupt them. They have to rely on private entrepreneurs to develop the hinterland." He pulled a folded paper from his jacket pocket and shook it as he explained, "All we need are at least 5 people in permanent occupation with their names written here. Whichever signatory delivers this claim and swears an oath of allegiance to the nation and people of will Quebec own 1000 square kilometers. He can sell or lease land, fishing rights, resource rights... anything. All with a clear title that Quebec not only will recognize, but will enforce on his behalf."

"Whoever out of the group delivers it? Like a bearer bond?"

"Yes."

"So four stay behind and one goes off to claim a barony."

"Yes."

"What do the four get out of it?"

"Normally the five signatories would make contractual arrangements among themselves before one of them delivered the claim."

"Normally. Let me be more specific. What do we four get out of it when you go to New York?"

"My good will. Don't worry, George, I will cut you in." This was the first time he had addressed me by my real first name. "Your status as a certifiable pre-deluge resident helps it look of legitimate, but don't think you are necessary. I'm offering you a deal, but I can do without you. We can tape the signing and take some Polaroids to prove the document is not a fraud."

"There are six of us here."

"Your math is irrefutable."

"Obviously you don't want Joelle's signature. Why not?"

"That French accent worried me before it worried you. I don't know what her status is or how it might affect my ownership claims, so why take a chance?"

Joelle smiled and distractedly fingered a window against which a hat sized moth fluttered.

"Sign, George," he demanded. "Don't make me go find someone else."

"May I ask why you didn't bring along one more crewman of your own so you wouldn't need me at all? That was sloppy."

"Well, I did. He met with an unfortunate accident. Terminal greed."

One of the sailors grinned.

"What if I should meet with an unfortunate accident after signing?"

"That would be tragic. It may make you rich." The humor left his voice as he demoted me for the second time, "Sign the paper, Colonel. I suggest that your options are limited."

He was right about that. I glanced again at his three goons and at the closet door in front of which they stood. I nodded.

Ulysses set up a video camera on a tripod and aimed it at the table. A sailor had retrieved a Polaroid camera from somewhere. Ulysses opened the claim document on the table. He pulled a pen from his pocket and extended it toward me. It was a fountain pen with an internal cartridge. I stepped up to the table and signed. I felt like John Hancock. The three sailors signed in turn, passing the camera as they did. A Polaroid flashed at each signature. Ulysses himself then signed with a bold sweep.

"Excellent. Now, Colonel..." Ulysses choked off as he looked up.

Joelle aimed the muzzle of a .32 automatic at him. It distracted me to guess where it had been. She waved the men back.

"Rewind the video, George. Start taping again just after our host signed."

I was ecstatic. Joelle and I were in this together. I rewound the tape. She handed her gun to me and walked to the table. When I touched the "record" button again, she added her own signature as I held her weapon on the others.

"Stop taping," she ordered when done. She then politely asked the crewmen to place the other photos on the table. They looked to Ulysses who nodded. They did as she requested. Joelle stuffed the pictures inside her dress.

"Give me the gun back, cher, take the tape out of the recorder, and then open the closet."

"Right." I was happy at the prospect of regaining my AK, but it was not to be.

"No, no!" she shouted as I reached inside the closet. She underscored her exclamation with a pistol twitch. "Put the tape on the floor, and then back away from the closet. Stand with the others."

With the constriction in the chest that one gets at such moments of betrayal, I backed up next to where Ulysses stood. He gave me a sour smile. Joelle sidled to the closet. Facing us at all times she managed to pick up the tape, sling the AK and the AR15 on her shoulders, and wrap the sidearm belts around one arm. The loose .45 momentarily had her stumped. She solved the problem by removing one sidearm belt from her arm and strapping it around her waist — no easy task one-handed. She then stuffed the .45 behind the belt. There was something fascinating about the performance. At the end, she was heavily and awkwardly encumbered.

"I think it would be best if I didn't hear any footsteps behind me from any of you. By the way, General," she addressed Ulysses rather than me, "you needn't have worried about my legal status. I am not a spy for Quebec or anything like that. I'm just a businesswoman. I happened to hear a few things in advance too. The foreign minister has tastes other than Monet, you see."

Ulysses poised to lunge as Joelle backed into the hallway, but I tugged on his sleeve as a message to hold back. He stifled an angry remark when he saw my expectant smile. He looked doubtful but stayed put. The crew waited for orders. Elevator machinery hummed and clanked. From the hall came a shriek and then a clatter. Ulysses flashed me his first genuine smile of respect.

Both of us hustled to the door and peered into the hallway. Ulysses' men scrambled around noisily behind us. The hall was empty except for two sidearm belts, a .32, an AR15, the claim form and the videotape, which were scattered on the floor near the elevator. Evidently, when the lizard charged, Joelle had dropped everything in order to unshoulder the AK47 as she ran. This was wise. The .32 would have annoyed the lizard.

My chance had arrived. I ran into the hall. To my surprise I was not racing Ulysses. Grabbing the tape and claim, I dove into the dark stairway by the elevator.

Bullets raked the swinging door behind me. There had been other firearms hidden in the suite. Ulysses must have judged me to be I was faster and opted to use his time to arm himself. He assumed he then could take the document from me by force.

I stumbled as the building shook from an explosion. My bomb had gone off by the generator. The building went black. I scrambled up to the landing where the steps reversed direction. There I stopped my ascent toward the roof and held my breath as the stairway door crashed open. The footsteps pounded in the logical but wrong direction: down toward the lobby. I hurried the rest of the way as quietly as I could. At the top step I paused long enough to set the timer on the explosives placed there earlier. I hoped I had given myself a few minutes delay but in the dark I couldn't be sure. I grabbed my Remington and exited onto the roof.

Gunfire inside the building was audible on the roof. It included the distinctive rattle of an AK47. I set the remaining charges on the microwave and satellite dishes for a short delay. I hoped this would block or delay the transmission to the outside of any tall tales about events in Morristown. I tossed the rope over the edge, shouldered my rifle, stuffed the document and videotape in my pants, and rappelled toward the launch tied up below. The roof and stairway charges made satisfying "crump" sounds behind me.

The rope ended about twelve feet short of the ground. I lowered myself as much as possible and released. I landed with a splat on the muddy bayou bank next to the motor launch.

Something large thrashed violently several feet away. I clambered aboard the boat without pausing to discover the source of the noise.

The launch had a key ignition. Ulysses, or one of his crew, had been kind enough to leave the key in it. One should never leave keys in a parked vehicle. That is an invitation to thieves. The engines started. I untied the mooring rope, backed up, reversed gears, and pushed the throttle lever forward.

I traveled as fast as I dared in the little moonlight that leaked through the clouds. It was almost too fast. I nearly decapitated myself on a tree branch that I simply didn't see because my eyes were focused on the water ahead. It brushed my hair and pulled several of them out. Had I been standing upright at that moment instead of leaning forward the branch would have caught me square on the forehead.

The yacht was still tied up prettily at the former Route 24 overpass. I pulled alongside and climbed up the rope ladder, which hung from the rail. Ulysses' lack of security astonished me. True, there probably was not another person for miles in any direction, but it was careless to rely on that assumption. Ulysses' rough and ready approach to life had its drawbacks. A little anal retentiveness is sometimes useful.

The big diesel engines of the yacht did not have a key. They started to purr merely at the push of a button. The big boat handled with ease, even in the narrow confines of the river. Ulysses always appreciated quality.

After the yacht exited the river, I was able to engage the autopilot and take a quick look around. Perhaps the yacht was laden with valuables. Every available space proved packed with artwork, precious metals and electronics that would trade well with the Quebecois. For that matter the yacht itself was worth a fortune and was far too big for my needs. The proceeds from the lot would be enough to recruit some permanent settlers including guards. I suspected the current residents of Morristown, if any were left, would be unfriendly toward their landlord upon his return.

Morristown didn't sound quite right for a town in Quebec. Maybe Morrisbourg would be better I thought to myself.

The yacht entered the Upper Bay as dawn broke. The green lady held up her torch of liberty. The skyscrapers of lower Manhattan loomed up out of the water. In font of them, a huge blue fleur-de-lis flew above the Battery.

CHAPTER 2

STARS

My pet 12-foot monitor lizard "Luggage" posed like a statue beneath the "Cave Saurum" sign atop the white marble steps. He didn't stir and his eyes trained fixedly ahead, but I knew he was aware of me. He preferred late afternoon when the direct sun bleached the steps. The length of his chain was open to doubt from the sidewalk so he discouraged idle visitors.

The tasteful masonry mansion atop those steps was built around 1910. It was once the post office in what was then Morristown, New Jersey. It is now both my residence and the Governor's Mansion in the proprietary colony of Morrisbourg, Greater Quebec. The federal style structure is remarkably well suited to the sweltering climate, which descended upon us when the sun went into overdrive. It is an oddity that Americans built more substantial public buildings during their leaner years. The last of the post offices built in the wealthy first years of the 21st century were flimsy aluminum and glass boxes.

I am George Custer. No relation to the cavalry commander of the same name. I'm the landlord and proprietary Governor of everything as far west as the Delaware River and as far south as the South Branch of the Raritan.

After a rough start the colony is flourishing. The smattering of tough survivors who had natural immunities to the tropical diseases that ravaged North America is leaving the hills and forests. Many are settling here, starting farms, opening businesses. Morrisbourg already numbers over 400.

At first I resented the loss of my solitude. I had grown accustomed to being the sole resident of the town of my birth, but the truth is that it is good to have people around again. Of course it helps when you are rich. I never had experienced wealth before.

All my memories of the time before the heat are dim. Once, northern New Jersey was home to millions. The four square mile town of Morristown alone housed 20,000. I am old enough to remember traffic jams around the central Green. It now seems fantastic that it was considered a small town even so. There are probably not 20,000 people on the whole Seaboard south of Cape Cod: that is, south of where Cape Cod used to be before rising seas and storms sliced it into islands.

I entered the mansion and marveled that I was really the Governor. My wife Joelle sat in an easy chair in the marble entry hall. She wore a bright orange two piece bathing suit. This pleasant vision suddenly turned disagreeable as I noticed an umbrella of blue haze hovering over her. She seldom was without such a cloud anymore.

She squinted at me while holding her breath. With a tightlipped expression she placed a pink bong with a happy face printed on it on a lamp table next to her. An empty bottle of banana wine lay on the floor at her feet. She finally exhaled a rich plume of smoke and then doubled over and coughed fiercely. The sweet smell of opium permeated the house.

"Good morning, Joelle."

"Hey." She lifted her head from her lap and assessed me with half-open eyelids. She looked away and shook her head. Once again I had failed to measure up to her standards. "I need some more weed and some more wine. Get them today. And the photocells on the roof need cleaning. Do it now! The fans are barely turning. I shouldn't even have to ask! You should take care of these things. You can be such an ass. And you leave me alone all the time! You don't care about me at all. I don't know why you married me."

Neither did I. There was no reason why she couldn't take care of those chores herself while I was out collecting the rents. Of course, that would mean getting out of the chair and putting her drugs aside for a while. Since descending into addiction, she had grown demanding, self-centered, unhelpful and mean. She had replaced her former powerful self-reliance with a tendency to bark orders to others. Those orders always involved some personal service that was quite within her own capacity to perform. Somehow she mistook this high-handedness for strength. It was, of course, a display of weakness.

Also, in contrast to her earlier self, she hated to be alone. I couldn't keep her company all the time. I had work to do and, to be truthful, staying home was unpleasant. She fought with all her friends so that they no longer came to visit. Yet she would not visit them unless they were throwing some party where she could drink herself into oblivion. I had tried hiring lady's maids to keep her company and to tend to her needs but none of them would stay. Joelle would lose her temper over some minor real or imagined mistake. The drugs, the alcohol, or the hangovers did the talking. She vented rage on those occasions so abusively out of proportion to the putative offense that the maids would quit. I knew just how they felt. This was not the woman I had married.

"Do you have to smoke dope right here in the foyer?" I asked quietly.

"What am I supposed to do? Lock myself in one of the boiling hot rooms upstairs and never see anybody? Not that we get much company anyway. I told you to get rid of that damned lizard! He scares everyone away."

"He is my pet." I didn't add that he was not the scariest member of the household.

"If I get a chance he will be my boots."

I tried make myself angry enough to order her out of my life, but once again failed. We once had known good times together. Besides, Joelle's looks were holding up well to the chemical battering and personal disregard they were suffering. Her pale blonde hair just touched her perfectly shaped shoulders, and she had not yet lost enough muscle tone to damage her figure. Even stoned, sweaty, rude and unkempt, she was beautiful. I again marveled how beautiful women make men stupid. Men themselves are well aware of this, but somehow that awareness doesn't change the response. This must help the survival of the species. It doesn't help individual men.

"I'll go fix the photocells."

"Don't break any this time! You're such a klutz! At least Ulysses didn't trip over his own feet."

Joelle was fond of comparing me unfavorably to Ulysses S.

Johnston. Ulysses, Joelle and I once had competed for possession of Morrisbourg. The competition involved the use of firearms. By virtue of a droplet of strategy, a cup of subterfuge, and a gallon of luck, I had jumped the claim and won. There was every reason to expect that one or both of them were lying in ambush for me when I returned to town with deed in hand. Accordingly, I returned with hired armed guards. Those guards still serve on the police force in Morrisbourg.

Ulysses had anticipated this precaution on my part and had motored away in Joelle's dinghy rather than stay to fight a lost cause. This didn't entirely surprise me. The man was adventurous rather than reckless. Joelle did surprise me. Instead of opening fire on me from some concealed sniper position the moment I stepped off the boat, Joelle ran to the landing waving her hand and greeted me with a smile. She actually respected my success. We were married a week later.

There was a prenuptial agreement with my bride that included restrictions on her inheritance of my estate. I don't mean to seem the cad, but when a woman has aimed a gun at you once, you hesitate to be worth more to her dead than alive. The truth is my Will negated the prenuptial by leaving everything to her, but I kept that little secret locked in a safe.

At first our life together was enjoyable and exciting. Together we built our colony and she had joined me in administration. Morrisbourg grew rapidly servicing the needs of a renascent New York City, recently reoccupied by Quebec, with food and raw materials.

English speakers just call the Quebecois "French" even though, or rather because, it annoys them. The French have done all right by me. After all, they enforce my ownership rights. I can't say I like them very much though. They are arrogant snobs and take national pride in being so. There is the whole matter of language, which is like something out of Sir Walter Scott's tales of Norman Saxon rivalry. Full citizenship is for French speakers only. Otherwise, you can't vote or be elected to office (my office was not elected). True, if you learn their language they don't discriminate against you as much, but Americans were never very good about foreign languages. If there are any Englishmen left they surely still complain we don't even speak English. Carpetbaggers from old Quebec dominate everything.

To give them their due, the French have re-introduced rule of law to our region. They have issued a declaration of principles that is passably liberal. In addition, they have a hydroelectric powered industrial base up North. Becoming part of their economic zone allows us to raise our living standards above the level of Tarzan and Jane. I suppose we could do worse. The real French in Europe do much worse under the Swiss.

Morrisbourg supplies New York with everything from fresh water to alligator skins. The key to our colony's success, however, is three cash crops, and Joelle deserves the credit for promoting all three. One is marijuana, a tough and versatile plant from which we make paper, cloth, rope and chemicals. The second is bananas. We sell the fruit of course, but the real money is in a dreadful banana wine labeled "Old Yeller, The Bananas That Bite." For some reason this foul brew became a fad throughout Quebec. Poppies are the third crop. We grow them not to make poppyseed bagels but to extract opium. The French are remarkably easygoing about this although they do restrict trade in opium to the territory south of the old Maine border. Perhaps they hope to keep their new southern colonies philosophical. Perhaps they want to starve criminals of revenues in the new lands. Perhaps they just like collecting the tax. Whatever their motives, the policy is a windfall for us.

The double edge of this particular economic sword cut into my own household when Joelle herself became a customer. The change in her was rapid and depressing. Joelle always had aspired to high position, to put it mildly, and she had the energy, ruthlessness and brains to get there. She was as dangerous as a leopard and as beautiful. I loved her that way. She scared me but I loved her. All her life Joelle schemed, plotted and fought to be Number One. Now she just wanted to stay at home and drug her mind into oblivion.

I realized Joelle's substance abuse and torpor were related to the misfire of her plan to own Morrisbourg herself. She felt permanently trapped in position Number Two. Marriage to the

Governor is not the same as the position of Governor. After the initial fun and hard work of getting things started, this distinction began to wear on her. For this reason I felt partly responsible for her current state.

I tried hard to think of a solution. I did not wish simply to sign the colony over to her. To be honest, this would have been hard on the residents including, I suspected, me. Joelle is not an easy boss. However, she needed to focus on some new ambition if she was to have any chance of abandoning her path toward self-destruction. While scraping fungal growth off the photocells I thought up some diversions for her. I hoped these would help, at least in the short run.

As usual, I was soaked in perspiration when I returned to the entry hall from the roof. I've almost forgotten what it is like to be dry.

"Joelle, I need you to accompany our next wine shipment to New York."

"Go yourself," she said sleepily. "And take a bath. You stink. Don't think I'd ever touch you when you smell like that."

"I can't. Go to New York, that is. This is a busy time of year. I need to collect the rents, go over the accounts, oversee production, and orient some new settlers. It would be helpful if you met with our major customers and politicos in the city for a few days. Go to parties with them."

"Parties?"

"Yes. I'll arrange for you to meet the Mayor and the provincial Governor. Make the society pages of the newspaper. It's good advertising, it's good politics, and you might even have fun."

She opened her eyes and looked as contemplative as her stoned state would allow. "Okay. I'll need money. And I mean enough money. When does the boat leave?"

"Take what you need. The boat leaves on Friday."

"Okay, but you owe me."

New York already numbers over 6,000 people and more immigrants arrive from the North and the hinterlands every day. This makes it once again one of the world's great metropolises.

Joelle must have liked the big city. Instead of a few days she stayed two months. To be honest these were relaxing days for me.

I got up, went to bed, went to work, came home, ate, and played entirely on my own schedule. There were no lists of chores. There were no arguments over my supposed transgressions and bad attitude. There was no emotionally unstable drug addict with whom I must live. I slept well and felt refreshed in the morning. I met some old friends for dinner without worrying that my spouse suddenly would fly into a rage and embarrass herself and me.

Yet for all that I missed her. I would be hard-pressed to explain why, but I missed her. It wasn't just that I missed sex, although that certainly was part of it. After all, I could have cheated on her; but even leaving the ethics and the wisdom of that aside, it wouldn't have been the same. Joelle was mine. Somehow it just felt appropriate that she be part of my existence. No one else could take her place, physically or any other way. Yes, I loved her.

Is love truly something positive or is it an insidious urge to self-destruction? I suppose it can be either or both. The ideal of mutually supportive helpmates is an all too rare reality. More common is the case of one partner unsuccessfully struggling to feed a black hole of need in the other. What is the motive of the feeder? Why the ingratitude of the fed? Why is it so hard for humans to be either together or alone? I have no answers. Perhaps someone does. No convincing explanations are to be found on the shelves of the local library, however. I have looked.

All vacations come to an end. One day I walked into my office and was startled and happy to see a familiar face behind the desk. She had sent no advance warning of her return. More heartening yet was the old fire in her eyes.

Yet something was missing. It took a moment for me to realize that she was not enveloped in pot or opium smoke. As I took my first step toward her for a welcome hug, Joelle fired off a curt question.

"Where are the distillery accounts?"

I halted. "Under 'B' for 'banana.' Have you found a discrepancy?"

"Not yet."

Some new game was afoot. I was thrilled. "Welcome back." I meant that in more ways than one. "Enjoy your trip?"

"Yes, actually. Enjoy yours."

"Am I taking one?"

"Yes, cher. Report tomorrow morning to Captain Le Clerc on the gunboat *La Salle*. She's tied up at the Battery in New York. You'd better catch the wine boat before it leaves."

"I don't think so! I have a colony to run here."

"No. I do. Your property is in trust until further notice. Guess who is the Trustee."

The thrill was gone. "We have a contract and a prenup..."

"They have been set aside in the national interest for the duration of the emergency."

"What emergency?"

Quebec is asserting its succession to the whole of North America."

"Really? What about Canada and the Republic of Alaska?"

"Except for them of course. For now anyway." Joelle gave me one of her enchanting smiles. It had been a long time since I had seen her smile. She still melted me with it. "Anyway we needed a powerful symbol of the new extent of our sway. The Prime Minister decided that the old US capital was perfect for the purpose. So, a Quebecois expedition occupied Washington, DC, a few months ago."

"What's to occupy? The city must be under water. Foggy Bottom was a swamp to begin with."

"Capitol Hill is dry."

"Well, OK. But the government was awfully quiet about something that was supposed to be so powerfully symbolic. There wasn't a word in the papers, unless the 'survey team dispatched to the coast' mentioned on page two a while back was the cover story. Isn't the whole point of a big symbolic gesture to make headlines?"

"If they're the headlines you want."

"Which brings us to the emergency."

"Right. They're gone."

"Who are gone?"

"The expedition! Who else? That is why things are hush hush. Radio communication with the first team quit a few days after they reached DC. There was no call for help.

They just stopped talking. A relief boat was sent out. The second crew sent back a message saying the place was deserted.

They turned up some evidence about what happened and then they quit talking too."

"Well, my guess is that some armed bandits attacked them. Some of the swamp dwellers are not nice people. The French probably were overconfident and sent parties that were too small to defend themselves."

Joelle smiled again. "You have a habit of referring to francophone citizens as foreigners instead of as your fellow countrymen. You are right, though, that we were attacked and that our teams were too small. Quebec views the matter very seriously. This time we are sending adequate forces."

The pointed use of the pronoun "we" did not escape me.

"Okay. But what is all this to me? And what is your part in this?"

"You're going to DC on the La Salle. That is what it is to you. My part is to be a loyal citizen."

I chose not to comment on her newfound patriotism. "I am not going to DC! Why should I? I don't understand why anyone would want me to go there. Whose screwy idea is this?"

"It was the screwy idea of the bandits, as you call them. They asked for you. Specifically. That was the evidence turned up by the second expedition. Finding it was not a masterpiece of sleuthing. A sign posted to the Capitol main entrance declared 'A state of hostility exists between our peoples.' It is not clear what peoples were meant exactly. The authors of the sign didn't identify themselves. The message then named you as the only acceptable emissary for a 'negotiated settlement.'"

I was totally taken aback by this news. "Well that is strange."

"Isn't it? I dare say the Prime Minister is suspicious of you. So am I."

"You met the Prime Minister herself? Anyway, this is all nonsense. I am not political."

"Oh no. That is why you run a colony, or did until today. You don't have a choice, George. You report to New York and follow your orders to the letter or you will be arrested as a spy. If anyone from the first two teams has been killed you most likely will be declared an enemy of the state and tried for treason and murder."

"Despite my having you as a character witness." She smiled again. "Is there something more to this story that you are not telling me?" I asked.

Joelle shrugged her shoulders.

"Well, I guess I'm going to DC."

"Wise decision," she concurred. "Pick me a cherry blossom."

"If I can find any I will. By the way, Joelle, what happens to Morrisbourg if I don't return?"

"I expect the terms of your Will to be carried out, which means I'll be stuck with this place. Don't trust so much in locks, George. Be careful down there, sweetie."

"Hmpf."

"Oh George?"

"Yes."

"There is one thing you might feel better about."

"Yes?"

"I'm pregnant."

Harbor water gently lapped the hull of the warship tied up at Battery Park on the tip of Manhattan. The French did not underestimate their enemies this time. The La

Salle was a beautiful diesel powered coastal patrol boat painted in elaborate blue, white and gray camouflage. She sported a 120mm gun and two .50 caliber machine guns. I didn't know any such vessel was left in service. The current economy can't support many like her.

Modern industrial civilization is an intricate web of resources, transportation, labor and markets. The collapse of the population and the subsequent end to significant world trade extinguished most heavy industry. As a result, with the exception of scavenged machinery, current technology is a weird mix of the 19th and 20th centuries. The auto and aeronautics industries are gone. Bicycles, horses and blacksmiths have made a comeback. Yet we have modern electronics. Computer chip design has more than stalled. It has rolled back substantially. Nevertheless, new, if less capable, chips are still available. The satellites are winking out, but while they last we have global TV coverage. There is a huge surplus of leftover war machines, but resources and skilled labor are too scarce to be wasted on maintaining them. The organized military forces remaining in the world consist overwhelmingly of small infantry units armed with automatic rifles.

I introduced myself to the French marine at the gangplank. Wordlessly, he grabbed the duffel bag off my arm, unzipped it, and dumped the contents on the wooden dock that extended from a concrete sea wall. He squatted and quickly sifted through them. He stuffed a pair of clean underwear, a pair of socks, a bar of soap and my razor back into the bag and tossed it back to me. A heap of clothes, books and spare boots remained at his feet. I sighed and walked past him up the plank.

I found the bunkroom below and slid my bag under a bunk next to three others. Rather than sit on a bunk to which some marine or sailor might have formed an attachment

I returned to the deck and found a place to sit on the bow in front of the main gun. Less than an hour later the plank was removed and the lines were untied. The ship backed away from the dock.

The sleek ship sliced through the calm New York Harbor water. The salt air blended with diesel fumes to form a heady smell. The La Salle probably outgunned any warship on active service on the North Atlantic. We cruised by the Statue of Liberty. Little of Liberty Island was dry. Water lapped at the bottom of the pedestal at high tide but the green clad lady herself remained proud and dry.

I actually would have enjoyed the trip were it not for the blatant hostility of the ship captain, a weathered choleric fellow who looked much older than his 30 years. He strode up to me on the bow. He obviously held me personally responsible for the loss of French personnel in DC.

"Mr. Custer!"

"Yes, captain."

"On this mission you will do what I tell you when I tell you to do it. Not one thing more or less. Not one minute sooner or later. Do you understand?"

"Yes, sir."

He spun on his heel and walked off. Restraining himself from tossing me overboard took a visible toll on him. My later attempts at communication only made things worse. On the back deck was a mysterious cargo as big as a medium-sized whale. It was tied down tightly under canvass by hemp rope. The rope was probably from Morrisbourg. I asked him about the cargo as we passed Cape May.

"What are we carrying back there Captain?"

"Mister Custer!" He almost spat the name. "I'll tell you what you need to know when you need to know it. If you poke your nose where it doesn't belong I'll chop it off and lock the rest of you below. If you signal anyone off this ship, now or later, orders or no orders you'll be breathing water. Do I make myself clear?"

"Crystal."

Except for the captain and medical officer, no one aboard spoke English. Perhaps everyone but those two was ordered not to speak it. With some 20 sailors and 40 marines aboard the vessel was crowded. The medical officer was also the only woman aboard. The Quebec military, like most others, remains very male-dominated despite desultory attempts at integration. I made little effort to exploit her language skills. One French woman in my life is quite enough. The fishing was excellent, however, and it was fun to sit by myself and watch the porpoises playing in the wake of the bow. With the end of overfishing by commercial fleets sea life has rebounded with a vengeance.

When night fell I could see the stars! I so rarely saw them back home because of dense plant cover, rainy weather and nightly haze. I stared at the sky for hours. Only toward the west was there a hint of a fog bank on the horizon. We re-entered the haze on the next day as we approached the tip of the Delmarva Peninsula.

The towers of the suspension sections of the Chesapeake Bay Bridge Tunnel were obscured by fog. Much of the old roadway formed a dangerous and barely visible reef.

Le Clerc did not throttle back the engines on this account. We cleared what must have been a tunnel section at high speed. If the captain was at all worried he had misjudged our position, he didn't show it. Soon we entered the broad Potomac, which had swollen far beyond its old banks. We cut back to a more cautious speed. Sailors took hand soundings to double-check the electronic readings. Others manned the guns as we neared the old

US capital.

The ambient heat was even more oppressive than in Morrisbourg. Back home the mist burned off by midmorning but here it was still as dense as a steambath. We rounded a bend where the Anacostia meets the Potomac and the Capitol dome came fuzzily into view. Jungle growth on the Alexandria and Arlington side of the river formed a wall of green except where broken by steel-framed high rises. DC was indeed flooded. The upper stories of decaying buildings rose out of the swamp. The Capitol and the Washington Monument grounds formed two islets barely above water level.

We maneuvered north from the main river channel and then turned 90 degrees starboard over a sunken Independence Avenue. We turned north again and slipped between the old Smithsonian castle and the Air and Space Museum. Spanish moss hung from the old castle tower. The former Mall formed a wide canal clear to the western side of the Capitol. We proceeded slowly taking soundings all the way. The hull gently touched bottom less than 20 feet from dry land.

Despite the brutal humidity, the French marines went over the side with admirable celerity. They splashed to shore and occupied the rear verandah of the Capitol in minutes. The sailors meanwhile tied up the ship and stretched a walkway of rope and boards to land. We waited as the marines entered the building and secured it — no minor task for a structure so large. The captain stood by the gunner manning the 120mm and watched intently. The weapon was not very useful support for his men inside but it could deal with threats from the opposite banks.

Two marines had been held back from the assault. They now were dispatched with radio gear on a motored raft to the Washington Monument. Le Clerc was unhappy about sending such a small team but he had no more troops to spare. The elevator in the monument was a rusted wreck. I didn't envy the marines the climb up the steps of the 550-foot tower. By afternoon, however, they waved from the top. It was an ideal observation post and sniper position.

The main force of marines spent the day searching the Capitol. They turned up no bandits and no survivors from the previous expeditions. Fortunately they found no bodies either. As night fell, men were posted around the outside of the building. Le Clerc ordered me below on the boat and posted a guard on me. I didn't know whether to be insulted or flattered.

After a fitful night's sleep I was awakened by a marine who spoke the first English words I had heard since the last time Le Clerc growled at me. "Follow me."

I badly needed a shower and shave. Nature also was calling me to perform some basic biological functions.

"Wait a minute, I'll be right with you."

The marine would have none of it. "Follow me!"

I followed him. I figured my bladder could hold out for another half-hour or so. As we walked over the patch of swamp grass that separated the ship from the Capitol I saw the first sign that we were dealing with unusual bandits. Horseshoe prints were plentiful, but where in the surrounding malarial mire would you raise horses? And why attack with them? We were on an island. Surely horses complicated transport beyond necessity.

We entered the Capitol through the Diplomatic Entrance on the ground floor. Our footsteps rang hollow in the hot dead air of the old stone corridor. We climbed a two-tiered staircase and passed through a short hallway. I looked up from my feet and found myself face-to-face with the mischievous countenance of Benjamin Franklin. This was

Statuary Hall, originally the House Chamber before the new wing was added in the 1850s. We moved on to the Rotunda. Even with the smell of decay and the spread of fungus the space was impressive. The dome soared overhead. On the ceiling was a bizarre painting of George Washington rising gloriously into the clouds above Roman clad figures. A winged woman with a sword, presumably Victory, carried a shield with the colors of the United States. Mildew had destroyed most of the large paintings in the wall niches but "The Declaration of Independence in Congress" and the "Surrender of General Burgoyne at Saratoga" were still recognizable.

The marine prodded me. "This way."

We walked north and entered a semicircular room with a half dome overhead. We were in the Old Senate Chamber where the

Senate met until 1859. This was the site of the historic debates of the 19th century on the great questions of freedom and slavery. I don't believe in ghosts but I almost could feel the presence of Hayne, Clay and Calhoun.

I approached Captain Le Clerc who sat at Daniel Webster's desk. Wordlessly he tossed a flag at my feet. It was the Stars and Stripes.

"This was flying on the east side," he explained at last with an expressionless stare. The east side was the main entrance even though it faced away from downtown.

"OK, so the bandits are patriots. What's that to me?"

"The very fact that you use the word 'patriots' tells me it means something to you."

I sighed loudly. "The USA is gone. I know that, even if the people who attacked this place don't. We'd be better off reunited, even under the French."

"We are not the French and 'under' is an insulting preposition. You are a citizen of Quebec. We treat everyone equally and if you just take the trouble to learn the language of your country even you could become Prime Minister."

"Whatever. I am not political."

Le Clerc looked at me with deep skepticism. "Let us call these people by their proper names. They are not bandits. They are terrorists. The terrorists left us instructions on how to proceed with negotiations. They take the form of an ultimatum. Their terms still are tacked up in front of the building if you want to read them — assuming you aren't the one who wrote them. We are to travel upriver. You are to be present. You will be our representative — which in my opinion is a case of the terrorists negotiating with themselves. There is no mention of hostages, but we must assume that they have them."

"I thought there was more than I had been told," I said.

"Don't pretend ignorance with me! Look, Custer. I think you and your buddies are cowardly scum. Taking hostages is low and despicable. If it were my choice I'd shoot you right here, ship in some serious artillery, and bombard the riverbanks with HE shells the whole length upstream. But the PM wants our people back even if it means negotiating with human trash like you. So cut the crap and let's get down to business. What do you want?"

"I want to go home. Le Clerc, you are way off base on this one. Honestly, I don't know who these people are. I certainly don't know why they asked for me. I don't know how they even know who I am. I'm flabbergasted."

Le Clerc exhaled in disbelief.

"So are we taking the *La Salle* up the Potomac?" I asked.

"Oh that would be just brilliant. Send our ship up a narrow river through dense jungle into enemy territory so your boys can blow us out of the water at will. No, Custer. I won't cooperate with you."

"I am not asking for cooperation. I have nothing to do with this. If you are not going to meet the bandits' terms, what are you going to do? I hope you have some more effective idea for negotiating with these people than threatening me."

Le Clerc reluctantly accepted that I would not speak for the hostage holders. He refused to accept the fact that I could not.

"Oh, we are going upriver; but we are going on my terms. That is the cargo you were so curious about. Come on."

Le Clerc stood up and led the way back toward the Rotunda. He left the flag on the floor. I almost picked it up, but instead I simply turned and followed. On the walk back to the west verandah we passed marines carrying crates of explosives. They were taking them to the Crypt below the Rotunda.

"We are prewiring the Capitol for destruction," Le Clerc explained. "If we have to abandon this site to attackers again, we are leaving it a pile of rubble. The explosives can be detonated by timer, by radio from the *La Salle,* or by radio from the Washington Monument. The snipers up there have the authority to use their own judgment. Your people have nothing to win here."

My people. Le Clerc seriously believed that I could somehow launch an army against him. I often have been underestimated, not least by myself. This was the first time I had been so seriously overestimated. I didn't like it any better.

I still believed we were dealing with bandits. Perhaps they were better organized than we expected. Perhaps they had stumbled into some Disney archive and watched too many reels of

Swamp Fox. But the raw, steamy, undeveloped jungle that surrounded us could not support any true threat to a power like Quebec. In terms of serious power politics, the bandits were ultimately only a nuisance. I merely hoped they were not a bloody nuisance and that there were no casualties among the first two French expeditions.

In a sense, the captain was right not to trust me though. The symbols of the Republic stirred the spirit of rebellion within me. Le Clerc had done nothing to make me like the French any better. I began to wonder if we Americans would be better off independent. Maybe we could rebuild on our own. Alaska was still a going concern even after the earthquake and tidal wave. If the Alaskans could push south to Oregon or someplace and then east while we in the East pushed west… but I was dreaming. The lower 48 were one big disaster area where only the surviving humans were more deadly than the climate, disease germs, and wildlife. What little law, order and, I had to admit, justice prevailed were contributed by Quebec.

The *La Salle's* secret weapon was unveiled. The Quebecois were returning to the skies and I had to admit the approach was both clever and consonant with economic realities. A small ultralight airship measuring scarcely more than seven meters in length inflated slowly on the deck. It was powered by a single 25 horsepower engine with a three-blade propeller. There was a small but serviceable gondola underneath with a cabin height of about six feet. Except for a forward plexiglass windshield the windows were open.

"She can handle three people although we are sending her up only with two. We are using hydrogen for buoyancy," Le Clerc informed me.

"Isn't that rather dangerous?"

"It is easier to come by than helium and it gives us 20% more lift. As for flammability, frankly I don't mind placing you at risk. I would regret the loss of a crewman, though, which is why I'm going with you myself."

"She is a pretty big target."

"This is purely a reconnaissance and diplomatic mission. Besides, these are your pals we are talking about. They asked for you. I'm bringing you. There are not even any weapons aboard except for this."

He patted the 7.62 on his belt. I caught the hint that this was primarily for use on me.

"Understand something Custer," he added. "If any harm comes to those Quebecois field personnel I am holding you responsible. I'll make you pay."

Actually, the prospect of flight took my fancy. It looked like fun.

"Fly now, pay later."

As the craft inflated Le Clerc explained the basics of airship operation to me. As with so many other apparently basic technologies, it is more complex than it looks. I learned, for example, that within the outer skin there were inner bags called ballonets that served to compensate for air pressure changes. These required constant attention.

As Le Clerc talked, a crewman brought a bottle and two glasses. It was Morrisbourg's horrible banana wine. To my surprise Le Clerc poured the two glasses full and handed one to me. I understood this to be a gesture of tentative camaraderie at the start of a mission. Given his suspicions and feelings, this was a major concession on his part. So, I clinked his glass and swallowed the vile elixir with as few facial contortions as possible. A marine gave us an intensely self-satisfied smile as he watched us drink. I wondered if he shared my opinion of Old Yeller.

We slowly rose above the sunken city. The engine started easily, and we nosed the craft upriver. Teddy Roosevelt's statue, standing in ankle-deep water, seemed to wave at us as we passed overhead. Linear breaks in the trees marked old major highways. I identified a long curving break as the Capital Beltway. For hours the scenery scarcely changed. There was mile after mile of thick steamy foliage split by a winding and swollen river. There were no signs of recent human occupation.

"What is the range of this thing?"

"We could make it to the Mississippi if we had to. We are not turning back until we make a full reconnaissance."

Slowly a change took place in the scenery below. Lowlands gave way to hills. The hills became mountains that our blimp barely cleared. We think of Maryland as a fairly level place which once hosted horse farms and well-to-do suburbs of DC and Baltimore, but the western counties are as rugged as anything this side of the Rockies. The foliage below changed with the increased altitude. The rain forest gave way to grasslands on the upper mountain slopes. While far from cool, the atmosphere this high was almost pleasant. The grasslands looked inviting and livable. They brought to mind photographs I had seen of the Kenya highlands in old atlases.

"We are running out of river, aren't we?" I asked.

"Why don't you just tell me what we are looking for and where it is?"

"I know you don't believe me, but I really have no idea."

Below was a broken and rotted but legible billboard: "Welcome to West Virginia. Wild and Wonderful."

We passed a bend in the river. Tied up at the bank was a line of wooden rafts. The bandit gang obviously was larger than I reckoned. Perhaps the French were right to consider them more than just a nuisance. We heard shouting from the riverbank.

"This must be the place. Are we setting down?" I asked.

"No, because this is where you want me to land. I'm going to look at what you don't want me to see. There is smoke from that ridge in the west."

I wasn't sure we had the altitude to clear the ridge but we did, barely. There were more shouts below and then the popping of rifle fire.

"Merde!"

Le Clerc full-throttled the engine. A hole appeared in the windshield. Some of the bullets penetrated the fabric of the blimp. We were above a plateau covered by farmland with fences and plowed fields. We passed over a white-painted farmhouse almost close enough to touch the chimney. The farm looked like a Norman Rockwell painting. A village center of sorts was on our left. Several barns had prefabricated chimneys that were clearly recent additions. The smoke that poured from them had the acrid odor characteristic of industry. I guessed the barns had been converted to makeshift factories or blacksmith shops. According to the map this was someplace called Aurora.

We were losing altitude from the leaks left by the bullets. At least we didn't explode. We attracted the notice of the residents. They were exiting their barns and homes to gaze skyward and point at us. Most were dressed in blue. We reached the western edge of the plateau without tangling with the trees beyond the fields. We were falling more quickly now but the mountain fell away at a rate that more than matched our descent. Jungle growth reappeared beneath us as we dropped.

"Call DC, Custer! I'm a bit busy here!"

I wasn't at all sure I wanted to call DC. A familiar symbol had caught my eye on the mountaintop. A US flag flew on a flagpole in front of the farmhouse we nearly had scraped. There was no need to draw firepower onto these mountain farmers. Surely they were guilty of nothing worse than defending their homes against people they viewed as invaders. They probably considered the French seizure of DC a threat. Furthermore, there would have been some justice to that view. Then there were the French captives from the first two expeditions to consider. Calling in the marines now might endanger them unnecessarily. Even if these people were using them as negotiating chips, the captives were more in the nature of POWs than hostages. The Aurorans' demand to use me as a negotiator began to make some sense too. They could have learned by radio news broadcast that I was Governor of Morrisbourg, a person of some importance in Quebec, who was not French. They assumed I would be a sympathetic envoy.

I perfunctorily fussed with the radio. "*La Salle.* Calling *La Salle.*"

"It will work better if you use the right frequency."

"Which one is that?"

"The setting before you changed it!"

Our descent was now alarmingly swift. As the valley floor loomed, a very bad collision with treetops seemed imminent. Our one chance for a softer end to our flight was a lagoon formed by some natural blockage in a small river. The river was probably the Cheat. Le Clerc revved the engine and steered us expertly toward the water.

"If we live through this, you won't live beyond it!" he shouted.

This threat no doubt made Le Clerc feel better, but it foolishly gave me fair warning. I grabbed his hair and banged his skull on the steering column. He sunk stunned to his knees. This gave me just enough time to slip the 7.62 out of his holster and throw it out the side window into the river. Le Clerc recovered enough to push me back and spin around. He managed to get a hand on my throat as we hit the water. Both of us went sprawling. The gondola submerged almost at once under the weight of the deflating fabric. I forced myself out the window against the inrushing water and swam to shore without looking back. I knew too well the sort of creatures that live in these hot waters. Among them was Le Clerc who, no doubt, was irritated with me.

I grabbed some roots at the river's edge and pulled myself out of the water and muck. Plunging into the dense foliage beyond, I felt I probably was safe. A passerby two feet away would have been hard pressed to see me. As a poisonous snake slithered by my ankle, however, it occurred to me that safe was a relative term.

Le Clerc was no longer an immediate threat, if he was still alive at all. I hoped he was. The Captain had an inflexible mind and his threat to kill me may have been sincere, but there was a sort of rough honor to the man. I almost liked him. Regardless of Le Clerc's well being, however, my own survival now depended on reaching Aurora.

That meant climbing the steep mountainside to the east. It would be best to reach the top before night. There were lots of sharp teeth in the jungle and I would be easy prey in the dark.

There is no need to recount in detail my painful ascent through vines and brush in the oppressive heat while having the blood sucked out of me by more insects than I ever knew existed. I have no wish to remember it. Suffice to say that I somehow avoided dying. Once upon a time, some people were desperate to save the last scraps of the world's rain forests. I hope they're happy. By nightfall I was near the top, but I had not broken out of the forest. I climbed a tree to sit out the dark, and hope I would not be eaten before morning.

I remember nothing until several hours later when I forced open my eyelids. The sunlight through the leaves hurt my eyes. Against my own expectations I had slept, although my sleep was of the kind that brought little reinvigoration. I was still exhausted, dehydrated, and in pain. My strength was nearly at an end, but I was encouraged by the quality of light to the east. I hoped I wasn't deluding myself into believing it indicated an end to the forest.

I dropped to the ground and forced myself forward. Emerging from the tree line I encountered a three-rail wooden fence. Beyond the fence was a field of grass with a scattering of peach trees. Horses at the far end of the pasture grazed peacefully.

My relief and joy were momentary. On the breeze wafted a smell even ranker than my own acquired odor. To my left on the ground was the carcass of something disgusting. It was the size of full-grown pig, but otherwise it resembled a half-eaten rat. I had heard of capybaras, giant rodents once native to Brazil, but I never had seen one. A rustle in the brush suggested that the animal hadn't died of old age. Something big had made this kill and I had interrupted its dinner. I regretted tossing Le Clerc's gun into the water.

I was far too tired to run. Besides, that might trigger a chase response from whatever was stalking me. A peach tree stood about 40 feet away in the pasture. I climbed over the fence and walked deliberately to the tree with as much confidence as I could fake. I felt eyes on my back the whole way.

A peach tree does not grow tall, but its profusion of branches makes it easy to climb. This merit quickly proved minor at best. As I settled into the upper branches a jaguar walked out of the jungle and leaped the fence at a bound. The big spotted cat would have been beautiful had she not been hunting me. She soft-pawed the 40 feet with the peculiar nonchalance of which only cats are capable. She sat at the base of the tree and stared patiently at me.

I stared back. She seemed to be enjoying herself. I didn't join her in that emotion.

I never have enjoyed, or even understood, killing animals for sport. It would be a lie though to say I felt anything but relief when a bullet dropped the jaguar. Ulysses S. Johnston's hand clicked the bolt on his hunting rifle. The reins lay on his saddle but his horse held steady.

The resemblance to General Grant, which always went far beyond his name, was now almost laughably close. Ulysses wore a blue uniform similar to that of a US army officer in the late 19th century. Five stars were on each shoulder, an unusual rank in any age. The uniform must have been terribly hot. He was guarded by two young cavalrymen. The cut of their blue uniforms also harked back to the 19th century, except they were made of cotton denim. The guards each wore an armband picturing a bald eagle clutching arrows. Between them on a donkey was a bedraggled Le Clerc whose hands were tied. One of the guards dismounted and offered his bay mare to me. I accepted gratefully.

"You should have walked up Route 50," Ulysses chided as we rode toward the village center. "I don't know how you missed it."

I probably hadn't missed it by more than a few feet.

"I prefer to take the scenic route."

I looked backwards at Le Clerc. The guard whose horse I had taken walked alongside the donkey. He loosely held a lead line tied to the halter. Le Clerc slumped sullenly on the animal's back.

"Are you OK?" I asked him.

Le Clerc's expression and carriage changed to alert anger when he heard my voice. He did not answer but seemed to be visualizing crosshairs on my torso.

"He'll be fine," said Ulysses. "He led us a merry chase before we surrounded him. His health must be good. Sorry about my boys shooting at you, by the way. You caught the troops off guard. We had sentries only two miles up the river from DC ready to greet you. Hell, we were expecting a boat. You always were full of surprises. An airship! That must have been fun."

"All but the last few minutes."

"'Oh, the humanity.'"

"Route 50 is really passable?"

"By horse and wagon as far east as Winchester and as far west as Parkersburg. It is our number one priority after the war effort. One day it will be clear from the Atlantic to the Pacific."

This struck me as an absurdly ambitious goal, but the work already accomplished was impressive.

Aurora would have been a small village in the old days, but by modern standards it was a world class city. The population was obviously greater than Morrisbourg's. Possibly Aurora rivaled New York. The absence abandoned city blocks hid its real size. The appearance was bucolic. We often forget that agrarian scenes belong to civilization rather than to nature.

I was taken with the look of the place. I was so accustomed to life as a fight against jungle growth and rising waters, that grassy Aurora was dreamlike. Here the farms, pastures, houses, and people seemed a normal part of the landscape. Clothes, of all things, were the jarring element in the scene. All of the men in view, and many of the women, wore anachronistic blue military uniforms. Even the children we passed wore uniforms: khaki shorts and blue tee shirts with red, white and blue armbands.

"I seem to have stumbled onto the set of F Troop except you're no Captain Parmenter." I commented.

"You're no Wrangler Jane."

"How have you done all of this? I'm guessing there are a few thousand people in these hills. That is a large number, but it really isn't large enough for major industry. You couldn't possibly manufacture everything I see here. Just making all these uniforms must keep your people working day and night."

"They don't need to manufacture everything." Ulysses flashed his fierce brown eyes at me. "There are still a lot of old shopping malls and warehouses to be scavenged if you know where to look. By the time they are picked clean we'll have more people and more territory and then we'll be able to make what we need. There is an old denim factory outlet only a few miles away, for example, with enough leftovers to last us for years; it doesn't take much to turn them into uniforms. In any case, a few thousand people are more than enough to do anything if you have national focus."

"'National focus.' Is that what you have?" I asked skeptically.

"Yes, that is what we have. It is all we have. You need to understand what these people have been through. After the world changed, this little community somehow managed to hold on. Immigrants constantly replaced the locals who succumbed to disease. Farming continued. The town lived on and eventually stabilized. Then things went sour. When I came here, George, these people were on the verge of losing everything. This little patch of the good life attracted human wolves. At first they would raid houses, steal food, terrorize folks, and disappear back into the forest; it was all a brutal lark to them. Then some of them didn't leave. They butchered a couple of families, except for the young girls, and the murderers took over their houses. They kept the girls of course. The local farmers were no match for these criminal gangs. In fact some of the young men of Aurora joined them. The gangs looted Aurora at will and then fought each other like dogs over dinner scraps. Anything made or grown here was free booty. Kids were kidnapped and tortured for fun. No one was safe. Decent folk one by one left. The jungle was safer. This would have been a ghost town in a year."

"So you marched in with a tougher gang and took over. That's called forming a government."

"Is that a joke?"

"Not at all. And don't make it sound so easy.

Suppressing the gangs was a hard fight. Of course, a lot of their members defected to us as soon as we began to win, but some of them mindlessly fought to the very end. You ask these people, George. They are grateful to me. They would die for me."

"And probably will."

"Is that a joke?"

"I truly hope so. Okay, so you're the man on top."

"They call me Chief, by the way, which I tolerate."

"'Chief.' So have you set up a real government, formed a legislature, written a constitution and all that, Chief?"

"They call me that among themselves. They call me General Johnston to my face. No, in answer to your question. This is not the time for liberal democratic tripe. That is what destroyed America to begin with. If there had been a true national government when the climate crisis hit instead of an electioneering pack of puerile panderers we might have held the country together. You must agree with me since, if I'm not mistaken, you run Morrisbourg like a medieval baron."

"An enlightened one I like to think."

"But that is your choice, isn't it? This is a military government.

Myself and my staff provide order and discipline. This town needed to pull together, to deliver

its punch as a single fist rather than as five fingers. I clenched them into that fist. Oh, I understand people are political by nature and they like to feel part of the process. A savvy leader needs to channel those instincts. Anyone here can join the National American Party, which is the one legal political organization and the surest path to personal advancement. The Party ensures that political activity is carried out on behalf of the interests of the state."

"'The state.' Once again, we are talking about a few thousand mountaineers."

"But we are focused. That makes us strong. Look, the 20th century taught us a few things. We learned that centralized states are not good at some things. For example, they were lousy at providing consumer goods to suit the individual mindless whimsies of stateless selfish sybarites. But they were very good at big, well-defined projects where the weight of the nation could be thrown against a single obstacle; they were good at building dams, exploring space, building roads…"

"Waging war."

"Precisely."

"You are planning a war."

"It is not a plan. We are at war. We have been invaded. America belongs to Americans."

"That didn't bother you when you expected the French to give you title to New Jersey."

Ulysses laughed. "You have a firm grasp of the obvious. Don't be offended. Few people grasp even that much." He dropped the tone of a committed nationalist.

"I'm glad you don't buy into ideology, really. We are more alike than you think."

"I am not political."

Ulysses laughed again. "Anyway, we'll let you get some rest and clean up. I'll get you a uniform."

"Have I been drafted?"

"Yes, as a matter of fact. Also, you and the French captain here are guests of honor at the rally tonight. Appropriate attire is required."

"I need to ask why you specifically requested me to come here. You nearly got me arrested for treason. I had a theory but it looks shaky now."

"Oh, you are quite useful. For one thing the request scared the French into thinking there was a conspiracy that included even the Governor of Morrisbourg. That makes them more hostile to anglophones who then will return the favor. That is all to our benefit. More importantly, it provoked them to commit their best forces to the occupation of a very vulnerable position; involving you made us seem a threat without revealing how big a threat. They remain overconfident. Finally, there is a certain propaganda value to your name for our side too. If the French arrested you, that would be one more crime for which to condemn them. If they sent you here, I assumed from that either you would be killed or that we would entice you over to our side. Dead you are an American martyr, at least the way we would tell it. Alive, you are a recognized authority who can lend legitimacy to the revolt against Quebec."

"I see. You are over-estimating my importance, I think, but your plan makes some sense in a Machiavellian sort of way."

"I can't claim credit for the idea. It was Joelle's."

This was a stunner. Why was a part of me proud of her? I had my own life to worry about, though, and Joelle was a deadly enemy at the moment.

"She just wanted Morrisbourg for her own, so she set me up."

"Of course."

"And she'll bend any way the wind blows to keep it. She'll turn on you the instant it is to her benefit. She may already have alerted the French to your plans. You shouldn't trust her."

"I don't. She doesn't know my plans, other than that I am challenging the French in DC somehow. She doesn't know my strength or my timetable, but I doubt she would say anything if she did. It is in her interest to be quiet and sit tight. If the French defeat us, they will let her stay on as Governor because she loyally saved Morrisbourg from you. If the Americans expel the French from our soil, I will allow her to remain as Governor as gratitude for her service to me. She wins either way."

"You would trust her?"

"No, I would allow her to be Governor. Ultimately, you see, she lacks ambition."

"What?!"

"She wants to be the big fish but she doesn't care if her pond is big or small. She will be happy running Morrisbourg. She won't set her sights higher. You are more like me whether you recognize it or not. You want the big pond and will face bad odds to get to it."

"Does my presence alarm you, what with my overweening ambition for the big pond and all?"

"Hardly. I am counting on your ambition. You will see that loyalty to me is your easiest path to power when I explain the facts. I know you prefer easy paths. You probably were spoiled as a kid."

"The middle 'S' stands for Sigmund?"

"Keep that quiet. It is not a name that suits a military man."

"So what are the facts? And what is at the end of this easy path down which you want to send me?"

"My job."

"Excuse me?"

"My job. If you cooperate, I am naming you as my successor."

This offer silenced me for several moments. He seemed to be serious.

"Why? I know nothing about this place or these people. Besides, you should hate me. I ruined your plans in New Jersey. It is a wonder you weren't killed that night. I assume Joelle missed."

Ulysses laughed. "Yes, she did spray some AK rounds my way, but her aim wasn't good. She was distracted by the big lizard you set loose on her. Actually, that whole improvised assault of yours is evidence you are qualified. It was clever and deceitful and for that you deserve credit. It also was absurd, but since it worked I suppose I can't quibble about that. What does worry me is that you displayed an element of hesitancy as though you weren't really sure you wanted to attack me. Your problem is that you have a juvenile sense of ethics that sometimes prevents you from taking sufficiently forceful action. That is a fine thing for a peon. We want peons to feel guilty if they disobey orders. It is a very dangerous thing in a leader. A leader has to set ethics aside and do what is right."

"When you say 'do what is right,' you mean 'do what is advantageous.'"

"For a leader the words mean precisely the same thing. Why didn't you simply shoot me? That is what I would have done."

"I wanted to give you the benefit of a doubt."

"That is a prime example of what I mean. You unnecessarily risked your life. You chose a ludicrous diversion over a direct attack because your conscience bothered you. You were concerned you might have misjudged me. That was stupid. As you are not a stupid man, you have no excuse."

"Are you seriously berating me because I didn't kill you?"

"Yes. To be sure, in that place at that time, your conscience was an affordable luxury. It was only your own life with which you were gambling, but when you exercise authority you need to be more responsible. I would like to feel more secure that, if you are left in charge here, you won't risk your people by giving a benefit of a doubt to outsiders. Fortunately, I don't think you are an absolute slave to your conscience or I wouldn't consider allowing you any rank at all. You pussyfoot annoyingly, but when push comes to shove you can be ruthless too. I am willing to take a chance on you anyway."

"Thanks for the benefit of a doubt."

"Don't dissuade me from granting you your legacy for the sake of making ironic comments."

There was some sense to this advice. I pondered my unexpected inheritance until another thought drove it out of my head. "Wait, when did you last talk to Joelle?"

"I wondered when you would ask. I met her in New York a little over a month ago. There are no walls and locked gates around the city, you know. I just sailed a small fishing boat into the harbor with some of my guards in civvies in order buy supplies and catch on the news. I read in the society section of the paper that Joelle was going to attend a party at the Waldorf with the mayor. I checked into the hotel and arranged to bump into her. She was surprisingly happy to see me."

"Yes, she is good about not holding a grudge." I had other

questions, but decided I really didn't want to know the answers. Instead I changed the subject.

"What about the French from the first expeditions? Are they all right?"

"You'll see a couple of them tonight. We are holding a rally as I mentioned. They will be there."

This was a relief. I risked my future with one more comment. "Ulysses, I am not political, but I do have a public relations suggestion."

"Which is?"

"Change the initials of the Party."

"Why?"

"Do you really want to be known as Nappies?"

Ulysses responded simply with an intense stare.

We approached the front of an old small two-story home with a porch wrapped around the front and left side. Four uniformed young people wearing Eagle armbands were on the porch. They snapped to attention. Ulysses knew at least one of the group by name.

"Weston!"

"Yes, Ch… Yes, General," she stammered.

"Show Colonel Custer here a room upstairs. You are his attendant until further notice."

"Yes, sir."

"What about Le Clerc?" I asked. "Is he coming?"

"The captain is a prisoner of war. He'll be quartered elsewhere. And you, Private," he addressed one of the young men. The guardsman ran up and saluted. "Wait at the dispensary. I'll give you a regular army uniform there to bring back to the Colonel. Go now."

"Sir!" The young man saluted and loped off.

I thought it odd that Johnston would take an interest in picking out my uniform himself, but I made no comment. I dismounted and said, "Until later, General."

He sat motionless in his saddle as though he expected more from me. I caught the hint and saluted. He saluted back and lightly tapped his horse with his heels.

I climbed the steps of the farmhouse. The young woman saluted.

"Please don't do that, miss. Not around the house anyway. Let's keep it informal."

"Yes, Colonel." She opened the door for me.

The interior of the house smelled of burned wood from the stove in the kitchen. It was a pleasant odor. At the top of the stairs on the other side of the landing was a bathroom. I peeked inside. A pipe with a showerhead extended above an old-fashioned claw foot tub on the far wall.

"Is the shower functional?" I asked my new attendant.

"Yes, sir. Will you be using it?"

The thought was delicious. "Yes," I answered emphatically.

"Shall I shave you afterwards?"

"What? Oh, no. I can handle that myself, miss, but if you bring me a razor I'll love you forever."

"Yes, sir."

The "cold" water was actually lukewarm, but it was still refreshing beyond description. My attendant walked in while I stood in the shower and placed a razor, shaving cream, toothpaste and a toothbrush on the sink.

"Will there be anything else?" she asked facing me.

"No," I answered with embarrassment. "That will be all, miss."

She picked up my clothes from the floor and left the bathroom. Moments later she re-entered with a bathrobe which she hung on the back of the door. After she left I did not hear her footsteps on the stairs so I presumed she waited outside. This was getting awkward. After shaving, brushing, and combing I slipped on the bathrobe and exited the bathroom. The young lady followed me into the bedroom.

"Will you be taking a nap, sir?"

"Yes, miss."

I lay face down on the bed. I remember nothing about the next several hours. When I awoke a 19th century style Colonel's uniform was folded on the bed next to me. My attendant still stood at ease by the door.

"Thank you, miss." I said somewhat groggily. "You are, um, dismissed."

"I am sorry, sir. I am under orders from the Chief himself to attend you."

"I see. Could you attend to me outside the door for a few minutes?"

"Yes, sir." She left and closed the door. I knew she stood directly outside.

I donned the uniform, which wasn't a bad fit. The boots were a bit snug. The rank was Ulysses' offbeat humor again. Colonel was the final rank of my ill-fated namesake. I looked at myself in the mirror, which hung on back of the door. I felt quite soldierly. It is amazing how a uniform can affect your whole worldview. I was an American soldier and I was able and willing to teach the French whose country this was. I opened the door.

"Excuse me, miss. Could you come in her for a few minutes?"

"Yes, Colonel."

I finally took the time to take proper notice of the young woman. She couldn't have been more than 19 years old. She was pretty in a tomboy sort of way with short-cropped dark hair and bright blue eyes that looked at me attentively and with respect. It had been a long time since a young woman had looked at me that way. In fact, I'm not sure one ever did.

"Tell me… Excuse me, what is your name?"

"Private Weston, sir."

"I wonder if you could help me."

"That's my job, sir."

"I just arrived."

"I know, sir."

"Everything here is new to me. I am trying to get my bearings both physically and, though I hate to use the word, politically. I need to ask some very basic questions.

They may seem dunderheaded to you, but then perhaps you expect that from an officer."

She didn't smile. "Ask away, sir."

"Let's start with that arm band you are wearing. What is it? Also, what is the story behind this total military mobilization? Is it because of Ulysses' planned war or did the mobilization come first? Is the war just an afterthought? Tell me, Private, what is going on here? I know nothing about this place and yet General Johnston already appointed me to be his successor."

"The Chief chose you as successor?" She was impressed enough to have missed the "sir."

"Maybe you shouldn't repeat that, Private."

"Yes, sir. Well, sir, the armband signifies the Eagle

Guard. We aren't regular army although we do fight alongside them. We are the armed wing of the Party. We act as the Chief's personal guards and we are sort of like police too. We enforce order, including political order. We are the Chief's primary weapons against anarchy and sedition. Are you sure you don't know this, sir?"

"Positive. It sounds like the SS."

"Sir?"

"Nothing. How did you become a member? Did you join or were you drafted?"

"I joined, sir. No one is drafted into the Eagle Guard. Only a few qualify for it. Sir, perhaps you don't know what it was like before General Johnston. There was no law. There were gangs of thugs and a protective association formed by ordinary folks."

"Vigilantes. Johnston didn't mention them. I suppose he put them down too along with the gangs."

"Yes, sir, and that was the right thing to do. They were almost as bad as the others. It wasn't outsiders who broke into my house one night and killed my parents. It was the vigilantes, as you call them. They accused my parents of collaborating with an outside gang, but the charge was false, of course. I don't want to tell you what happened to me. An arrogant awful boy from the group spent a couple of hours with me though. I had snubbed him kind of rudely a couple days earlier, so in a way I felt it was my fault. He accused my parents in order to get back at me."

"It wasn't your fault, Private. The boy deserves to be shot."

"Thank you, sir, and I'm pleased to hear your judgment about the boy, sir. Anyway, General Johnston rode into town with some very well armed men and put down the gangs and the association. The Chief had an armored personnel carrier that he must have found in a Reserve armory. I'm not sure even now how he got it here through the woods. Some of the local boys fought back but the toughest members defected to Johnston early on. Soon he had things in hand. Now we have law. We have order. We have peace. I don't bother to lock my door anymore."

"What happened to the boy who ... um ... hurt you?"

"I told the Chief my story and the boy was arrested and

brought before me. General Johnston gave me his gun and told me to do with the boy whatever I thought was right. I was free to choose any punishment or to show clemency and let him go."

"What did you do?"

"I shot him. The Chief said that when I turned 17 I could have a place in the Eagle Guard. I would die for General Johnston."

"Yes, I suppose you would."

"As for your other question, sir, the mobilization came first. It was what brought us all together."

As I suspected, Ulysses had forged an army first. He used defense against outsiders as his rationale and as emotional motivation for his troops. Now he was eager to find another use for the army.

The rally was held in an open field just after twilight. The stars were bright and a warm breeze blew gently. A rustic wooden stage was lit dramatically by four well-placed bonfires. A primitive but effective loudspeaker system was wired to a car battery. At least 3000 people were gathered in the field, most of them in uniform. I don't recall ever having seen so many people in one place.

Ulysses walked on stage to a drum roll. Applause and shouts came from the crowd. He held his right arm back toward me. I took the hint and walked on stage with him. He held back his left arm. A Guard escorted Le Clerc onstage. Le Clerc's hands were still tied behind his back. Ulysses waved for quiet.

"We have with us today, Captain Le Clerc of the French naval vessel *La Salle.* His plans to destroy us have been defeated."

A roar of approval came from the audience.

"Also with us is George Custer, the legitimate Governor of New Jersey, now in exile. By his order New Jersey is returned to the Union." There were more shouts. "The days of the French invaders in the United States are numbered. I also have appointed Custer to be the Commissioner for the Recovered Territories."

This was news to me.

"Care to say a few words?"

I thought frantically. I leaned into the microphone and uttered something ambiguous.

"I am deeply impressed by all you have accomplished here. I hope to accomplish everything you expect of me, and more."

Restrained applause came from the men and women in blue. Ulysses smiled at me and gestured with his hand. I took the hint again and walked backstage. The guard led back Le Clerc as well. Ulysses continued with a tone of determination in his voice.

"Here in Aurora we know what it is like to have our freedom wrested from us by hoodlums. We know what it cost us to win it back. Now we face a threat from the largest outlaw gang of all: Quebec. We have paid too high a price and struggled too much to allow our way of life to be destroyed by these new invaders. We will roll back the French all the way to the St. Lawrence River and restore America to the American people!"

There were more roars from the crowd, but they seemed to me less universal.

"This is not just a patriotic crusade although it is that too. This is a war for higher culture and the future of mankind." Johnston warmed to his subject. "The French are at the root of all that is rotten and corrupt. They always have been the weak link in Western Civilization. French values undermine health, decency and family values. French high art is simply decadence with a good conscience."

Ulysses held up a copy of *100 Days of Sodom* by the Marquis De Sade.

"Books like this deserve only the bonfire. French values are effete vales. They weaken us."

He tossed the book into the nearest flame.

"America saved Western Civilization once by regaining its roots on the simplicity of the frontier. We are the ones who fought for independence while Quebec sat comfortably under the British yoke. It is time to cleanse our continent of the French corruption and rebuild a healthy world for the minds, bodies and spirits of our children.

"My fellow Americans. We are on the verge of a great moral and military victory. We will regain what is rightfully ours, first in Washington, DC, then in New York City, and then on the whole continent. One day we will link up with our Alaskan brothers and restore our nation to its rightful status."

This voicing of my own earlier thoughts put a knot in my stomach.

"This is no time for internal political squabbling. We must be united. Whoever is not for us is against us. America belongs to Americans. The French have taken our lands. They have corrupted our culture and oppressed our people. In the occupied territories they deliberately destroy American lives with unrestricted trade in opium and other drugs that they ban north of the Maine boundary. This is a deliberate policy of genocide.

"Now we in the free territories face the bullets of our ruthless and murderous foe. French marines are camped downriver at this very moment and their objective is Aurora. Our culture, our heritage, the future of our children, the very lives of our children, depend on what we do here in the next few weeks. We can be slaves or a free people. We meekly can suffer French boots in our faces or we can fight back.

"We live in the proud state of West Virginia which never failed to fight under our great star-spangled banner when our nation was in peril. Once, as part of Virginia we led the rebellion against the British to create our nation. When the Civil War threatened to destroy that nation, we chose the higher good of the Union and refused to join sedition in Richmond. We have contributed more than our share to the defense of our homeland in every war since our nation has fought. We are proud of our heritage. The time has come again to save our land. This time we are fighting on our own soil for our own homes. We shall prevail. We shall drive the alien forces from our land.

"I know we have sacrificed much to build our military strength. We have labored long and hard and we have consistently chosen guns over butter. It was the right choice. Remember that guns are muscles while butter is merely fat.

"The greatest danger to our success is not the French army. I have every confidence in our brave men and women on the field of combat. The danger is subversion from within. Only Americans can defeat America. The Eagle Guard is our defense against treason. The Guardsmen are our best and brightest. When not fighting at the front they are political soldiers protecting our rights at home. They will weed out traitors, pacifists, and

French sympathizers. Help them in their task however you can.

"We have here two French spies from an earlier invasion force."

Two grim prisoners were led on stage. These were the first members of the earlier expeditions I had seen.

"The rules of war state that military personnel out of uniform are spies rather than Prisoners of War and may be treated as such."

An Eagle Guardsman withdrew his gun and unceremoniously shot each in turn execution style. I was stunned. Le Clerc attempted to rise to his feet but was shoved back with a rifle butt. He glared at me with deep hatred.

As the bodies were removed from the stage, Ulysses directed the crowd.

"Please join the singing of our national anthem."

An extraordinarily beautiful red-haired woman in the uniform of the Eagle Guard walked up to the microphone. She stood in blood. In a very sweet voice she began to sing.

"Oh say can you see..."

The rally attendees joined in weakly at first, but by "the bombs bursting in air" all were singing forcefully.

Other speakers followed the red-haired singer. All found something to hate about the enemy. Ulysses joined me backstage during some fellow's denunciation of French cooking. He sat down on a wooden bench.

I spluttered. "What was the purpose of those murders!? They were just two field biologists from Montreal. Surely that atrocity shocked everyone. Don't you think you shook the support for this war of yours, and for this whole blue machine?"

Ulysses frowned. "Just the opposite. By not objecting to that 'atrocity' they become participants in it. They then must accept the argument that our program is for the higher good in order to justify to themselves their participation."

"There is no justification. Your followers may be caught up in the moment, but most of them will have second thoughts. If they don't object, it is only because they are afraid to object."

"The Aurorans will see things my way. Believe me, Custer, they by and large will get with the program or seize on legalisms rather than force themselves to wonder if they are cowards."

"Legalisms?"

"The French were in civilian clothes. That made them spies."

"I was … am … a civilian too."

"Then you may profit by their example. Anyway, what do you think of my speech?"

The easy change of subject threw me, but I struggled to respond.

"Irrational. The Quebecois, as they so often tell me, are not the French. They are not invaders of North America. Their ancestors probably were here before ours. You called them effete and dangerous. They cannot be both. As for corruption by drugs, I'm more responsible for the opium trade than they are. Moreover, the real French were not a weak link in Western Civilization. To a large extent they were Western Civilization. The Marquis De Sade is a giant irrelevancy who was jailed by his own people. By the way I kind of like his play *Justine.*

"The true legacy of the USA is the principle that the legitimate purpose of government is to protect individual human rights. Quebec incorporates more of that heritage than you do."

Ulysses finally stopped me. "Come, come, my boy! I wasn't asking you if the speech made logical sense and I wasn't asking you to recite the Declaration of Independence. I was asking about its effectiveness as a propaganda speech. When you are talking to the masses you are talking to a dumb brute. Any message more complicated than 'Our side good, their side bad' just confuses them. A public speech must be judged on its emotional appeal."

This put Johnston in a different perspective. Unfortunately, it wasn't a better one.

"So you are not a fanatic ideologue who believes his own drivel. You're not some overgrown boy adventurer like I used to think either. What is your real motive? Joelle?""Sometimes you disappoint me, George. Is that the best your limited mind can come up with?"

"Okay, so you are not a romantic either. What is your problem, Johnston? Are you just a plain old psychopath?"

"Pfft. Psychopaths are interested only in their own short-term sensual and material satisfaction. They don't think beyond themselves."

"And you do?"

"More than you do, George. Unless you make yourself part of this movement, when you are dead it will be as though you never lived. You are nothing except what I have made you! I'm 47 years old."

I quoted Oscar Wilde, "'You look weeks younger'." Actually he looked a decade younger. There was not a hint of gray in his black hair and beard.

"I feel years older. I need to leave something of myself behind."

"And you figure a fascist state and a continental war are just the thing?"

"They'll remember me, George. Even if the Aurorans are defeated one day, I gave their miserable lives meaning. I gave them an ideal to fight for. Their personal liberties are a small price to pay for meaning."

"'Humans will accept any how provided they have a why.'"

"Nietzsche."

"Yes. He wouldn't have approved of you though."

"I don't approve of him. He didn't have the courage to be as immoral as his philosophy."

"So all this is because Ulysses S. Johnston is afraid of death?"

"Don't be a fool. You can't taunt me with that. Every person with an ounce of sense fears death. So do you or you wouldn't have survived this long. You are going to prove that very point by joining us 'fascists' as a VIP. Your alternative is to join those dead Frenchmen. Look, Custer, this moralistic outburst of yours is precisely what I meant when I complained about your juvenile sense of ethics. Get over it. Join us or join them. You have to decide now, George."

Ulysses' case was persuasive. These West Virginians were going to war. I didn't approve, but didn't see how my execution would help anything. It certainly wouldn't help me.

"Okay, I'm in. Maybe I can meliorate this group from the inside."

"There you go. No weasel of a Congressman could have rationalized better. In two days we occupy the Capitol. Then we sail into New York Harbor pretty as you please on the *La Salle.*

Defenses in New York are all but nonexistent. I worked out an occupation plan while I was there on my last visit. The English speakers will rally to us."

"A third of them will. A third will accept whoever is in authority. The remaining third will oppose you but they will take note of your firepower."

"See, you can Machiavellian when you try."

"Don't think your support in these hills is much deeper than what I just predicted for New York despite all your uniforms and rallies. All of your officers want your job. Without the Eagle Guard you wouldn't last a week before one of them took your place. Aurora fundamentally is fragile. You actually need the French as an enemy to keep all this going. The Aurorans would tire of military preparedness to no purpose."

"Well, I better not disband the Eagle Guard then," Ulysses responded, "and I'd better keep stirring up hate against the French. As for the officers, they plot against each other more than against me so their ambition is to my advantage. Each tries to ingratiate himself with me and turn me against the others. You are the one they view as an obstacle to power at the moment."

It occurred to me it was a bad sign that Ulysses was willing to discuss his war plans in front of Le Clerc. Le Clerc's attitude of fatalistic courage showed that he recognized this too. He spoke up.

"There is a flaw in your war plan, Chief."

"What is that my dear captain?"

"My sailors and marines. Not one of your barges will get within 500 meters of the Capitol."

"Oh I think they will. Are you an oenophile, Captain?"

"Why does that matter?"

"Several months ago we found cases of some marvelous

chardonnay in the ruins of a restaurant in Clarksburg. I was somewhat surprised. Anyway, your marines are sure to have discovered them by now. We left them in a chamber just off the Crypt in the Capitol."

"What have you done to the wine?!"

"Yes, that would offend a Frenchman. Well, among the multifarious new bugs, of which we are all so fond, is a little fellow who just loves to live in wine. The alcohol doesn't bother him at all. He even improves the taste, some have said. Unfortunately he secretes a rather deadly toxin. Mortality is about 80% within two days. The survivors are in no condition to fight. I suspect we will be facing only a handful of teetotalers."

"I don't care if only one man is left, you bastard. He'll know how to use the 120mm. You'll never take my ship."

"Well that would be a shame because I really like the *La Salle*, but we can do without her if we must. You see, we left some very big charges underwater all around the Capitol. If we get any fire at all from the *La Salle* she is going to the bottom. I'm not a fool Le Clerc. You'll also be happy to know we repaired the holes in your airship. We even rigged up machinery to produce hydrogen with electrolysis. What is the lift capacity of the airship?"

"A crew of two barely."

"Three easily," I corrected.

"When you are lined up against the wall, I'm volunteering for the firing squad," Le Clerc snarled at me.

Ulysses laughed. "So what shall we do with the Frenchman?"

"Take him with us. French survivors may surrender if they see we have him. They may wonder what is up and not fight at all."

"Logical, although I suspect you just lack the stomach to shoot him. You don't mind if I keep him tied, do you? For now, also, you travel without a firearm."

"I rather expected the former, and everyone seems to feel that way about the latter."

Back in my room I was supposed to rest for a few hours but I tossed fitfully instead. The juvenile sense of ethics that annoyed Ulysses so much was making my life miserable. I have no love for the French but the avid patriots of whom I was second in command were poised to carry a reign of terror to the North fatal to anyone with the wrong accent. After a sleepless hour I heard a tap on the door.

"Yes?"

My attendant peeked in. "I'm sorry to bother you, sir, but I could hear that you were awake. May I enter, sir?""Yes, Private. What is on your mind?"

"Permission to speak freely?"

"Of course."

Private Weston entered the room and sat on the corner of the bed where I lay covered only by a linen sheet. This was a little freer than I expected.

"I told the truth when I said I joined the Guard out of loyalty to the Chief and out of patriotism, but it doesn't hurt that it is a good career move."

"Of course it doesn't."

"You are Governor of New Jersey?"

"Morrisbourg."

"New Jersey, sir."

"What's in a name?"

"The authority of the person who gives it, sir. What is New Jersey like, Colonel? What is New York like?"

"Morr... New Jersey is a wealthy piece of jungle that supplies the city with a variety of foods and commodities. It is a comfortable place. New York is spectacular. The skyline takes your breath away. The Urban Homestead Act allows new settlers to own entire buildings so there are tremendous opportunities..." I decided to halt my praise of a Quebecois law.

"When we take it back will you show me around, sir? You will need an attendant there if you are next in line to be Chief. I think you are a good choice."

The young lady did indeed have an eye for her career.

"Private Weston…"

"Judy."

"Private Weston, I realize you have suggested a purely professional relationship, but I think you should know I am married."

"To a Frenchwoman?" she sneered disdainfully.

"Yes."

"Do you love her? Does she love you?"

"Yes to the former. As for the latter … well, actually I think she is trying to kill me."

"I won't do that, sir."

"That is most appreciated."

"What I will do is give you my support and loyalty. Is there anything I can do for you tonight Colonel George Custer?"

It took me a moment to be sure the offer meant what I

thought it did. "Uh, no Private. Perhaps we can resume this discussion in a few days, though."

"Yes, sir."

"I think I can sleep now. Wake me up in time for the war, would you?"

"Yes, Sir." She left, not altogether displeased with herself.

I did not sleep. I am sufficiently in love with my homicidal wife to have regretted accepting the young lady's offer. Yet truthfully I regretted not accepting it too. These thoughts drove politics out of my head for a while.

The barges set off downriver at night in order to arrive in DC at dawn. Our blimp would catch up with them in time for the assault. I felt it was reckless of Johnston to place himself inside of such a big target, but the man really did have much of the boy in him. He wanted to fly in an airship. Le Clerc sat morosely on the floor of the gondola. We rose into the sky high enough to glimpse the sun on the horizon. We began the leisurely flight downriver. Embarrassingly, at last I fell asleep. Ulysses kicked me awake as we floated over Chain Bridge.

The river broadened out below Georgetown and the barges full of soldiers and horses spread out for the attack. I was about to warn Ulysses of the snipers Le Clerc had sent to the Washington Monument, but the view ahead startled me into silence. The *La Salle* was gone. The city looked desolate.

For the first time since we left New York, Le Clerc smiled. "Did I neglect to mention that I left standing orders to pull out if there were a risk of losing the vessel? You may have poisoned some of my men but they were smart enough to realize what was going on. You chased your prey away, Johnston. Your plan has misfired."

"Well, that certainly is a setback, but not a fatal one. We have taken DC, and this time we are staying. We have agents in New York who can sink the *La Salle* with a mine easily enough when it gets there. Quebec still doesn't bother with adequate security. We can take New York with the boats we have. Yes, we have boats, Le Clerc. It is far too soon to gloat, captain. By the way, without any French occupation force with whom to negotiate, we have no need of you anymore."

The barges grounded on Capitol Hill and a blue human wave rushed toward the building. It was surely empty but the West Virginians would be as thorough as the Quebecois had been. The scene before us brought home to me what the future truly held. The military success shaping up below portended a major war — a continental bloodbath based on nationalist hate.

I am not political, but there are times when a human being must choose sides. The Nappies were a perversion of the symbols they exploited.

Damn it all, I had to back the stinking, arrogant, miserable, nose-in-the-air French, may they all choke on their nasalized vowels!

On the theory that one should stick with a winning strategy, I grabbed Johnston by the hair and rammed his head on the wheel. Ulysses must have had a harder head than Le Clerc. He pushed back on me and spun around with his handgun already drawn. He surely would have shot me had not Le Clerc kicked him with both feet. Ulysses stumbled against the side window. I grabbed his feet and pulled up. He tumbled over the side. The gun discharged as he fell. The bullet penetrated the fabric of the blimp. This time we were not so lucky. A white ball of fire erupted above us. I since have learned that the remarkable fact about the famous *Hindenburg* crash was the number of survivors. It is the nature of hydrogen to burn rapidly up and away from anything beneath it. At the time this was no comfort. We fell out of the sky as something like a blast furnace hovered over us. I managed to free Le Clerc's hands before we hit the water.

"*Deja vu*!" I remarked.

"About time you started speaking your country's language."

Both of us dove beneath the river surface before the flaming fabric enveloped us. Don't try swimming in full uniform with boots. It is harder than you think. Eventually my hands touched bottom and I pulled myself up on the shore of the hillock containing the Washington Monument. The rank smell of riverbank mud was overpowering, but I felt too tired to lift myself out of it.

Two powerful hands wrapped around my neck and the knee of a heavy man jammed in the small of my back. The world began to go black before the hands and weight lifted. Le Clerc had pulled Ulysses off me. The two wrestled on the wet ground while I forced myself to my feet and made a dash for the Monument entrance. There wasn't much time before the blue-coats would arrive to rescue their Chief. There are 897 steps to the top of the Washington Monument. I had cleared fewer than a hundred when a voice boomed below me.

"One of us dies today, Custer!"

I suspected Johnston was right. Both of our footsteps echoed loudly inside the all masonry obelisk. He was catching up. I could see nothing in the black interior. My lungs were raw and painful and no amount of panting was enough to catch my breath. My feet resisted each aching move. Before long I was crawling. My lungs rasped worse with each breath. 897 does not sound like an overwhelming number, but I felt as if I had spent a lifetime on those stairs. At long last my hands pushed open a door and light washed over me, but my vision was badly clouded by lack of oxygen. I heard a loud wheezing behind me.

As I had hoped, a transmitter was still in place at the observation port facing the Capitol. I made one final lunge for the box. My vision was still cloudy, so I felt around desperately for an obvious switch or button. Almost by accident my right hand found and pressed a plunger.

Even with my fuzzy eyesight the Capitol dome rose noticeably. Then the 9,000,000 pounds of iron crashed into wreckage. Other explosions ripped through the House and Senate Wings. These must have been from incendiary devices because fires leapt up almost at once.

The wheezing behind me turned to coughing. My vision cleared as I turned. A mud-covered Johnston lay on the floor a few feet from me. His face, where it was exposed, was as red as any I ever have seen. Saliva dripped from his mouth and he gripped his left arm with his right.

"This could have been yours, you total fool!"

"Does that mean I'm no longer Commissioner for the Recovered Territories?"

"I'm going to get you, Custer. Somehow I'll get you."

"You shouldn't threaten me from your present position."

"You don't have the guts to kill me, you spineless wimp."

I considered this. "You're right, Ulysses. And you know what? I'm proud of it."

I walked down the stairs. My lungs still hurt badly and my legs felt rubbery. Two hundred steps or so later an explosion roared overhead. Huge masonry blocks missed me by inches. A 120mm round had taken off the top of the structure. The *La Salle* was back. At least a few of the crew must be alive and they had spotted our blimp from downriver.

I quickened my descent. The reports of gun and machine gun fire were the sounds of serious damage being done to the remaining West Virginians. I felt sick about the fighting and I hoped it would end soon. I also wanted to visit the botanical section of the Smithsonian's Natural History Museum.

The next day the *La Salle* motored past the Chesapeake Bay Bridge Tunnel. It turned out we owed our survival to the age-old dispute between marines and sailors. The marines hadn't shared the wine.

A badly battered Le Clerc looked at me and said, "I still don't know whether to shoot you or give you a medal."

"Neither. I am not political."

"Their nest in Aurora should be rooted out."

"No. They won't recover from their losses. Besides, all fascist states are personality cults and the personality is gone. They'll go back to fighting among themselves now. With luck they'll do it with words at town meetings arguing over things like local zoning and the school budget. They really aren't a barbarian horde bent on conquest. They're just mountain farmers who went on a binge. Most of them probably are ashamed of themselves."

"They should be. They murdered civilians. They need to be placed under occupation and brought to justice."

"They already had a lot of justice dealt to them. What they need is a trading post, not a military occupation. It should be someplace other than Aurora but nearby. It should be someplace other than DC too. The symbolism there is too in-your-face."

"Harper's Ferry?"

"Le Clerc, that was almost a joke. By the way, what is your first name?"

"Maurice."

"Oh. Sorry. Maybe I should stick to Le Clerc."

"I'd appreciate it."

The Quebecois authorities were accommodating upon my return. My Morrisbourg estates were returned to me although I am in the process of transferring title in fee simple to my tenants at very reasonable prices. I also have petitioned Quebec to transform Morrisbourg from a proprietary colony to a full Territory with an elected governor and a representative assembly. I have asked for a limited waiver of language laws for voters and office seekers within the Territory. Representative government is safer than one-man rule even when I'm the one man. A year ago you would not have convinced me that the folly of many is less dangerous than the ambition of one, but it is true.

Joelle accepted the defeat of her schemes with her usual good grace. When I returned home, my monitor lizard was nowhere to be found and Joelle had a new reptile skin vest. I didn't ask. Some questions are better left unanswered. She disappeared before her treason trial even though I think I could have gotten her off with probation.

She left behind the dried cherry blossom I had brought back from the Smithsonian. She also left our newborn son. I love him dearly but I wonder where he got those fierce brown eyes. Mine are hazel. I can't help but picture his face with a full black beard.

CHAPTER 3

SAND

CONFIDENTIAL REPORT TO QUEEN ANNE
RE: TRIAL A. CUSTER
FYEO, FROM AGENT 4 (Hello, cousin)

ANALYSIS: Testimony presented at the trial has caused some diplomatic embarrassment to Her Majesty's government. The Alaskan government appears unconcerned about the matter, but our ambassador to Canada may receive a formal protest. He also may receive an extradition request for one resident alien. Military or economic sanctions directed against Her Majesty by either power are unlikely.

RECOMMENDATION: Accept any protest without comment. Comply with extradition request if one is made.

REPORT METHODOLOGY: As requested, I have tried to capture the sense and flavor of the events surrounding the trial in a narrative style in order better to convey the attitudes and reactions of the participants and of the Alaskan public. I understand that this will supplement the ambassador's formal report to you. I have made much use of the trial transcript, which is surprisingly useful in this regard. For events to which I was not a witness, I have relied on information supplied by our paid informants and by forensic evidence. I have made some conjectures based on my knowledge of the individuals whose actions (and sometimes whose thoughts and motivations) are described.

REPORT: It was yet another warm and sunny day in Juneau, Alaska. A gentle breeze nudged the leaves of the palm trees lining the streets. The air was clear to the eye but an acrid smell from some distant conflagration was unmistakable. The mountains towering over the center of town blocked any view of the offending wildfire.

There was a festive spirit on Fourth Street. Women in sundresses stood and chatted, men in tee shirts talked to each other about the women in sundresses, and children ignored both sets of adults while playing games of their own making. A street vendor sold cotton candy. The focal point of the crowd was the architecturally uninspired brick building that served as the Capitol of the Republic of Alaska. Inside, the most notorious international criminal of the age faced the legislature. He was not one of the legislature's own members.

Inside the building the infamous Aeneas Custer, formerly of Greater Quebec, listened quietly to the roll call of votes. The only suspense was regarding the size of the majority. When the roll call was finished, 57 legislators had voted for indictment and three had abstained. All those abstaining were from Fairbanks where, by some quirk of local political psychology, there was an undercurrent of sympathy for the accused. Truth be told, even in Juneau nationalists had little hate for Aeneas. Few would say so openly however. It was hard to make such a statement sound respectable.

One fellow without any concern for respectability was expressing himself at that very moment outside on Fourth Street. "Hey, I don't approve of what he done," said the unshaven man to his buddy who sat next to him on the curb. Each had a beer in his hand and three under his belt. "But shit, the man just stood up for himself. The French should have left him alone. And, hell, he did Alaska a favor."

"Yeah, I know what you're saying, Bill, but we can't just let him go. The French are people too, kind of," observed his broad-minded football-jerseyed friend.

"So give him back to the French then. It ain't our business to judge him."

"They'll just shoot him."

"Well, that ain't our business neither."

Bill's views did not carry much weight politically. Certainly, no career in the Capitol chamber could be based on a vote for acquittal for Aeneas Custer.

Aeneas sat quietly through the next vote but this time he didn't bother to listen. It didn't concern him. The second vote indicted *in absentia* the second most notorious criminal on earth, Selena Custer. The indictment was mere posturing. Selena was still at large. The second vote was unanimous.

The indictment was the first step in an irregular and ad hoc process. "Crimes against humanity" was not a formal charge under existing Alaskan law. When Aeneas was taken unexpectedly into custody the governor and the legislature quickly had cobbled together a procedure that gave an appearance of legitimacy. There was a sound argument for extraditing Aeneas. However, the Alaskans trusted their own judgment over that in Quebec City; and Alaskan politicians were unwilling to forgo the publicity the case brought them.

Since the outcome of the vote to indict was never in doubt a three-judge panel already awaited the accused in the Courthouse across Fourth Street. Alaskans pride themselves on swift and often rough-handed justice.

The crowd outside awaited a chance to glimpse the embodiment of evil as he was escorted from the Capitol to the court. News photographers waited to capture digitally Custer's steps toward the trial of the century.

A hush came over the street as the moment arrived. Aeneas, wearing no handcuffs and flanked by only four police, emerged from the building. Bill, the beer drinking sympathizer, rose unsteadily to his feet. He took one look, snorted and sat back down. He was disappointed by the ordinary appearance of the accused. He was not alone in this reaction. A slightly overweight young man of average height and pleasant expression, Aeneas Custer appeared to be anything but a menacing super-villain.

"Four cops!" harrumphed Fred. "Maybe they're hoping one of us will spare the state the expense of a trial."

Bill shrugged.

If in fact this lack of caution was a deliberate exposure of the prisoner to his enemies, the authorities too were disappointed. No one in the crowd made a threatening move. Even the reporters kept a respectful distance and did little more than shout questions as Aeneas passed. Aeneas did not respond to the queries. The five walked unmolested across the street and past the statue of a bear, a symbol of Alaskan frontier ruggedness and a reminder of the role Russia played in Alaskan history.

Long ago during snowier days, the statue had replaced an unloved abstract piece named *Nimbus. Nimbus* was banished to a seldom-visited museum where it remained. There still were bears to be found in the mountains so the statue had not become an anachronism.

The courtroom was no larger than the average. Most of the seating was taken up by an international assemblage of newspeople. The remaining 18 seats were reserved for the general public. They had been awarded by lottery.

The three judges were among the most famous in the country. Sitting at the head of the table was the Chief Justice of the Supreme Court of Alaska. Alfred Hirisawa was a stocky man of 50 years with tawny complexion and a full head of mixed black and silver hair. Eccentric in style and dress, his past decisions were an odd mix of libertarian principles and authoritarian enforcement. He was widely respected for his intelligence and enjoyed a reputation as a character. Several of his opinions were required reading in most of the local high schools because of their literary qualities. On this day he wore a flowered Hawaiian shirt.

To Hirisawa's right sat a fortyish woman with red hair wearing a traditional black robe. Her name was Jeanette Wilson but she was better known as Judge Jeanie, a television personality who acted as the judge in a show featuring real cases. She was known for insight, impatience, and a quick sarcastic wit.

On Hirisawa's left was a soft-spoken and dignified man of frail frame and 90 years. One of the founding fathers who wrote the Alaskan Constitution, Michael Maggio used his years to advantage. It amused him to dissect the faulty reasoning of young attorneys; their instinct to associate senescence with senility would be shattered by the display.

The prosecuting attorney was the ambitious Alexander Proudfoot. Proudfoot was thrilled at the career opportunity this case presented. Custer's legal counsel was an undistinguished and pudgy man who smelled faintly of scotch. His expertise was in the handling of traffic cases. He was not destined to be famous, nor would his name be remembered.

Aeneas sat down next to his attorney. He seized the attaché case that lay on the table in front of the lawyer and slid it in front of himself. He unsnapped the clasps and began to examine the papers inside. His aromatic companion looked surprised but made no comment.

Within 15 minutes of Custer's arrival in the courtroom, the bailiff called the court to order.

Hirisawa smiled at the television camera. His colleagues avoided looking at the lens. Judge Jeanie did so with the professionalism of an actor and Justice Maggio with the disdain of a jurist who often had argued against the presence of cameras in courtrooms.

The persistent shortage of technological goods has caused a recrudescence of manual professions in Alaska as elsewhere. Even stenotype has been displaced by shorthand in the courtrooms. Functional tape or digital recorders are too scarce to be wasted on most trials. This case was sufficiently important to be an exception, but the shorthander was at her post next to the recording device anyway. As a matter of law, her record is the basis for the official transcript. The tapes nevertheless are stored in the national library and are available to scholars. The only serious objection ever raised to the transcript of the shorthand writer was came from Judge Wilson. She complained of the persistent identification of herself as Judge Jeanie. Cynics suggest that Judge Wilson was prompted by her publicity agent to complain.

Considering the charges, the trial took very little time. As the record shows, the panel of judges valued speed.

TRANSCRIPT *ALASKA VS. CUSTER:*

CHIEF JUSTICE HIRISAWA [to prosecution]: State what we are here for and keep it brief.

PROUDFOOT: Your Honors, the man before us today is accused of crimes against humanity: murder and mayhem on a scale that almost defies comprehension. We will show that he committed these crimes and that he did so with foreknowledge, intent, and without excuse.

The defense surely will argue that these crimes were committed in the context of a war. Yet it long has been settled that the phrase "*c'est la guerre*" is not a license for murder. Moreover, initiating the war was itself a crime.

We are not dealing with some oppressed rebel or some patriot with a noble cause. We have before us a spoiled scion of the most influential family in the Southern Territories of Greater Quebec. His future would have been one of wealth and power had he only refrained from unleashing his vicious brutality. He brought immeasurable harm to his country and to the world, a world that has been harmed enough already. He deserves no more mercy than he meted out to his hapless victims.

HIRISAWA: That will do, counselor. How does the defense plead?

AENEAS CUSTER [Out of order]: Your honors! I wish to fire dispense with counsel.

HIRISAWA: That is beyond foolish, Mr. Custer. This is a capital case.

AENEAS CUSTER: Understood.

HIRISAWA: If you wish, a change of counsel I may consider the request, although you had more than enough time to make that request earlier.

AENEAS CUSTER: No, sir. Frankly things don't look good for me even with the best counsel in the world. If I'm going to crash and burn anyway, I'd rather pilot myself.

HIRISAWA: This is not a kangaroo court, Mr. Custer. We are prepared to give you a fair hearing. Whether a fair hearing is of any help to you is another matter.

AENEAS CUSTER: I understand that too. I don't mean to impugn this court's fairness, but I still rather would speak for myself in my own way.

HIRISAWA: Suit yourself. Sit down, counselor. You will remain there, however, in case the defendant changes his mind. So, Mr. Custer, how do you plead?"

AENEAS CUSTER: To a charge of crimes against humanity? Your Honors, what can I say?

HIRISAWA: Guilty or not guilty is traditional. Pick one.
[delay] Mr. Custer?

AENEAS CUSTER: Not guilty as charged.

HIRISAWA: In that case you again should reconsider your refusal to accept counsel.

AENEAS CUSTER: Thank you but no thank you, your Honor. I simply wish to tell my story. My defense succeeds or fails on that alone. I have no wish to argue points with the learned prosecutor over there or to have them argued on my behalf by the gentleman beside me.

PROUDFOOT: Your Honors, the defendant should not be allowed to dominate the structure of this trial. This is not his own private theater.

AENEAS CUSTER: Your Honors, this trial is very much theater. If I am not the star of the production, who is?

HIRISAWA: Facetiously stated, but not without foundation. [Pause while Justice consults colleagues.] If the defendant wishes simply to make a statement and then shut up, we are inclined to let him to do so. How long will this take, Mister Custer?

AENEAS CUSTER: I don't know. A couple hours maybe.

HIRISAWA: Go ahead.

AENEAS CUSTER: I wish to read into evidence the journals of my father, the former Governor...

PROUDFOOT: Objection! Relevancy, your Honors. The father of the accused is not on trial.

AENEAS CUSTER: The prosecutor brought up my family, your Honors.

HIRISAWA: So he did.

PROUDFOOT: But your Honors, we are familiar with these documents anyway. They have been published in the papers every day for the past week.

HIRISAWA: True, but the media are not the courtroom, except for my learned colleague. [Hirisawa gestures at Judge Jeanie.] Go ahead, Mister Custer.

AENEAS CUSTER: Thank you. These journals are largely responsible for my presence here. They originally were published, some of you may know, in the English language version of *Pierre Roulant,* which translates somewhat strangely as *Rolling Stone.*

INTERRUPTION OF TRANSCRIPT BY AGENT 4:

The shorthand recorder struggled to keep up as Aeneas Custer read George Custer's account of the founding of Morrisbourg into evidence (see attached copies of George Custer's first two memoirs). Aeneas' reading was initially deadpan but it grew increasingly animated. By the time he described the party in the Headquarters Plaza his left arm was flailing. At the end of the first memoir he paused, wiped his brow and poured a glass of water

The prosecutor took advantage of the pause to speak up. "Your Honors, I applaud the defendant's thespian talents. His expressions, gestures, and voice imitations — especially Joelle's — are wonderfully entertaining. Yet once again we must question the relevance of these memoirs. The adventures of the defendant's ancestors have nothing to do with his own offenses. The defendant wasn't even born when Quebec annexed the Atlantic coastline."

Judge Jeanie wagged a finger. "Please don't refer to yourself in the plural, counselor. It annoys me. You may represent the state, but you speak for yourself."

"I apologize, your Honor."

"Don't apologize. Just don't do it. As for you, Mr. Custer, the prosecutor has a point. Explain how this memoir has anything to do with the case."

"Your Honor, the context of my actions are my only defense. This is my way of providing that context."

"I have a roomful of this killer's victims ready to testify as to the context," interjected Proudfoot.

"That hardly seems possible," commented Aeneas.

"This is no joking matter!"

"Both of you are to speak to the bench, not to each other," reminded Hirisawa.

"Your Honor, you said you would allow me to tell my story in my own way."

"I know what I said! Is there more to these memoirs?"

"Yes."

"Are you mentioned in them?"

"Yes, sir."

"Proceed."

"Your Honor," spoke up the prosecutor.

"I said he may proceed!"

The prosecutor sat down.

Aeneas read George's account of the Auroran War. At the conclusion of the memoir, Aeneas poured another glass of water while staring at the prosecutor. Proudfoot stared back, but remained silent. Aeneas looked at the judges.

"That was the last memoir that George Custer completed. He began a third..."

The prosecutor was on his feet again. "Your Honor, we have no way to authenticate this supposed third memoir. Even if we did he has yet to establish relevance. The defendant has read to us the Governor's suspicion that he is not a Custer at all, but the bastard child of the rogue Johnston. That is all very well and good for any genuine relatives of George Custer. No they doubt are happy to disown this madman, but parentage is not the issue here. Few of us can be altogether certain of our ancestry, after all. Cuckoldry is no excuse for wreaking havoc."

"Your Honors," responded Aeneas, "this copy of the memoir was forwarded here from Quebec City. I don't think the folks there would have edited it in any way that would benefit me. They appear to be unaltered. This is the memoir to which I appended my so-called threat. The threat has been published in the papers but the memoir has not. One cannot be understood without the other."

Justice Maggio leaned to his left and whispered to Hirisawa. Hirisawa conferred Judge Jeanie. She answered loudly, "That seems quite relevant to me."

"To me too," said Hirisawa. "We, if I may use the plural," said Hirisawa with a wink at Judge Jeanie, "will consider any questions regarding authenticity of evidence presented to us by the defendant at the appropriate time."

Judge Jeanie raised an eyebrow in her well-known way. This elicited a chuckle from the audience.

"Thank you, your Honors."

"Don't thank us yet, Mr. Custer, if that is what you prefer to be called. You may just be tying your own noose. Proceed."

TRANSCRIPT *ALASKA VS. CUSTER*:

AENEAS CUSTER: I need to place this memoir in context, sir.

HIRISAWA: Contextualize away.

AENEAS CUSTER: Okay. Well, the pivotal event that changed my life and the lives of all of us here occurred 11 years ago when I was 16. It was the night of a beachside bonfire in Asbury Park. The junior class of Morrisbourg Central High School was celebrating the onset of summer vacation. This was an annual tradition that had replaced the old "proms", whatever they were exactly. The event always was held on the eve of July 4 because that date annoyed the French speakers in the southern parts of Greater Quebec. A few of the French always showed up at the bonfire though. Hey, it was a good party.

That year the party was one of the best ever. Flames from our fire leapt 30 meters into the air. We fueled it with timbers from the abandoned buildings of the old town, most of which was overgrown and in ruins. The music was loud and assonant enough to chase away most adults. There were a few exceptions who had volunteered as chaperones. These were the usual 35-year-olds desperately trying to be teenagers. We teased them mercilessly of course. They either didn't notice or didn't mind. They were as drunk as we were, which probably made them more tolerant than they otherwise might have been.

All of us, young and old, dipped our mugs freely into the open kegs of Old Yeller banana wine that some party-capable students had brought to the beach. We carried on in the manner you might expect. By midnight a fair minority of our class had passed out. The remainder sang, danced, chased each other, mock fought, and not-so-mock necked. The tales I had heard of wild orgies from previous bonfire veterans proved to be fiction however. If there was any real coition going on I missed it. My nearest encounter was when one classmate flashed her breasts at me. Afterwards, though, she wouldn't even talk to me. Perhaps she had mistaken me in the dark for someone else.

PROSECUTOR [wearily]: Your Honors, the defendant's sex life, or lack thereof, surely does not pertain to the charges.

AENEAS CUSTER: On the contrary, Your Honors, it is central to them.

HIRISAWA: This I have to hear. Unless my learned colleagues disagree, you are over-ruled, Prosecutor.

AENEAS CUSTER: Thank you, Your Honors. Anyway, more revelers dropped out as the night went on. By 4:10 AM only a few of us remained awake. I wanted to see the sunrise. Given my condition this was an ambitious design, but I was well motivated. True, I had seen sunrises before but a very pretty and mildly drunk brunette wanted to see the sunrise too. So, I fought the heaviness of my eyelids until the night neared its end.

As the quality of the night sky hinted at an approaching dawn, the brunette walked almost to the to the edge of the dry sand. She sat down cross-legged and faced the sea. I obligingly sat down next to her. She uplifted her arms as though willing the day to break. I hoped against hope she soon would prove willing in other ways as well. She took deep breaths of the sea air. I forced my eyes away from her heaving chest long enough to take in the sky. The overhead haze was exceptionally thin, and light from a number of stars leaked through. My eyes were drawn back when the brunette took another awesome breath. She placed her hands back down on her thighs for a moment and then waved them upward once more.

Blinding white light engulfed us. When my vision returned my surroundings were as brightly lit as if it were noon. The distant sky was pale blue and overhead the haze was a painful white. A visible wall of compressed air rushed toward us from the eastern horizon. It hit hard enough to knock me flat on my back. Grit and salt water stung my body. I sat up dazed. The brunette was sprawled in the sand. She lifted herself up shakily on one elbow. A wave high enough to be impressive, though not high enough to be truly scary, struck the beach and washed past us a good three meters. Both of us clawed at the sand against the backwash. I was soaked. The brunette, dripping water, stood up and ran for higher ground.

The sky darkened, but there was still a glow on the Atlantic horizon. A mushroom cloud took shape. Newspapers called it the July 4 Firecracker.

JUDGE JEANIE: You were an eyewitness to the Firecracker?

AENEAS CUSTER: Yes, ma'am.

JUDGE JEANIE: Hmm. Go on, Mr. Custer.

AENEAS CUSTER: Yes, ma'am.

Anyhow, the Firecracker could have been a lot worse. It was too far out at sea to do significant harm on shore. There were some casualties though. A few fishing boats and coastal traders failed to return home that day.

Government officials were in an uproar. Fearing a second and more deadly blast, they mobilized the military. This was scant reassurance to the public since the military was at a loss as to how to respond or to whom. Many New Yorkers fled town.

Days passed. Then weeks. There were no further explosions, and no foreign power claimed credit for the bomb. No credible threat or blackmail note came from any terrorist group. A few muddle-headed radicals pretended to have something to do with it, but they were arrested quickly and shown to lack the technical expertise to have delivered anything more sophisticated than a spitball. Fears eased. With an odd sense of anti-climax civilians returned home. The troops stood down.

There remained a political need in Quebec City to bring some sort of closure to the incident. A Parliamentary committee, without a single scientist on it, quickly announced that the explosion was accidental. This was what the public wanted to hear. There was even some logic to the position. A modestly competent witness called to testify before the committee estimated the explosion's yield at 200 kilotons. Another witness, a munitions officer with the rank of ensign, testified that this yield was consistent with thermonuclear warheads carried by the submarines and surface ships at the beginning of the century. The committee accordingly concluded that a live warhead on some aged sunken vessel had destabilized in a remarkably unlucky way and had detonated. This theory was reasonable and satisfying. It was also dead wrong.

The Firecracker produced fallout far more serious than a little strontium 90. It set in motion a chain of events that destroyed my life and the lives of my countrymen.

The prosecutor was not wrong when he alluded to my pampered upbringing. My mother, Joelle Perrault-Custer never returned to Morrisbourg after she fled prosecution for treason over the West Virginian affair, but George spoiled me enough with the help of maids and nannies. He lost the election for Governor not long after I was born, but we remained the wealthiest family in the territory.

We were not in the public eye very often once we were out of politics. There was no mention in the papers of our trip to Montreal shortly after Parliament published its report on the Firecracker. There was no mention when George publicly declared his plans to explore the Midwest. There was a three-paragraph article on the front page of the *Morrisbourg Daily Record* when I announced some time later that George had failed to return from an excursion into the ruins of Chicago, but that was because it was a slow news day. No police in Montreal or Morrisbourg ever questioned me about my story even though, as sole heir, I arguably had a motive for murder.

There was, however, plenty of official interest in my property. As soon as George officially was declared missing, a court placed the family assets in trust for me as I was still a minor. The judge was an appointee of the new Governor and he immediately appointed political friends of the Governor as administrators. They rapidly declared my estate bankrupt and sold off the assets to pay their own fees. My complaints before several other judges that the administrators simply stole my inheritance were to no avail.

As it happens, I had lied about George. George had not gone exploring and he was not missing, but it would not have saved my property had I told the truth. Therefore I let the lie stand for 11 years. It was then that I received a fateful visit from a *Pierre Roulant* reporter named Boris Fontaine.

The 25th anniversary of the incorporation of Morrisbourg colony had arrived. The celebrations were bigger than expected because of the victory of the Jersey Giants over Montreal in the baseball playoffs. As a result, anything relating to Morrisbourg was in the news. The locals still preferred to call Morrisbourg "Jersey" even though scarcely any knew the origin of the name. Boris saw the opportunity for a story about me.

Boris did not have an easy task finding me. I lived in the one small patch of rain forest I could call my own. It was the gift of a successful West Virginian businesswoman, a trader named Judy Weston. Though I never had met the woman before, she looked me up in my rooming house and told me some tales about the war that George had left out of his memoir. Embarrassingly for me, she felt sorry for my plight. The day after our meeting a courier handed me a deed. I wasn't too embarrassed to accept the gift.

The deed was to a 300-year-old two-room log cabin with dirt floors in a place called Jockey Hollow. By pure luck it had survived the jungle growth that had engulfed and destroyed most of the wooden houses built before the climate change. According to a plaque on the wall, it originally belonged to a man named Henry Wick. His daughter Tempe, the story goes, once hid her horse in the house from George Washington's troops. It is a pleasant story and for that reason I don't believe it. The house was modest, but it was mine.

Boris lacked social skills to a degree that was awe-inspiring even for a member of his profession. I first saw him through the window as he sat on his horse and examined my house. When I walked outside he did not introduce himself. As he looked at my impoverished surroundings his first words were, "The Custers were the wealthiest family in the Southern colonies and now you're down to this. This is great!"

I didn't think it was great. When I loudly enunciated "Go away!" he just smiled at me. I repeated myself and waved a pitchfork for emphasis. Boris was not intimidated though his horse pitched his ears forward and eyed me warily. Boris then told me his plans. Boris wanted to do a human interest story on the rise and fall of the Custers. He said that the Custers were a colorful family as well as the founders of Morrisbourg. He nearly choked on his own enthusiasm.

"We can lead with a photo of this cabin next to one of the Governor's Mansion," he added. I was about to use my pitchfork when I thought about old family records in the bedroom trunk. Perhaps they were worth something. I asked him how much his publisher would pay for George Custer's secret memoirs and journals. As it turned out he was willing to pay a lot.

I never properly thanked all those connected with the magazine for their generosity. They were too generous for all of our good. It would have been better if they had cheated me out of it. George's memoirs of the Foundation and of the Auroran War pretty well spoke for themselves, so I left them unembellished when I read them into evidence. However, since George never finished this third one, for the benefit of the court I will add commentary during the reading.

HIRISAWA: The court thanks you, Mr. Custer. Recorder, enter the defendant's reading into evidence as JOURNAL OF GEORGE CUSTER PART III.

JOURNAL OF GEORGE CUSTER PART III—

The government dismisses the Firecracker as a unique mishap, a random short circuit in an abandoned weapon. My instincts, however, tell me this is wrong and that another fuse is lit and burning. Scribbling about it helps me think. Perhaps the poor fishermen who were killed by the explosion were the last casualties of last century's cold war, but maybe they are the first casualties of a hot new one.

The act of writing reminds me that I would have been happier as a writer or professor of history than as an active participant in it. I'm really not ambitious enough to have sought the life I have led. Ulysses would have made a competent Proprietary Governor of Morrisbourg, and if he hadn't threatened me so convincingly I happily would have supported him for the job. The Auroran business could have been avoided too. Why didn't he just leave me alone?

The accident theory applied to the Firecracker is just plain wrong. I am sure of this even though my technical expertise in the field is limited. All I know about nuclear engineering is what I have gleaned from some very general books in the Public Library. However, these books were enough to convince me that a thermonuclear warhead just doesn't explode all by itself. For starters it must be armed deliberately. Triggers on those old weapons consisted of precisely shaped conventional charges designed to implode plutonium or uranium cores. The resulting atomic fission would then, in a series of steps, initiate hydrogen fusion. As a safety measure the conventional charges in the trigger were kept misshapen so that if they went off accidentally they simply deformed the core. In order to arm the weapon the charges needed to be repositioned properly.

Conventional charges inside unarmed nuclear weapons exploded on several occasions in the 20th century. Two triggers went off at the same time once when a B52 crashed in Greenland. The same thing happened when a bomber went down in the Mediterranean. No nuclear detonation followed in either accident.

It is not credible that a weapon could be armed by accident. Early nuclear devices used a keyed arming system. The keys had to be inserted into the bomb and turned simultaneously. No single individual was allowed to carry both keys. Later warheads were armed electronically by a two-part access code. Once again one person was allowed to possess only half the code.

This indicates to me that the Firecracker was armed deliberately and at least two people participated. The real question is when. It is, of course, technically possible that this was done several decades ago, but it seems unlikely. Why would someone have armed a weapon and then not used it right away?

Then there is Aeneas' eyewitness description. True, eyewitness reports always are somewhat suspect. People remember things inaccurately even when they don't lie outright about what they have seen. Still, he describes something more like an air burst than a submarine explosion. That, in turn, suggests a deliberate act by present day people.

So, let us assume the Firecracker was not an accident. Who did it and why? Did some enemy aim at New York City and miss? Was the bomb dropped right on target: someplace visible but not too destructive? This would be the method of blackmailers, but where are they? No one claims credit. Is the government hiding something from us?

Some big piece is missing from this puzzle.

For some reason the document in the safe nags at me. I haven't looked at it in a year. There is no reason to draw a connection, but somehow I feel there is one. Yet, the document was given to me personally. It surely is megalomania to believe the explosion was for my benefit in any way.

INTERRUPTION OF JOURNAL:

AENEAS CUSTER: It apparently was megalomania to believe it, but not to suspect it.

"The document", your Honors, was a note written by Ulysses S. Johnston. George found it in the pocket of the uniform given to him by Ulysses during the Auroran War when George and Ulysses were briefly on the same side. If my benefactor, and Auroran War veteran, Ms. Weston is to be believed, George went over to the West Virginians for a time rather more enthusiastically than he admitted in his journal. To this day I find it curious that George did not hand the note over to Le Clerc the moment he discovered it on the voyage back to New York.

Anyway, at the top of the document was a pentagram. The text in Ulysses' own handwriting read, "I'm twice the man you are you two-faced panderer." Following in very small type was an apparent cipher consisting of fifty strings of numerical symbols such as >171.74+76.23. After each of these symbols was a list of ten other strings of letters and numbers such as QKJY4567, VCKO5489, and so on.

By the way, my account of the Firecracker is not suspect. It is accurate.

JOURNAL OF GEORGE CUSTER PART III—

The meaning of this cryptogram, if that is what it is, continues to elude me. Quebec's experts might be able to figure it out, but I remain reluctant to give it to them. I have tried rearrangement, substitution, and using the initial statement as a key, all without result.

Johnston was trying to tell me something. I suppose he didn't want the meaning to be instantly obvious to just anyone who saw the document but he really did expect me to make sense of it somehow. He gave me too much credit.

Johnston was a strange fellow. I never understood why he appointed me heir to the Auroran command after our history as adversaries. I still dream about the artillery strike that killed him and nearly killed me.

Two days have passed since my last entry. I am an idiot.

INTERRUPTION OF JOURNAL:

AENEAS CUSTER: George had rare moments of insight, your Honors.

HIRISAWA: Try to keep your commentary pertinent, Mr. Custer.

AENEAS CUSTER: I'll do my best, your Honor.

THE JOURNAL OF GEORGE CUSTER PART III—

The only balm for my ego is that my subconscious mind was on the right track. The breakthrough came this morning when Aeneas knocked on the door and entered.

Aeneas is 16 and already is bigger than I am. He must shave daily to keep back a beard. His robust figure easily could become rotund if he doesn't exercise enough. I have little room to lecture about that since middle age spread now shows on me.

While taking in the boy's unsettlingly familiar features yet one more time, it at last occurred to me that Ulysses tried to secure the future of Joelle's child when he appointed me his successor in Aurora. Am I really that slow? I wonder if Aeneas shares my opinion about his paternity.

INTERRUPTION OF JOURNAL:

AENEAS CUSTER: No I didn't. I guess I'm slow too.

JOURNAL OF GEORGE CUSTER PART III—

Aeneas brought me the mail and wanted to chat.

"What are you working on, Dad?" Aeneas asked.

My eyes were suffering strain from examining the document for the thousandth time. "Here, you may as well look at it. It's a family treasure, but I have no idea what it is."

Happy to be included in a family secret, Aeneas snatched up the paper eagerly and began to pore over it.

His face soon acquired a frown. "What's this pentagon on top?"

"Pentagram. It's an occult symbol... or maybe it is a pentagon. Maybe it's The Pentagon and the occult symbology of the five-pointed star is just to obscure that meaning. I've pursued the idea before but it doesn't explain enough."

"Wasn't the Pentagon the old American military headquarters?"

"Yes, which might mean Johnston dug this up in Arlington. Maybe I'll have to go back there and poke around. Do the letters and numbers suggest anything to you?"

"Well, I don't know. Could they be directions to someplace — maybe someplace inside the Pentagon?"

"Possibly. I doubt it though. I'm not sure how intact the building is. There seems rather too much information for just a corridor map anyway."

Aeneas sat on the lounge chair and stared at the paper. He plainly was pleased to provide help. Perhaps I should ask him for some more often.

"This came from Johnston? Ulysses S. Johnston?"

"That's the one."

"Did he give to you or did you steal it?"

"He gave it to me, after a fashion. He gave no explanation other than the insulting note on top."

"So he wrote it specifically for you. Maybe we should start there. Why would he write such a thing?"

"In order to get my goat. Also, it must relate somehow to the cipher. Perhaps it is all some joke. We could decode the document and discover it is just another banal insult. That wouldn't surprise me much. The man had an idiosyncratic sense of humor."

Both of us were saved from further embarrassment to our reputations as detectives by the morning post.

"Here is the mail, by the way," Aeneas said off-handedly as he tossed the letters toward my desk with his right hand and continued to study the document in his left.

Most of the letters were bills. It is surprising how little real mail a washed-up politician gets. Since my last defeat for Governor most people have forgotten me. At the bottom of the pile was one personal letter. It was stained and wrinkled as though hand-carried through severe weather. I ripped it open. The interior paper was in similar condition. The letter was dated July 4. The message was written in block letters:

DO I HAVE TO DRAW A MAP FOR YOU PANDERER? TRY TRAVELING NORTH BY NORTHWEST. BRING THE BOY AND NO ONE ELSE. YOU HAVE 30 DAYS. TELL NO ONE OR YOUR TIME IS UP IMMEDIATELY. THE WORD OF ULYSSES S. JOHNSTON IS GOOD.

I was stunned. How possibly could Johnston have survived that artillery strike in Washington? Besides, he was having a heart attack at the time. Yet, here was this letter. Would I never be free of this man who has plagued the majority of my adult life? Why doesn't he leave me alone? My sluggish synapses finally sparked.

"Why are you holding your hands over your face, Dad?"

"Because the voters were right to toss me out. I don't deserve to be governor. Bring me an old Atlas from before the heat. There's one on the second shelf. Look up South Dakota if you would."

"Why South Dakota?"

"Because Ulysses always called politicians panderers,

Mt. Rushmore is carved with the faces of twice two of them, and Cary Grant hung off one in *North by Northwest*."

"Who?"

"Never mind, just bring the map."

I knew Mt. Rushmore was in the Black Hills somewhere in the southwest of the state. The first place name to leap out at me from the lower left-hand corner of the map was the town of Custer, and just above Custer was the Crazy Horse Monument. I knew I was on the right track now. These locations shouted the mocking humor of US Johnston.

INTERRUPTION OF JOURNAL:

AENEAS CUSTER: George has no right to comment on the humor of others after naming me Aeneas, your Honors. I've also learned about Cary Grant in the years since then.

HIRISAWA: Don't make me repeat myself.

THE JOURNAL OF GEORGE CUSTER PART III—

Mt. Rushmore National Memorial appeared on the map slightly northeast of Route 16. The note rudely offered to draw a map. I picked up a pencil and reached for the document. Aeneas handed it over with visible reluctance.

Using Mt. Rushmore as a starting point, I drew lines in accordance with the first set of numbers. I guessed that the "greater than" symbol meant east and the following number was distance in kilometers or miles. My instinct was that they were miles: Ulysses had old-fashioned values. The "plus" symbol I took to mean north. On the map this indicated a spot somewhere above Pierre. Pierre almost surely was a ghost town.

Either my analysis was very wrong or this location was very odd. Even before the climate change there wasn't much in that area but pasture. Current world maps mark it as a desert. What could be of economic or strategic value to Ulysses out there? Having phrased the question to myself that way, the answer was suddenly obvious.

I dug out a book from my library shelf. It was a history of US strategic planning, and it confirmed my fears. During the Cold War the USA developed a complementary triad of strategic nuclear weapons: manned bombers, land-based missiles, and submarine based missiles. The centerpiece of America's land-based ICBM force was the Minuteman. The larger Peacekeeper had been phased out early in the 21st century as part of an arms control agreement. The last ICBM model to be deployed in substantial numbers was called Minuteman VI. There were 500 of them. Each missile was tipped with three independently targeted warheads. There were fifty dispersed control rooms. Each control room commanded a squadron of ten missiles. The missiles were heavily concentrated in the two Dakotas.

I was certain Ulysses had discovered a list of control room locations and had given me directions to them. The other symbols on the document, consisting of letters and numbers, almost certainly were the complete access codes for arming the nuclear warheads.

I knew now that the July 4 Firecracker was a calling card addressed to me personally.

INTERRUPTION OF JOURNAL:

AENEAS CUSTER: Even megalomaniacs are sometimes considered important by others.

HIRISAWA: Mr. Custer…

AENEAS CUSTER: Yes, sir. Anyway, George shared none of this with me until it was too late. By the way, Your Honors, in the spirit of public responsibility I falsified the sample directions and access codes I gave earlier."

PROUDFOOT: What else did you falsify?

HIRISAWA: Mr. Prosecutor, there will be time for that later.

THE JOURNAL OF GEORGE CUSTER PART III—

"Aeneas, there is no time to lose. Pack your bags. We are going away, maybe for months."

"Months?"

"Arrange for someone to feed the pets. Pack light. Take informal rugged clothes."

"Where are we going?"

"New York. Then Montreal."

"Informal rugged clothes? Are we camping in the park?"

"Just do what I tell you. We leave tonight. Pack for me too. I have a stop to make while you are doing that."

I exited the old Community Theater that once again had become my home after I left the Governor's Mansion. I still call my building the Theater even though it has been my private home for years. It is an appropriate abode for me even though I wish my life were less Shakespearean.

INTERRUPTION OF JOURNAL:
AENEAS CUSTER: Polonius?

HIRISAWA: [Clears throat.]

THE JOURNAL OF GEORGE CUSTER PART III—

Keeping roads open for traffic is an unending task. I am glad this is no longer one of my responsibilities. The rapid growth of vines and tendrils constantly creates snares for hoof and wheel. Roads are cut off frequently. Without boats and barges Morrisbourg would be in serious trouble. I was fairly confident, however, that the land route once known as Columbia Turnpike was passable for the short distance I needed to go.

The nearest stable is located on Bank Street, and both my horses have stalls there. My chestnut mare named Hobo, short for Hoboken, is only 14 hands which technically makes her a pony. I learned early on that smaller is better. My other animal, a paint named Goblin, is almost too big at 15 hands. The taller the horse, the more branches one has to duck. Also small animals shed heat better. Hobo groaned as I tightened her girth. After a brief resistance with clamped teeth, she accepted the bit into her mouth.

Despite her size Hobo handles my weight well. She has one more advantage over most other horses. Her unusual coloring consists of pale gray stripes against a yellowish base. These are signs of her zebra crossbreeding. Zebra blood helps her to remain comfortable when other horses sweat and languish.

We traveled east on Madison Avenue past the old hospital and then cut over to Columbia Turnpike by way of Normandy Parkway. These are grandiose names for routes that are scarcely more than trails. My eyes adjusted to the dark when the sun was cut off by the jungle canopy. Eventually Hobo debouched from our tunnel in the foliage into an area of tall grasses. We approached a faded sign with the legend "General Electric", presumably a singularly uninspired name for some bygone corporation. We followed a narrow path to the right until we approached a concentration of low-rise masonry and glass buildings. The grasses around these buildings were crudely cut to thigh height, probably by the sickle bar of a farm tractor. This wasn't pretty, but it was adequate lawn care to protect the structures from damage by encroaching greenery.

We were on the grounds of an old research laboratory complex that was home to one of the most colorful characters in Morrisbourg. Living here by himself was a crotchety old man named Melvin the Nerd, whatever "nerd" means. It is not in my Webster's. I do not know when Melvin arrived in town. Perhaps he was here even before I was born. I became aware of his existence a few years into my proprietorship of Morrisbourg. The very day a new immigrant had opened a well-stocked general store, Melvin showed up to trade for supplies. He must have known about the new store but I don't know how.

Melvin is an electronics genius. His skills are a valuable rarity in today's world. Processors and computers are not what they used to be. The best of the new ones are scarcely better than the old Pentiums from the turn of the century. Our marginal and fragile communications network means the internet just barely operates. Usually, connections are disrupted before one accomplishes anything useful. Melvin, however, is wired (and capable of wiring) like few other people on earth. He has salvaged superb equipment and has access to a vast library of data. He uses his retained programming skills to full advantage.

Melvin earns money by distributing news and entertainment locally from satellite broadcasts. Many satellites have lasted far beyond their designed operational lifetimes. This is fortunate since they cannot be replaced. Global communications are destined to deteriorate seriously over the next several years as the surviving links wear out. Perhaps in a decade or two earthside industry will have recovered enough to reverse the slide. We will not be returning to space anytime soon though. We will have to rely on new line-of-sight relay towers, cables, and short wave radio.

Powerful diesel generators hummed loudly from a small concrete block building. There probably was enough diesel fuel stored in tanks on site to meet Melvin's lifetime needs. There is plenty of petroleum to supply earth's tiny population, of course, but distribution is a problem.

One building in particular bristled with radio towers, microwave transmitters, and satellite dishes tilted up toward objects in geostationary orbit. Fans whirred audibly on huge air-conditioners set inside cubes with concrete sides and a steel grid top. This was Melvin's primary lair. He was home.

I replaced Hobo's bridle with a halter and tied her loosely enough to let her graze. As I approached the building, a TV camera above the door followed my movements. I was still six feet from the door when a speaker shouted. "Go away! I'm busy!"

I closed the distance and spoke into an intercom set in the wall. "I'm George Custer and I need to speak to you."

"I don't care if you are Emperor of Tibet. Go away!"

"This is about the Firecracker. It wasn't an accident."

"I know that, you idiot!"

"There will be another one unless you help me."

"So what?"

"The second one will be a whole lot closer. What do you think the electromagnetic pulse from the explosion will do to your equipment?"

Actually, the next explosion will be so close that EMP need hardly concern us, but I intuited that Melvin would rather die than live without his computers. Threatening his machines was more effective than threatening him.

Nearly a full minute of silence passed. Then an electric lock unbolted with a loud snap. I opened the door and walked down a long hallway. It was illuminated by a single fluorescent light. Melvin had given me no interior directions but a camera blinked a red light at me from above double-hung steel doors at the end of the hall. This looked promising.

I pushed through the doors. The large room on the other side was darker than expected. Most of the light came from display panels. The room was crammed with mainframes and PCs. Wires interconnected across the floor in a spaghetti tangle. Active screens displayed a bewildering variety of data and images. One showed a real-time weather satellite image. Another played the *I Love Lucy* episode where she misses her ocean liner.

Melvin sat at a desk. Disconcertingly he wore only a pair of shorts. He was a bald, skinny old man with bulbous joints and wisps of white hair on his chest. A virtual reality helmet lay on the blotter in front of him.

"Don't you politicians know how to do anything but blow things up?" he snapped.

"No. We can't even do that without help from fellows like you. That's why I'm here. What do you know about computers for aiming ballistic missiles?"

Melvin intently assessed me carefully before answering. At last he replied with the overloud annoyance of a man who has been bothered with a question beneath the dignity of his talents.

"Simple machines. Electronic morons. Ballistic principles are very basic even with the Coriolis effect and gravitational anomalies thrown in. There are a lot of numbers but any half-wit can add them up."

"Could I bug such a machine so that it displays one set of target coordinates to the operator, while it actually sends the missile somewhere else entirely?"

He assessed me again and answered more quietly, "It will display anything you tell it to display. The machine doesn't care. Access to the program should not be much of a problem assuming you actually get to sit at the console. Precisely because only authorized people use weapons systems, the security on the electronics typically is amazingly rudimentary. What's your game?"

"Do you really want to know?"

"Am I one of your targets?"

"No."

"Then, no, I don't really care. I do need to know what missile you want to monkey with."

"Minuteman VI"

Melvin nodded.

"Of course. There is a good chance most of them are operational: solid fuel and self-contained power system. The fuel cells may not even need recharging. The Firecracker was one?"

"Yes, I think so."

"Where did the other two warheads go?" Melvin asked.

"I don't know. Makes one wonder, doesn't it?"

Melvin squinted at me.

"OK, maybe I should care about this. One, can you get to all of the ballistic computers and, two, what are your targets?"

"One, I hope so, and, two, anyplace harmless. I don't want to destroy anything except the missiles themselves."

"Then why not just dynamite them inside the silos?"

"There are 500 missiles and I don't know exactly where they are. I do know where the control rooms are."

"Dynamite them."

"That would leave the missiles intact. Could you jury rig some way to fire one off if it were disconnected from its control room?"

"Of course."

"Maybe someone else can too. Besides, if I'm caught blatantly destroying a control room, my opponents will launch whatever they have left from the remaining facilities. I prefer a more insidious and less noticeable sabotage. If I'm simply caught inside a control room, I have a chance to make up some credible lie about what I am doing there. Lying is a politician's skill too."

"Agreed."

"If I'm not caught, then they'll have only blanks to shoot whether they get trigger happy or not."

"Who are they?"

"You wouldn't believe me if I told you."

"And no doubt with good reason."

I shrugged. "By the way, it would be best not to mention this to anyone."

"What about the police or the army?"

"Especially the police or the army."

"You want me to trust you."

"Yes."

"And you trust me."

"Yes."

Melvin smiled. "How quaint. Very well. I don't expect to see you again anyway. Say hello to your charming opponent for me."

"You know who that is?"

"I think so. It makes a human kind of sense — which in turn explains why I dislike humankind. Don't tell me though. If I'm wrong the truth must be even more disappointingly banal. Okay,

I'm going to make a CD for you that can be run on each targeting computer. It will lock in target coordinates on the control rooms themselves. The control room terminals will display any target the operator wishes, but the missiles aren't going anyplace other than right at him. Any launch will be an act of self-destruction. Do you like that idea?"

"Yes."

"Do you have those coordinates with you?"

"Yes. I mean we can work them out from the information I have."

"You are making me work Mr. Custer. I expect you to be caught, so I recommend a red herring. I will include on the CD a simple block on the firing controls that should be easy for any mildly competent person to fix. That way anyone suspecting you of sabotage will look no further.

"Good thinking."

Melvin was insulted by my praise. "I'm glad you approve," he said with annoyance.

"Hey, why not just set detonation at a high altitude so it doesn't hurt anyone on the ground — not even the people who launched?"

Melvin was shocked at the suggestion. "A high altitude air burst would damage the satellites."

"Ah yes. Of course."

Still visibly shaken by my reckless suggestion, Melvin added, "Let me call up some data about precisely what machines we are dealing with so I can glitch them appropriately. Then I want you to leave me alone."

Somehow it didn't surprise me he would have ample data available to him on Minuteman VI equipment.

Melvin stood up and walked to an oversized flat screen computer terminal. Despite his hunched posture he moved spryly.

While he fussed with search programs I couldn't resist a quick peek in the VR helmet. A very graphic porn program was in progress. Melvin knew what I was doing even though he didn't look.

"Don't change any of the settings!" he growled.

INTERRUPTION OF JOURNAL:

AENEAS CUSTER: George wrote the above pages in a notebook that he left in the safe at home. I found them a couple months after I got back. The rest of the journal that I'll read to you now was written in a small leather bound book that he kept tied to his belt. I'll explain how I came into possession of that in due time.

THE JOURNAL OF GEORGE CUSTER PART III—

Captain Le Clerc, retired, rents an apartment on the fourth floor of 30 Central Park South in New York City. The elevators in the building are not on line. Ever since I climbed the Washington Monument during the Auroran War I have hated stairs. Aeneas sat outside on a park bench while I trudged up to the fourth floor and banged on the door of 4A.

Le Clerc opened the door as far as the chain lock would allow. Even through this crack I could see that he was unshaven, his clothes were dirty, and he was getting a paunch. His breath smelled of banana wine.

Le Clerc had not advanced in rank in the 15 years he had remained in the navy after the last time we met. I do not know whether the deterioration in his personal habits was caused by his stalled career or vice versa. I do know I feared my visit was a big mistake.

"Do I know you, sir?"

"Yes. You expressed your intent to shoot me, and you said you would give me a medal. You didn't follow through on either promise."

"George!"

The door slammed shut. Le Clerc unlatched the chain and flung the door open so that it banged against the doorstop. Le Clerc grabbed my hand and shook it hard. He pulled me inside. The apartment was messy. It was not yet filthy, but seemed well on the road to that condition. The view out the window of the park, even in its overgrown state, was beautiful.

"I've meant to visit you a hundred times over the years, but I didn't want to impose on a big shot governor."

"Ex-governor. I introduced elections to Morrisbourg and right away the people voted me out of office."

"Excellent! That restores my faith in democracy! Come, have a drink."

"Thank you. Maurice, but this isn't just a social call."

He grimaced at my use of his first name.

"I need your help," I stated flatly.

"I'm a retired man on a scandalously small pension, but what I have is yours. Our action together in DC made my career and broke it on the same day. That has to count for something. What do you need?"

"I need your professional help. Ulysses is back."

"Nonsense. He was killed when my gunners shelled the Washington Monument."

"Apparently they missed."

Maurice waved his hand dismissively and poured himself another glass of wine. He did not pour one for me.

"Absurd! They blew off the top 20 meters. He couldn't have gotten out of there. You were on the stairway below and he didn't run by you, did he? Hell, you were nearly killed by the debris yourself. Besides, George, even if he did escape, which he didn't, he would be an old man. How much harm could he do?"

"He isn't much older than we are."

"That's what I mean. Assume for the sake of argument the old geezer does stir up the Aurorans again. Why come to me? The military can handle it. Zede, my old ensign, commands the *La Salle*, I think. I'm retired."

"It's not the Aurorans. And what do you mean by old geezer? I'm no geezer. I still can be dangerous: on purpose, I mean, and to someone other than myself. So can Johnston. Besides, you don't need to be an athlete to push a button."

"What are you talking about, George?"

"The Firecracker."

"You think he set that off?"

Le Clerc plainly thought I had developed paranoid dementia in my old age.

"He wrote me a note. He has more nukes, Maurice."

"A note?" For the first time Le Clerc considered the possibility I was right.

"Merde! Have you notified anyone? If this is true, let's call the Defense Ministry. We'll take him out for good this time! Where is he?"

Le Clerc's health appeared to improve as he focused on a new military objective.

"No I haven't notified anyone but you, and I'm taking an enormous risk doing even that. He wants just me and Aeneas. I think I can get away with bending his conditions enough to bring you, but I'm sure any attack on him by armed forces would provoke nuclear retaliation."

"George, this doesn't concern only you. The government needs to be told right away."

"No! He may have agents in Quebec, maybe even in the

Defense Ministry. I've underestimated this man before. I don't want to do it again. We can't afford to take that risk."

"So what do you suggest we do? Wag a disapproving finger at him?"

"I have a plan."

"You have a plan for countering a nuclear-armed crackpot. All by yourself?"

"No. You can help."

"Just the two of us."

"And Aeneas. Three of us don't look very threatening.

Besides, I don't think he will harm Aeneas if he can avoid it."

"The three of us don't look very threatening for a good reason, George. What is this plan? It doesn't involve lizards in elevators, does it?"

I regretted having told him that old story.

"No lizards. I can't tell you everything yet. I'm sorry, but you seem too eager to go running to the authorities. I'll tell you this much though. I think I know where Ulysses is. Maybe we can hijack one of his own warheads and drop it on top of him."

"I like the sound of that, but I'm a little concerned that he might shoot first. Look, if you are right about any of this, we need to plan a real military strike instead of some half-baked commando raid by two old fogies and a kid."

"Then he definitely will shoot first. We don't want that, do we? I mean to deal with this situation in my own way, with or without your help."

"Suppose I make a phone call and have you arrested and interrogated in the interest of national security?"

"Then we all vanish in a thermonuclear fireball. Even if Ulysses does not have spies watching me he gave me a time limit by which I must surrender myself to him."

"Or he nukes Quebec."

"Yes."

"He rates you rather highly."

"Yes."

Le Clerc sat on the sofa and considered what he had heard. After a few minutes he relaxed and sat back with a skeptical smile on his lips.

"OK, I'll go along with you. For one thing you are wrong about all this. I'm sure of it. You are gullible and I am embarrassed to have been caught up in your ridiculous alarmism even for a moment. I plead a mind befuddled by wine as my excuse. What is your excuse, George?"

"This is not a joke."

"Yes it is, and you are the butt of it. Someone is playing a hoax. Yes, it must be. Someone took advantage of the Firecracker to play a big joke on you. Ulysses simply can't be alive. He can't be. But my life has been boring lately anyway. I've been vegetating."

He swigged more Old Yeller, sighed and swirled the wine in his glass.

"Or fermenting."

"Wise ass!" Le Clerc retorted as he put down the glass. "All right. I'll go on a camping trip with you if you are paying the bills."

"I am."

"Fine. And a camping trip is all it will be, George.
Or is it a sailing trip? This time you're the skipper.
Where do we go and what do we do? Back to DC?"

"No."

Le Clerc's analysis had shaken my confidence more than I let on. Was I in fact the butt of a practical joke? If so, the writer of the note had to know about the coded document. Perhaps some Aurorans did know about it. Any veteran of that war had reason to hate me. Perhaps I was totally off base and the note had nothing to do with the document at all. Maybe the "north by northwest" in the note referred only to High Point, New Jersey. What if I traveled all the way to South Dakota only to discover there were no control rooms at the locations I had determined. What if I was wrong about everything? I disguised my doubts.

"I can't tell you where we are going yet," I said firmly, "but we'll spend time both on land and water."

"I see." Le Clerc looked genuinely amused.

"Our intermediate stop, though, is Montreal. You'll find our trip nostalgic."

"I'm from Drummondville."

"That's not what I mean. We'll be recreating high old times."

INTERRUPTION OF JOURNAL:

AENEAS CUSTER: There is a gap in the narrative here. I should fill it.

After a brief stay in New York, Le Clerc, George and myself took a steamer up the Hudson. There was a short portage to Lake George. The next boat took us to the northern tip of Lake Champlain. They told me I wouldn't get seasick on a lake but my stomach disagreed. I spent most of the trip leaning over rails while surrendering my breakfast. Then we took a shuttle down some other river to the St. Lawrence. We got in yet another boat, and when we arrived in Montreal I needed to be held up under each arm in order to get off the boat. I was so nauseated I don't remember how we got from the docks to the hotel. George and Maurice left me there. I slept for 12 hours.

THE JOURNAL OF GEORGE CUSTER PART III—

Montreal is a subtropical paradise. Palm trees line the streets. The climate is much like that of Miami a century ago, although art deco and pastels have not taken hold. The metropolitan area is home to an astonishing 50,000 people. This makes it second largest city in the world. Only Llasa in Tibet is bigger. Outside the city is an industrial park that for some reason is called Expo. Our first objective was a factory located there.

Inside a large geodesic dome were the offices, warehouse, and assembly plant of *Dirigeable Fabrique Nordique*, manufacturer of ultralight airships including the one that had given Le Clerc and myself such good service over DC.

The company had not been a financial success despite the expertise and dogged persistence of the owners. The Defense Ministry had purchased a few of the craft for reconnaissance and VIP travel but the Auroran War showed that airships were vulnerable to ground fire. Storms were a major concern for potential commercial buyers. Bad weather can handle airships roughly. There also was a problem with limited cargo and passenger capacity. A few well-publicized disasters scared off buyers too. At the time of our arrival *DFN* had entered "reorganization" in order to hold off creditors. This was one step from full bankruptcy.

The owners' names are Jacques and Charlotte Le Pen. They are a bitter middle-aged couple. They live in the dome amid a huge jumble of airship parts. Despite incessant bickering, the two are inseparable. Perhaps only unquestioned spousal commitment makes such sparring possible. It would put an end to any less secure relationship. The source of the bitterness, unsurprisingly, is the financial strain produced by the crippled business.

Manufacturing continued on the site, albeit slowly. Two airships were complete but unsold and uninflated. These were stored in a large tent outside the dome. One more was under construction.

The peculiarities of company financing require that new airships be built as security for any further draws on the sole remaining line of credit. Without these draws the Le Pens would have no money on which to live. Of course, without sales this only deepens their debt. Enough spare parts are on hand to build two additional craft. After that the Le Pens will need new customers or their business will go under.

After all my years in politics I still don't speak more than a little French. This may be why I am unsuccessful in politics. In any event, I needed Le Clerc to serve as translator. I rely on his account of the conversation in the dome.

For reasons best known to himself, Le Clerc chose that day to wear his old military uniform even though it was too tight. Right from the start the uniform annoyed Charlotte who was angry at the military's reluctance to place new orders. The anger escalated to fury when she recognized our names.

"You two get out of here!"

"Why? We want to purchase one of the blimps."

"Do you have 400,000 francs?" asked Jacques.

I understood the gist of that sentence. "Terms," I prompted Le Clerc.

Charlotte began to shout again, this time at her husband.

"Never mind whether they have it or not, Jacques!

We're not selling to them!"

She spun on her heel, stuck her finger at Le Clerc's nose, and declared, "You are the reason for all our hardships!"

"Why?"

"'Why?' After that debacle of yours in Washington the navy canceled a dozen orders. The army canceled two more!"

"I was hoping for terms on the 400,000 francs," Le Clerc answered Jacques. To Charlotte he explained, "Flaming the blimp wasn't our idea. That was in combat. Besides, weren't there a couple of crashes other than ours?"

She scowled and turned her back. Jacques answered for her.

"Yes, yes. Just after you swam in the Potomac an army craft was hit by lightning while tethered to a steel pole a few miles from here. We warned them to keep it in a hanger in bad weather. That was pure carelessness on their part. It made headlines anyway. It was an election year so the newspaper editorials made a fuss about taxes. They called our airships a dangerous waste of taxpayer money. That's a lie, of course. Airships are the best investment the military can make. The truth didn't stop the politicians from canceling orders. For 15 years we have had to scrape by, mostly on private sales."

Le Clerc remembered something else. "Didn't one go missing some years back too? Some high profile fellow was on board."

"Yes, Quebec still owes us money on that one. A politician, named Delacroix, took a new experimental model on some secret mission and never came back. He said the government would pay the bill. His party had just won re-election so I had every reason to believe him. It was the biggest ship we ever built: over 30 meters. It cost us a fortune."

"I told him to get paid up front!" Charlotte interjected. Jacques ignored her.

I understood little of this at the time, but the name Delacroix caught my ear.

"Wasn't Delacroix the foreign minister who disappeared in one of their blimps years ago?" I asked Le Clerc. "Ask them more about that."

"Tell me more about the foreign minister," he requested dutifully.

"Well, he wasn't the foreign minister then. He had held that post the previous time the Conservatives were in power. He told me he was a 'special envoy.' After he disappeared I tried to bill the Treasury for the airship. The folks there actually laughed at me. They told me Delacroix was on the outs with the new PM. They said he had no connection with the Administration at all. They said they knew nothing about any special envoy or any airship or any mission. I'm sure this is a lie. I think he was involved in some secret game that turned out badly — maybe some spy thing over Canada or something. Whatever it was, the government denied knowing anything about it. Bastards. I voted Conservative too!"

"I warned him about that," harrumphed Charlotte.

"I'm PQ myself, Madame," said Le Clerc ingratiatingly.

"That doesn't win you any points with me!" she snapped back.

"Was Delacroix alone when he flew away?"

"No, but I didn't meet his traveling companion. They boarded and left at night. Anyway, his disappearance made the papers. Once again a lot of buyers were scared off. They still are after all these years.

"We hoped to win our reputation back with our new Z16 model this year," Jacques continued. "Then some fools at the aerial billboard company bought one and didn't hanger it during the heavy winds last month. It was destroyed on the ground. No one was hurt. Still, I don't know if we'll ever sell another one now."

"We want to buy one."

"No."

"Good." Charlotte nodded approval at her husband.

"Just take one," Jacques offered.

"What? Jacques are you insane?"

"No, I'm not. We are going bankrupt anyway. This is a chance to turn things around."

"You're crazy! Hopeless! I give up on you!" Charlotte stormed off to her office where she banged drawers loudly and slammed items on her desktop.

Jacques turned his attention back to Le Clerc. "Take the craft and bring it back safely. Since you are responsible for our bad publicity in the first place you can undo some of the damage. If you endorse the machine when you get back it will help us."

"OK, that's a deal, but it may be a long trip."

"The longer the better. Just bring it back."

"Tell him we need acetylene and dynamite," I prompted.

Le Clerc looked exasperated at this new demand but he translated it. Le Pen frowned, but he answered "I'll see what I can do."

Le Clerc was hugely proud of himself for the deal he had negotiated. After he bragged about it to me I praised his skills. I understood, though, that the terms of the deal had been Le Pen's idea entirely.

More exciting to me than our free airship lease was what Le Clerc told me about Delacroix. Two decades back Ulysses had bribed this same Foreign Minister Delacroix with a salvaged Monet. That was how Ulysses had learned in advance of Quebec's annexation of New York. It all fit together. Ulysses and Delacroix probably flew to South Dakota together and built up whatever little army they could. Is it possible their army still numbers only two? Could we be that lucky?

It took two days for Le Pen to ready the new Z16 craft for us. During that time I accompanied Le Clerc to every bar in Montreal. I was afraid to leave him alone lest he be overcome again by the urge to inform the authorities of our mission. He didn't. He didn't believe there was a mission and he was having far too good a time to reconsider the matter.

On our last night, ten vodkas and a series of lap dances by a chokingly beautiful stripper put Le Clerc in an amorous mood. After we were thrown out of the bar, we were approached by a young lady on the street. Despite my protestations he readily agreed to her proposal. I waited in the brothel's anteroom while Le Clerc and the object of his affection attended to their business upstairs. I meekly brushed away offers from the lady's co-workers by explaining I was broke. This was untrue, but I didn't want Le Clerc to slip away from me while I was preoccupied.

There was no risk of this as it turned out. After a half-hour Le Clerc's date, whose name was Mona, came downstairs to ask for my help. Maurice had passed out on the bed. Mona helped me get him dressed. She was pretty nice about it. He must have tipped her well. We roused him sufficiently to get him to the door with Mona under his left arm and me under the right. Once on the street I was on my own. I struggled to hold him up as he staggered all the way back to the hotel room. There Aeneas helped me guide him to a bed on which Maurice collapsed face forward.

"That brand of perfume doesn't become either of you," was Aeneas' only comment. He went back to reading his book.

When daylight came a few hours later we received a call from Jacques Le Pen. The airship was ready and waiting for us at the airport. Le Pen had flown it to there on a test run from the Expo grounds.

Aeneas and I pulled an unshaven and aromatic Le Clerc from the bed. For a French chauvinist he displayed an admirable command of Anglo-Saxon. He looked miserable during our horse-drawn taxi ride to the airport. His eyes stayed shut and he intermittently heaved. Before long we pulled up beneath the silver-colored machine.

The airship was larger than the one I had flown in DC but was not the behemoth that Delacroix had taken. This one measured 10 meters and cruised on two small diesel turbine engines that boasted a phenomenal range. Le Pen insisted they could take us all the way to the Pacific. The engine propellers were cased in aluminum shrouds. One was located on each side of the gondola and could pivot on an axle to provide directional thrust. This allowed it to hover and land almost anywhere, even without a ground crew. The craft was ideal for exploring the great empty spaces of the West. The Z16 even had its own electrolysis kit to replenish lost hydrogen. The Le Pens had remained wedded to hydrogen despite its fiery history. This was not entirely their choice: helium had become a rare and expensive commodity.

Aeneas looked as appalled as Maurice looked sick. Perhaps I should have warned him about the airship, but I wanted it to be a surprise. It was. Given his obvious dread, he deserves some credit for having climbed into the gondola after me. While he was doing it, he had the expression of a man climbing the gallows.

Le Clerc pulled himself in wearily. Still convinced I was chasing fairies, he viewed the whole expedition as a sightseeing trip. He awaited the opportunity to say, "I told you so," and to wax smug on the journey back home.

Melvin had given me a few electronic navigation aids. I unpacked these carefully. As Le Clerc sat back comfortably as was possible with a hangover of those dimensions, I started the engines and Le Pen released the lines. We rose smoothly into the balmy skies of Montreal. Within half an hour Aeneas was enjoying himself. Le Clerc, on the other hand, looked even sicker. He deserves credit too because I had presumed it beyond his capacity to look worse.

The skies were not balmy for long. Ominous clouds loomed ahead and the wind began to pick up. Soon water drops obscured the windshield. The windshield wipers were powered by a hand crank. This was reliable but tiresome. It hardly mattered anyway because the clouds themselves enveloped us. We were flying blind, and our compass was finicky. Without the receivers given to me by Melvin we would have gone far off course. These receivers picked up signals from the bare bones remains of the Global Positioning System. They were enough to provide our position within ten or fifteen meters.

Over Lake Ontario the weather turned from harsh to brutal. Lake Erie was even worse. We were buffeted by heavy winds and drenched by rain driving through the unglazed side windows of the gondola. Lightning flashed from cloud to cloud around us. Through all this Le Clerc began slowly to recover, but Aeneas grew ill again.

INTERRUPTION OF JOURNAL:

AENEAS CUSTER: This is an understatement of breathtaking enormity.

THE JOURNAL OF GEORGE CUSTER PART III—

Moisture from the lakes was the main cause of our problems. It would have been shorter to fly over southern Ontario and the weather might have been better, but the Canadians are unpredictable. There aren't many of them but they are fiercely determined to keep Quebec at bay. At the very least they would have complained formally to Quebec. I didn't welcome the thought of creating a diplomatic incident with its attendant publicity. At worst they might have shot us out of the sky.

The buffeting precipitated a potentially serious accident. The airship was hit by a particularly strong gust and lurched sideways. Our supply trunk of food and water strapped atop the fuel tanks broke free and plunged out of the starboard window.

Le Clerc recommended that we turn back. I was sorely tempted to do so, but the deadline in the note dissuaded me. There was no guarantee of calmer weather before our time ran out. I insisted we persevere. Le Clerc held up his hands in an "as you wish" gesture. He probably didn't want to admit fear. Male pride has its uses and, when it is my own, its drawbacks. Aeneas was in no condition to make any comment.

Whether or not my decision was wise, we survived it. At length the rain diminished and the winds eased. We neared the Lower Peninsula of Michigan. We were still flying blind. For hundreds of miles we remained in a thick fog that prevented sightseeing of the land below. It didn't dissipate until we were over Lake Michigan. Despite the shaking we had endured I was pleased with our progress. Aeneas began to look as though he felt better again. By the time the skyline of Chicago loomed into view the sky was a crystal blue.

When at a loss for words one has a tendency to announce the obvious. "I think we are through the worst of it," I opined.

"If you are referring to rain I have to agree," replied Le Clerc, "but we still are out of food and water."

"That's a pretty big quantity of water underneath us. We should be able to replace the rest of our supplies in the city."

"It's supposed to be empty."

"Of people, yes, but they must have left stuff behind."

"Okay. Where do we shop?"

"State Street I suppose. The old travel catalogues from before the end say it was a pedestrian mall."

"Good. I hate traffic."

As the Z16 nosed over Lake Shore Drive we could see that drifting sand had infiltrated the city. Dunes were heaped up on the western side of buildings, cars, and other obstructions. The searing sun had bleached everything pale resulting in an odd art deco effect. There was no sign of life. The silence of big empty cities always has disturbed me. Chicago was a very big one.

"Think there will be a line at the checkout counter?" asked Le Clerc.

"Won't those stores already have been totally ransacked?" asked Aeneas more seriously. He had a point. The urban centers were heavily looted as the economy broke down and deliveries of new goods stopped.

INTERRUPTION OF JOURNAL:

AENEAS CUSTER: George needn't have been so surprised that I had a point, I have been known to have one occasionally."

JUDGE JEANIE: This is not one of those occasions. Please get on with it.

THE JOURNAL OF GEORGE CUSTER PART III—

"Maybe so, but it is worth a look. If the shelves are empty we can head out to the suburbs. There is always something to be found out there."

We crossed over Michigan Avenue and cruised past the John Hancock building. The building looked intact but in this sun the interior must have been an oven. We turned north and passed the watertower that survived the famous fire and survives still. Just ahead of us was Watertower Place, a multi-story indoor shopping mall.

"Let's give it a shot," I proposed.

The directional thrust of our turbines allowed surprisingly effective control. A typical airship actually needs to be caught on the fly by a fairly sizable ground crew. Except in bad winds we didn't need anyone. We could alight wherever we chose. We chose to hover above the street.

I tossed a grapple hook to a nearby lamppost. It was a lucky toss. The hook wrapped around the pole and secured us. I tossed another rope over the side and lowered myself to the street.

"I'll be right back if the stores already have been picked clean!" I shouted.

A brief gust blew sand in my eyes and face. It was difficult to resist rubbing my eyes, even though doing so risked scratching them. One of the doors to the mall was wedged open by a pile of sand. Most of the windows were badly shattered and the sun's rays glinted off the broken glass. The ground level looked as though it had been bombed. I walked up an immobilized escalator. A Goodie Chocolate outlet was on my right, but the shelves were empty. All of the clothing stores had some stock on the racks and even more on the floor. I spotted a sporting goods store and picked up some large thermos containers. We would need them for water. There wasn't any store of a type that would carry canned food. Besides, something about the mall gave me the willies.

I hurried back to the airship, tied the rope from the gondola around my waist, and climbed the lamppost in order to release the grapple. This was harder than I expected. After some struggle the grapple hook broke free. The airship immediately floated away and pulled me off the lamppost.

"Somebody grab the controls before we drift into a building!" I shouted while dangling from the rope. Le Clerc steadied us as Aeneas helped pull me on board.

"Where to next?" asked Aeneas.

This near accident worried me. I realized a little carelessness could strand us permanently. I managed to control my temper and my fear.

"Lake Michigan I guess. The water should be pretty clean. No one is dumping sewage in it anymore. Then let's look for a mall outside of town. One with a supermarket."

A gentle wind helped blow us south toward two towers that looked like giant corncobs. I tried seriously to admire the pale orange thing that stands in front of City Hall. With all due respect to Picasso, the sculpture is ugly. Le Clerc gently revved the engines and turned us toward the lake. We hovered over Grant Park. This time I grappled us to a fountain. The fountain was dry.

If there is anything more eerie than the streets of a deserted city it is a park in a deserted city. One almost hears echoes of children, dogs, lovers and dope dealers. I instinctively looked for traffic before crossing Lakeshore

Drive to Lake Michigan. I quickly filled our containers in the lake and lugged them back.

While standing on the fountain handing up containers to Aeneas in the gondola I noticed that the park had ceased to be deserted. Twenty wild men emerged from the parking garage beneath the park. They were naked except for green paint and spears. They seemed upset.

"Machine! Machine!" they shouted. Then they charged waving spears over their heads.

They apparently had an eco-message of some sort for us. They were sincere about it too. However, as the time was not auspicious for discussing such matters, I unhooked the blimp and we took our leave.

INTERRUPTION OF JOURNAL:

AENEAS CUSTER: Your Honors, George's understated bravado seriously misrepresents this scene. George yelled "Oh shit!" and clawed unsuccessfully at the rope knots. I'll give him credit for pausing long enough to toss two full thermos jugs into the gondola before pulling out a knife and cutting the taught grapple line. He managed to hold his grip on it somehow while shouting "GO! Get the hell out of here! NOW! Shit! Shit!"

Le Clerc took him at his word and throttled the engine hard. George swung below us as we accelerated away from the park. He owed his survival only to the bad aim of the green people. One fellow was probably only 5 meters away when he tossed his spear, but he missed George by several centimeters. George several times swung dangerously close to the whirring propellers. Had the rope been slung in front of them instead of behind, he might have gotten sucked in. By the time we pulled George inside he was drenched in sweat and shaking. He couldn't speak for ten minutes. He was hardly nonchalant.

HIRISAWA: You judge harshly, Mr. Custer. That is my prerogative.

AENEAS CUSTER: I apologize for encroaching upon it.

HIRISAWA: Pardoned.

AENEAS CUSTER: A full pardon?"

HIRISAWA: No.

PROUDFOOT: Your Honor, I object to the tone of levity in these proceedings. We are here to consider crimes that are truly unspeakable.

HIRISAWA: They had better be speakable or the defendant will be released for your failure to state a cause of action.

PROUDFOOT: Your Honor…

HIRISAWA: And don't think for a minute that anyone on this panel takes murder less seriously for being able to smile in its face. Please do not attempt to correct our attitude again. Go on, Mr. Custer.

THE JOURNAL OF GEORGE CUSTER PART III—

We picked up altitude and speed as we passed the Sears Tower. Through a broken glass panel on the 90th floor I could see inside one of the business offices. The phone was off the hook and lying on a desk as though an administrative assistant had left momentarily to check a file.

I was surprised to notice a handgun in Le Clerc's belt. He must have pulled it from his luggage when the green people appeared. Gun laws are pretty liberal in Morrisbourg and other frontier regions, but in Old Quebec the restrictions on gun ownership are severe. Le Clerc's status as a member of the Reserve may have made it legal for him to carry the weapon to Montreal, but I doubt it. While fundamentally pleased no one was hurt in Chicago, I can't help but wonder why he didn't shoot at the wild men when the spears were flying my way. Perhaps he was too occupied at the controls. I hope so anyway.

About 15 miles west of downtown we spotted a Food Lion in the suburb of Elmhurst. I was reasonably sure that this time we truly were in a desolate region.

We lowered the blimp down over a sand-covered parking lot and once again tied up to a lamppost. This time we were lucky. Ample stocks of canned goods still lined the shelves. I also noticed the remains of a house neighboring the mall. After replenishing the food supply on the blimp, on a hunch I strolled over to the house. Sure enough the fill pipe for a heating oil tank stuck up from the sand in what had been the front lawn of the house. I removed my shirt and used it to insulate my hand from the searing hot metal. The lid came free. I removed my belt and used it as a dipstick. The tank was nearly full. Since #2 heating oil makes fine diesel fuel I signaled to Le Clerc to maneuver. the airship over my position. He did so. Aeneas dropped the fuel hose to me, and the on-board pumps did the rest.

With our tanks topped we left the metropolitan area behind. The Great American Desert stretched out ahead of us as far as we could see. The land below us was once America's breadbasket. Now it barely feeds a few lizards. The landscape below was not the brush filled desert one sees in old movies of the American West set in Nevada or southern Arizona. It resembled the old Sahara more.

After hours of glaring sunlight we approached a large trench in the sand. The once great Mississippi River was reduced to a wadi. Recently cut sharp edges in the sides testified to occasional sudden floods. On this day the only sign of dampness was a darker shade of brown near the centerline of the trench. The sky remained blue as the sun sank into the horizon, but the distant western sand grew pinkish. As the last piece of sun slipped out of sight, day turned to night almost as if someone had thrown a switch. The stars were as bright as I ever have seen them.

INTERRUPTION OF JOURNAL:

AENEAS CUSTER: Your Honors, several pages of entries are missing at this point. The lost entries covered the period of time we spent sabotaging Minuteman VI missiles. My guess is that George tore out the pages, which recorded these events as soon as we spotted some live South Dakotans. This was sensible. In the event we were taken prisoner, it would have been unwise to let our enemies know what we had done. It was even more unwise to reveal that we hadn't finished the job. Disposing of the journal entirely surely would have been the most sensible option of all, but I like George a little better for not doing it.

JUDGE JEANIE: Why didn't you finish the job disabling the missiles?

AENEAS CUSTER: The fact is, ma'am, we didn't have the time or the resources to visit all fifty sites. It was more difficult than you might think. Most of the control rooms were covered with sand. Even when we dug out an entrance, often we couldn't get in without an acetylene torch or dynamite or both. Therefore George chose to sabotage only the 10 sites closest to Mt. Rushmore. This task was monumental enough for the three of us. He gambled that Ulysses wouldn't travel any further from his home than necessary if he chose to initiate another launch.

JUDGE JEANIE: Big gamble.

AENEAS CUSTER: Yes, ma'am.
Le Clerc worked very hard with us through all this but he continued to argue that our trip was unnecessary and Ulysses was long since dead. However, he did agree we were doing something useful. It certainly didn't hurt the security of Quebec to render these missiles harmless regardless of Ulysses' condition. He argued less when one site showed clear evidence of recent tampering. One of the squadron's missiles had been launched.

"That could have been done in some test 60 years ago!" Le Clerc pronounced with a wave of the hand.

I don't think he believed his own words though. I think Le Clerc was convinced that George was right.

George never expressed any doubts to us, but he certainly looked relieved when the first control room was located where his directions said it would be. George's long shots usually came in. His gamble that the sites would be unguarded paid off too. This surprised me. It seemed a very unmilitary omission by an opponent who once took on and nearly defeated Quebec.

At each location George reprogrammed the targeting computers himself. He refused to let me or Le Clerc help. I didn't learn precisely what George did to the targeting systems until I read the notes George left in Morrisbourg about Melvin's CD. At bottom, Le Clerc must have trusted George. After all, as far as he could tell George in reality might have been targeting Montreal.

After sabotaging 99 missiles in this way we proceeded to the Black Hills. They are no longer black, if in fact they ever were. They are brown. As we neared our final objective Le Clerc grew agitated. He abandoned all pretext of skepticism. He said a nuclear threat to Quebec clearly existed regardless of who actually launched the Firecracker. He apologized to George for not taking him seriously, but then he shouted angrily about our minimalist response.

"The missiles must be destroyed!" he insisted. "Every last one of them! I don't understand why we don't bring in some help and do it! You are the one who said there is a deadly enemy out here. OK, you are right. Why are we flying straight into his trap? If we notify Quebec about this a real expeditionary force can hit all the missiles in very short order. You know where the control rooms are. Please, before it is too late, hand me whatever you removed from the radio and let's call home! Now!"

"That means you already tried to call home despite your explicit agreement to do things my way."

George removed the missing part from his pocket and tossed it over the side.

"Are you crazy?!"

"Probably. But I'm still right about this one. Listen, Maurice," explained George quietly. "Ulysses only has to fire one missile to wreak untold havoc. Just one. If he sees the whole airborne forces of Quebec coming after him he surely will try to do just that. Quebec doesn't have 40 airships. It has maybe six or seven and might be able to commandeer a few more. Their seizure of the control room sites will not be done in 'short order' in any sense that matters. Ulysses will have time to respond."

"He could respond to us too."

"He could, but I doubt he will. We are just one small aircraft. Probably we have eluded detection so far. Even if he has spotted us he probably doesn't think we are much of a threat. Our presence shouldn't set him off. I hope."

"Okay, George, how about this? Let's lob one of these missiles at Ulysses himself and eliminate his threat that way. You can do that, can't you? You once suggested it yourself as I recall."

"Well, it may yet come to that; but there is an old saying, 'If you plan on injuring your neighbor, better not do it by halves.'"

"More Nietzsche. Speak clearly."

"I'm only guessing about where Ulysses is. If we miss him he is sure to shoot back. Besides, I have some ethics even Ulysses doesn't. He once complained about that."

"Maybe he was right. Anyhow, what is unethical about shooting at this man?"

"What if he isn't alone? What if there is a town or village out here somewhere? I'm not going to launch a missile against what might be a civilian site. We don't know what we are up against yet."

"You are over-thinking. This is a time for action. If you must wallow in thought, though, change philosophers. Switch to DesCarte — or maybe La Rochefaucald if you must be a cynic. German philosophy didn't do the Germans any good. I'm pleading with you, Custer. Let's do a quick recon. You actually may be right about that if only to help us acquire the appropriate target. But then let us use that information to fire a missile that won't miss."

"We need to assess the situation thoroughly before we fire anything at anyone."

"Why did you bring me along when you fight me on everything?"

"Because you say the things out loud that I think to myself. The thought of nuking Johnston and his boys satisfies me too. But when I hear you voice it as a recommendation, I know it is right to reject the idea. You remove my doubts and make me feel better."

"Glad I'm such a comfort to you. So where are all the civilians whose noncombatant status we so ethically respect? All I've seen so far is sand. How can anyone live here?"

"I don't know. There may not be any civilians. There are people of some kind in the Black Hills somewhere though. I don't know how many. Maybe they live underground. Mount Rushmore is the reference point on my directions."

"Thank you for finally clueing me in."

"You are welcome. I suggest we start our search there." As we cleared a ridge, George sat back in his seat and sighed, "Or then again we can start the search here."

George pointed ahead toward a huge blackened area. As we passed overhead we could see that clumps of sand had been fused into glass.

"Wind Cave should be down there somewhere according to the map. Looks like someone used it for target practice."

Before long we came within sight of the Crazy Horse Monument. The rock sculpture was either wind damaged or deliberately modified.

"It looks almost like someone has been feminizing the features," I commented.

"Yes, it does," answered George pensively. The journal picks up again from this point.

THE JOURNAL OF GEORGE CUSTER PART III—

The faces of Mount Rushmore loomed ahead of us. They were painted with colors one expects to see only in comic strips. All of the complexions were shocking pink. Washington seemed to be wearing lipstick. Jefferson's hair was fiery red. Lincoln's black beard was streaked with gray. In spite of myself I laughed. I wondered idly if the eye colors were right. My laughter was curtailed by what floated below TR's chin. It was an airship: a big one. It too was painted. The paisley design looked fresh. Perhaps the paint job was added after the ship delivered the note to some mailbox near Morrisbourg. Surely that was how the note reached me.

At the base of the mountain were movements and dashes of color. As we neared them, the moving patches resolved themselves into camels and garishly dressed people.

"There are our civvies," I remarked.

Le Clerc grunted in response.

Some of the people pointed at us and shouted. Others jumped up and down and applauded like children. When we had closed to within 100 meters of the other airship, a tall white-robed young woman in its gondola waved to us with an air of authority. She directed us by arm movements to the east.

"What do we do?" asked Aeneas.

"We go east, I suppose."

As we veered to the east, smoke signals went up from Washington's noggin. Presumably an announcement of our approach had just gone out. It seemed unnecessary. We were hard to miss.

Soon we approached a cluttered outpost. Clusters of solar panels reflected brightly on the hillside. Their arrangement seemed artistic rather than industrially efficient. Their frames were painted, which gave them the appearance of mechanical flowers. Long rows of transparent plastic sheets stretched over flatter spots of ground; garden vegetables grew beneath them. I recognized this as a desert farming technique developed in the Middle East. The plastic forms a kind of flexible greenhouse that preserves moisture and controls sunlight. A handful of gardeners walked between the rows. In other spots canvass sunscreens were held up by poles. Beneath them were picnic tables. Several windmills churned in the light breeze. They supplied the site with mechanical power for pumps or for nighttime electric power generation.

I heard a click as Le Clerc chambered a round in his handgun. "Put the gun away, Maurice. I mean away, not just in your belt." Le Clerc shook his head, but he packed the pistol inside his duffel bag.

"I agree you are in command, but you are going about this all wrong," he advised.

"Opinion noted."

We hovered over a large sandy flat area next to a hill. The remains of lampposts and stretches of exposed curb revealed it to be an old parking lot. Out of a tunnel in the hillside suddenly emerged scores of young men and women with abominable fashion sense. Their clothes included sarongs, loincloths, bikinis, togas and gauze wraps. The fabrics were bright with painted flowers, stripes, and tie dyed patterns. The gardeners and picnickers joined them, and they all waved, applauded, laughed, and smiled.

"These folks don't look much like nuclear terrorists, do they?"

"I can't say I have met enough nuclear terrorists to judge."

Privately, I wondered how Ulysses possibly had related to these people. Something was wrong in my analysis of the situation.

"Where the hell are we?" Le Clerc asked.

"Beautiful Rushmore Cave."

"Is that an opinion?"

"No. According to the map that is actually the name of this place."

We lowered our craft slowly and dropped ropes over the side. The prancing throng below skillfully fielded the ropes as though they did it for a living. The gondola touched ground. Our new friends lashed the ropes tightly to four steel rings mounted in concrete posts. Probably this was an alternate port for the paisley airship.

"Let's go."

We three slid over the side and instantly were mobbed by attractive young men and women with leis. Despite the Hawaiian neckwear the ethnic mix was primarily Caucasian and Indian, probably Sioux, with a small sprinkling from other groups. This reflected the pre-disaster regional population. A rhythmic shouting began. "Custer! Custer!"

"They seem to know you. What's going on, George?" asked Le Clerc with deep suspicion.

"I honestly don't know."

"That's what you said in DC."

"I was telling the truth, wasn't I?"

"How should I know?"

We were picked up by our admirers and carried toward the tunnel entrance. Beside the opening a young man sat in a lotus position playing a strange string instrument. I believe it was a sitar, although I never have seen one before.

"Is Ulysses here?" I asked one of my bearers.

"Ulysses? No, of course not. You are joking with me, Custer. Mother is waiting for you. We all have been waiting a long time. The circle is complete and everything will be happy now."

The gardens were more impressive seen from the ground. Cannabis, tomatoes, grains, potatoes, beets, turnips, and yams grew under plastic. Dates and figs grew in the open. The gardens were served by a complex network of PVC pipes supplying drip irrigation. The pipes were tied together into a 20cm diameter main line that disappeared into the tunnel entrance. Inside it was mounted along one wall. A water source was surely somewhere in the cave.

We entered the tunnel, once the tourist entrance to Beautiful Rushmore Cave. It was wheelchair accessible. Multicolored party lights lit up the interior in a deliberately tawdry display. A naked couple made love by the wall with unashamed abandon. They glanced our way long enough to shout "Custer! Custer!" They returned to their passion after we passed. I noticed the couple copied the position of a couple in a mural above them. Other painted scenes on the rock walls were impossible to describe politely. Aeneas gawked at the couple and the paintings in a salaciously adolescent manner. I'll have to talk to him about that.

INTERRUPTION OF JOURNAL:

AENEAS CUSTER: And he leered like a dirty old man, your Honors. Give me a break.

THE JOURNAL OF GEORGE CUSTER PART III—

The temperature dropped as we walked. The subsurface of the earth is a constant 56 degrees Fahrenheit at modest depths. Perspiration cooled on my khakis. For the first time in years I actually felt chilly. It was wonderfully refreshing.

We entered an enormous cavity. This space, called simply the Big Room, was decorated by nature with baroque stalactites and stalagmites. The locals had added to nature by carving many of these rocks into playful statuary. A variety of lamps and colorful fabrics were strung from the ceiling. In the otherworldly light, children played and adults worked or relaxed in a friendly chaos. One woman was giving a puppet show to a mixed-age audience. The puppeteer made one of her figures call the other one George. The referenced puppet didn't look like me, however.

INTERRUPTION OF JOURNAL:

AENEAS CUSTER: Yes it did.

HIRISAWA: Mr. Custer…

THE JOURNAL OF GEORGE CUSTER PART III—

Elsewhere on the floor a man sat amidst a pile of cloth and sewed something that looked like a bra with a sunflower painted on each cup. I don't know for whom he intended it. Our arrival in the Big Room also interrupted an enthusiastic game of Twister.

Our bearers carried us into another passage and through a string bead curtain. The rest of our entourage hung back. The second room was smaller but still far from cramped. Leather living room furniture gave the space a homey appearance. Beyond was a bedroom set with what looked like a waterbed. Somehow this touch of domesticity was comforting.

At the far end of the room was a large chair or throne carved out of the rocks and covered with padding. Two scarcely dressed female guards, who would make any normal male eager to surrender, flanked the throne. They were armed with spears. The spears were the first weapons we had seen among our hosts. On the throne, clothed in a flowing white silken robe, sat Joelle. Even at 40 something she was stunning. A garland of flowers lay on her pale blonde hair that had yet to gray or darken.

"Hello George."

"Joelle."

"Hello boy."

"Say hello to your mother, Aeneas," I prodded.

"You're my mom?" Aeneas asked.

"The Mother is mother to us all," a pretty woman who had helped carry him answered.

"Yes, and it is Mother, not 'mom.' And who is this?"

Joelle gestured at Le Clerc.

"This is Maurice Le Clerc, he was captain of..."

"The *La Salle.* Yes I know who he is now and I remember what he did to me!" She stood up and shouted, "Why is he here!? I told you to come alone!" This display of anger clearly surprised the locals. Joelle caught herself. Her demeanor abruptly calmed. She sat down and continued in a normal voice. "No, don't answer that. Maybe it is for the best." Joelle smiled. "Everyone leave us please."

Our livery service left tittering and chattering. "You too," Joelle said to the guards. One guard looked surprised and hesitated as though to be sure she heard correctly. Joelle nodded. Both guards exited the chamber.

"You named him Aeneas?" Joelle asked me. "You have a dark sense of humor, George. It almost makes me suspect you are sharper than you appear to be, but the length of time it took you to get here argues against that conclusion. My people were beginning to doubt me about you, even though they didn't say so to my face. I nearly went and got you myself."

"Why didn't you make the directions clearer? Your letter was cryptic to say the least. It was your letter I presume."

"Because someone else could have read it, George. You were the only one who would know what it meant, I hoped."

"So where is Ulysses?"

"Ulysses? Why, he is still dead I suppose. You and the sailor boy here killed him in DC if you recall."

"But your note..."

"Said he was an honest man, not a live one."

"Very misleading, Joelle."

"Sue me." Joelle crinkled her nose cutely. This rarely is effective for a mature woman, but somehow it still worked for her. "You insult me, George. Ulysses! Please! Ulysses wouldn't have prevailed here even if he had escaped DC. His plans always were too big. He always over-reached himself."

"And you didn't?"

Joelle smiled again. "Not always. I don't mean to dismiss Johnston's abilities either. The man was intelligent and imaginative, so his plans always were worth a listen. They just needed to be implemented with a soft touch rather than with ham hands. For example, I wouldn't have attacked with rafts a town defended by a warship. While I give him credit for identifying the possibilities of this place he would have made hash of it."

"Whereas you have made a soufflé?"

"You had plenty of opportunity to do some baking with me. I can't believe that for 15 years you couldn't make sense of that document he left you about this place."

"You knew about the document?"

"How many times have I warned you that locks can be picked?"

I suspected Ulysses also explicitly told her about his plans for the Dakotas when they had their fling in New York, but I kept that thought to myself.

"Then you were the one who flew here with Delacroix. Right. I forgot that you once bribed him too."

"'Rewarded' is a more appropriate term than 'bribed' and 'repressed' is probably a more accurate one than 'forgot.' Do I still disturb your psyche that much, sweetheart?"

It was annoying that after all these years Joelle so easily could make me jealous. It was more annoying still that she knew it. There was no sense denying it.

"Yes. So where is Delacroix?"

"He had an accident during the flight."

"A fatal accident?"

"Yes."

"An accidental accident?"

"There are accidents and then there are accidents. This was one of the latter."

"Well, you seem to have done pretty well without him."

"Yes, thank you for noticing. I had good people and excellent resources."

"What resources? This is a desert."

"Yes, but the geology is very special, you see. Delacroix and I packed the right tools to exploit it."

"Explain."

"Well, to begin, the Black Hills are a really big granitic outcrop in the middle of an enormous doughnut of limestone. For the past several million years, water has drained off the granite into the limestone. The result is an elaborate ring of caverns laid out around the Hills almost like slashes on a clock face. There is enough water in the lower depths of the caverns to support irrigation on the surface. The caves also provide plenty of natural shelter. The desert sun offers a surplus of power for solar electric panels."

"And then there are the Minuteman missiles."

"So there are, but I don't want to talk about them right now."

"OK, then let's talk about all your admirers out there with the circus clothes. Where did they come from?"

"Natives. That was just luck. The caverns already were occupied when I got here. I had hoped to find maybe a few people so I wouldn't have to be a hermit, but I was amazed to find hundreds. There were scraggly bands of young people who lived on bats and lizards. Their lives were pretty awful. Short too. Boys from one cave would kill boys from another for their food and their girls. The population was diminishing. They were running out of food. They were desperate. They would have followed anyone who gave them hope."

"I once heard a similar story in West Virginia. Johnston's solution was fascism. You seem to have worked out something that at first glance is less brutal."

Le Clerc spoke up. "Less brutal? Have you forgotten the Firecracker already? And what about that fused glass we passed over some miles back? Do you think that was just target practice?"

"Quite right, Le Clerc," answered Joelle with equanimity. "I'm not ashamed of using force where force is needed. I'm pacific, not pacifistic. There is a time for gentleness and a time for ferocity. When I came here it was no time to be gentle. To my delight I had a huge windfall. My appearance in the sky was dramatic in any case; but I discovered the folks here were in superstitious awe of my married name. A lot of places around here are named after someone named Custer. The people seemed to think I was that person and I saw no reason to dissuade them."

"I noticed the place names. I'm sure Ulysses did too. He probably started to think about the potential of this area precisely because the name Custer caught his eye on a map."

"Maybe so. It never caught your eye, though, did it? Anyway, this aura around my identity meant my orders were followed with far more enthusiasm than would have been likely otherwise. I organized this one cave rapidly and took stock of the total situation in the Black Hills. I armed the boys here with the assault rifles that Delacroix had been kind enough to pack for us. We set out to take over the other caves."

"Very pacific," Le Clerc growled.

"I united these people, Le Clerc, and that has reduced violence. We put an end to anarchy."

"I haven't seen anyone with rifles," I observed.

"No, of course not. I took back the guns after unification. We don't need them anymore. This is a peaceful place. My people love me. I gave them a better life. In addition to assault rifles, Delacroix had packed seeds of crops from Quebec's agricultural labs that had been bred and engineered for desert environments. We planted them almost at once. The first year of my rule was pretty lean. We hunted and gathered what we could. Ever since the first harvest, however, the family has had more food than it needs. As you can see our crops do spectacularly well."

"Making the desert bloom is all very nice, but you had another option. You could have ferried the locals out a few at a time to Quebec," Le Clerc suggested. "That would have given them an even better life."

"My life would have been a jail cell, wouldn't it? As for the rest of the family, ask them if they want to leave. They prefer what they have here.

"Oh, at first we lacked some machinery and some finished goods, but the airship made it easy to scavenge those things. More than enough hardware and textiles are out there for the picking in the local ghost towns. On one of those forays after our first harvest we even discovered townspeople hanging on in Rapid City. They provided us reconditioned manufactured goods in exchange for fresh vegetables. That trade set us up with our electric power and furnished materials our mechanical needs."

"How many people live in Rapid City?"

"It doesn't matter. We don't need to trade with them now. We are self-sufficient. What we don't make ourselves we can scavenge.

"I saved these people, George. I really did. I saved them physically and spiritually."

"Spiritually? I hesitate to ask."

"Don't hesitate about that because you were a big help."

"How did I help?"

"I told them George Custer would come when they had advanced far enough along the path of enlightenment. They really think you are the Custer for whom everything is named around here. The 'Custer is coming' line had messianic value of surprising force. It helped me give them an ethos to live by and a communal sense of extended family."

"So you run some kind of cult."

"Call it what you wish."

"The Crazy Horse Monument is being reworked to look like you, isn't it?"

"I try not to interfere with artistic expression."

Le Clerc spoke up. "Unless that expression undermines you. Mademoiselle..."

"Try 'Madame', sir. George and I are married. But actually you can just call me Mother."

"Madame, I wonder if you could divert yourself from enlightening your people long enough to enlighten me."

"I'm not sure we have that much time left in our lives, but let us give it a try. What is your question?"

"Why did you set off a 200 kiloton explosion in the

Atlantic when a simple greeting card to your husband would have sufficed?"

"You should understand a show of force, Captain. I needed to bring George here with Aeneas. I also needed to deter him from attacking me. George is normally mild mannered and lazy. You are wrong, though, if you think it is safe to provoke him without scaring him sufficiently. I made that mistake twice before. The warhead gave me 'credibility' as they used to say in Cold War days. I figured it would scare him enough to do what I ordered without a fight."

"It seems excessive."

"It worked. Besides, there was a matter of timing. I had two enemies in South Dakota who needed to be removed just then. The Minuteman had three warheads and it seemed a shame to waste the third. In a way, George was a target of opportunity. Perhaps I would have been a little more subtle otherwise."

Joelle paused for a moment and then shrugged. She continued with air of someone noble enough to admit a human flaw.

"Okay, maybe it was excessive. You have me there, Le Clerc. I must admit to having been motivated in part by revenge, by *Schadenfreude*, and by my wish to solve a mathematical puzzle."

"Madame? I understand the revenge aspect of your attack, though in truth you are the offender against George and against Quebec, rather than the reverse. I have no wish to understand German. But what puzzle?"

"I refer to the challenge of programming a proper trajectory for the three warheads to include two nearby targets and one in the Atlantic. The wide target spread posed an intriguing problem. Perhaps my satisfaction at finding a solution clouded my judgment about using it. I'm glad I didn't miscalculate and cause the warhead actually to hit you."

"Not as pleased as I am, Madame. Was one of the nearby targets just to the south of here?"

"Yes, at Wind Cave. A breakaway gang of ruffians set up shop there. You know the type, Le Clerc: sadistic thugs and the imbecile women who love them."

"Why would I know the type, Madame?"

"Because they were just like you, but without the self-delusions. To that extent I liked them better. You truly believe that your violent world outlook is about honor and justice when it is just about pride and greed. Your uniform is no different than the colors of any outlaw gang. The Wind Cave boys didn't bother with your pretenses. They liked thieving, cracking skulls, and raping women; and they said so openly. We couldn't allow that, of course, but I did admire their honesty."

"I'm pleased to be excluded from your admiration."

"Then I expect you will be pleased quite frequently during your visit here."

"You accuse me of thuggery yet you vaporized your own people."

"They were no longer my people. We had to eliminate the Wind Cave boys despite my kind appraisal of them. Raising troops again to fight them would have upset our social harmony. I solved the problem instantly, cleanly, and with minimal bother.

"But you do have troops. There were two guards in here when we entered."

"There are a handful of young ladies who do not carry firearms."

"I suppose frying Wind Cave at a distance made an impression on your subjects too."

"Yes, as a matter of fact it did, but they are not really my subjects. We are a family. I am simply the head of the family. This is a near-perfect society. We live as human beings not as wolves. Not as hyenas either. I didn't let the Wind Cave boys destroy us and I won't let you do it either."

"I didn't know I was poised to do that, Madame. What was your third target?"

"Rapid City."

"Self-defense again?"

"Yes, though that was more in the nature of a preemptive strike. But we can talk about that later. Let me show our family to you and show you to our family. George is a celebrity and the newest addition to our clan. He needs to wave to his fans and kiss his cousins. You, my dear captain, are an educational tool."

"I'm not sure I understand that."

"You will."

Joelle led us on a tour of the cave. Everywhere we went we met smiles and applause. The commune was impressive, if unconventional. The members had built and maintained functional plumbing and electric power systems. They also tried to be artistic with their technical competence. This explained the ersatz floral arrangement of the solar collectors. Art for the sake of art bloomed too. The Dakotans made rock paintings, wove fabrics, cut and dyed clothes elaborately, and carved sculptures of all sorts. We saw many more reliefs with frankly sexual themes cut into the rock walls.

The family did not neglect the liberal education of the young. We observed classes. The schools appeared effective if unruly by the standards of Quebec. The teachers often were as playful as the children.

Beautiful Rushmore Cave, we learned, was a cultural center for the extended commune. Joelle insisted that we see some of the region firsthand. We traveled by camel to a nearby cave containing factories and warehouses. These helped fill the fairly simple needs of the commune. Despite a casual approach to work the family already had produced a surplus of textiles, mostly from cannabis fiber. Dye and paint production was more than adequate.

At another site Joelle showed us the beginnings of a durable goods industry. Small but functional furnaces for melting scrap metal and firing ceramics operated in the open air. Inside a neighboring cave we watched the output of the furnaces turned into photoelectric panels. Other workers made machine parts from scratch using the classic disappearing wax method with sand molds. Joelle did not want some critical piece of equipment to fail because a minor spare part was unobtainable. She wanted artisans capable of manufacturing the mechanical parts the family needed.

Everywhere the people seemed happy. Hardly anyone worked more than four hours a day. Because there were few personal possessions there was no need to encourage higher productivity. Even living space was communal. Only Joelle, her guards, and the love priestesses had separate apartments. Most people slept on mats in communal rooms.

I conceded that Joelle had adapted the population to as pleasant a life in the caves as was practical, given the natural limitations of the place. I wasn't totally sold on her claim that life here was preferable to life back home however. Life was more individualistic and more cosmopolitan in Greater Quebec. To me that meant better, and I said so. Joelle let me talk; she smiled and shrugged.

We rode back to the main cave and Joelle led us to her chamber. She belatedly addressed my arguments.

"We've done something new here, George. Or maybe something very old. Anyway it is different from the way of the world for the past few thousand years. You can't judge us by the standards of the East Coast. We have conquered the enemy within."

"Am I supposed to understand that?" I asked.

"Yes, when I'm done. Don't feel too dull-witted for not seeing it instantly. I had some help understanding it too. Freud, Jung, Reich, and the other shrinks I had to study in school turned out to be useful after all. They were men of their times, and also just plain men, so they made some errors of perspective; but some of their insights were on the money. The problem, honey, is you."

"Me personally?"

"No. Men. All men. Men created civilization. Don't mistake that for a compliment. Civilization is organized domination. Some domination, some repression, is inescapable in any social group, but men overdo it."

"Occasionally. Not always. It depends on the man."

"Always. Every man." Joelle infused her lecture with an ideologue's tone of conviction. "Humans are motivated by Nirvana and Eros."

"I remember that was the theme of a book I saw in the library back home. It was written, I think, by some neo-Marxist psychologist. The title was something like *Eros and Civilization.*"

"Did you read it?"

"No. I sort of skimmed through and went on to something else."

"You should have stuck with it, because the author was onto the truth. Nirvana is escape from the pain of life, the desire to return to the womb. It is why people get drunk. It is why they are destructive to themselves and others. Ultimately it is a death instinct. The life-engaging motive is Eros, the search for pleasure. Limiting pleasure — which for men can be summed up pretty much as food, sleep, and sex — is a domination technique. When the supplies are limited, men compete for them, fight for them, deprive each other of them. They become warriors, form warrior castes, build empires, and dominate and repress each other and their women beyond all sense and reason. This is a bad idea. One result is the array of Minuteman missiles that worries you so much. I'm sure you see how the death instinct ties into those too."

"OK, you can look at it in that framework I suppose."

"Can you look at it honestly in any other?"

"Yes, in many others, but let's just stick to your viewpoint for now. What is your solution to the social problems rooted in these instincts?"

"For one thing, men here are not deprived of pleasure except for the very few hours per day they're required to work."

"Are you telling me that you are forestalling repressive civilization by making sure your men eat, sleep, and get laid regularly?"

"That is a crude way of putting it, but it is not entirely wrong."

Aeneas, to my irritation, looked rather pleased at this.

"We are building an alternative culture," she continued, "a matriarchal one, built on nonviolent principles."

"Women fight too, Joelle."

Joelle gave me one of her winsome smiles.

"Oh, of course they do. We're ambitious too. That is why women can and do thrive in a repressive male war culture. Some thrive by acting like men, in which case they are no better than men. A particularly female method, though, is to exploit male sexual and emotional deprivation. It is possible to use sex and affection to dominate wealthy and powerful men for the benefit of oneself and one's child at the expense of others. You should know something about that. While such women are personally endearing — to men anyway - they reinforce the whole patriarchal system powerfully.

"One key to building a matriarchy is to stop women from using this tactic. We all are better off without it. I have created an ethos and a social order in which the tactic brings no advantage. Sex has no scarcity value here. There are no private fortunes so there are no wealthy and powerful men. If some men are still more desirable for biological reasons, the better ones belong to all of us, not to one woman. Our children's needs are met regardless of who happens to be the father.

"We don't have couples here. We don't have nuclear families. We have a single, big extended family. All the men are fathers to all the children. All the women are mothers to all the children. We have no private property aside from a few personal items."

"I can see by your own possessions and living quarters that some people are still more equal than others," I responded skeptically. "Surely you can't eliminate greed and jealousy just like that in either men or women. As you yourself just admitted, there is natural inequality. Some folks are beautiful. Some are ugly. Some are talented. Some are inept. The unattractive ones are sure to be unloved and, according to your own analysis, dangerous."

"Natural inequalities are acceptable. We try to celebrate what we are rather than moan over what we are not. Most of us are talented in something. As for ugly men, they actually may have an advantage because the love priestesses see to their needs."

"Love priestesses?"

"The pretty women you see in white robes."

"Officially sanctioned prostitution," grumbled Le Clerc. "This gets better and better."

"There is no cause for sarcasm, Captain, and even less cause for moralizing. For one thing, the work of the priestesses is charity and therefore not prostitution, but there would be no shame even if it were. After my father died when I was 15, I survived in Montreal by that honorable trade for years. Among my clients were many sailors. In fact, I have to say there is something familiar about you. Do you have an explanation?"

Le Clerc looked uncomfortable.

INTERRUPTION OF JOURNAL:

AENEAS CUSTER: Not as uncomfortable as George looked, your Honors.

THE JOURNAL OF GEORGE CUSTER PART III—

Joelle turned her attention back to me.

"And yes, George, of course there are some inequalities built into our social order. The family understands this. Ordinary folk don't begrudge an aristocracy so long as it does its job without being needlessly abusive or overbearing. The love priestesses, for example, get special benefits for their special sacrifices. The warriors are also compensated because there are social costs to their job too."

"The warriors are all female?"

"Yes. This is so men don't ever get accustomed to dominating women with force. There are times even here when persuasion fails and a little armed authority is necessary, so I must have some soldiers. It doesn't happen often though. This is a happy place. Champions are a third case of inequality. You'll see them later."

"Is there another case?"

"You, sweetie."

"I have a question," chirped Aeneas.

"Yes?"

"What about gay men?"

"What about them?"

"Are there like love priests for them?"

"No, not necessary. The social dynamic of same-sex lovemaking is a bit different. Same sex bonding has survival value for the species, which is why the trait doesn't die out. We have no problems with any form of affection among adults. You'll find that people categorize themselves less around here anyway."

Joelle stopped abruptly and looked concerned.

"Why? Don't you like girls?"

This classic homophobic taunt surprised me in its context.

"Sure. I was just curious."

Joelle relaxed. I comprehended then that Joelle did not have a sudden episode of prudery. She had political plans for Aeneas. Those plans included marriage, or whatever passed for marriage in this strange place. Perhaps a more biological terminology would be nearer to the truth. For the moment I chose not to explore this.

INTERRUPTION OF JOURNAL:

AENEAS CUSTER: Of course not. My future was expendable.

HIRISAWA: You have made clear your filial hostility, Mr. Custer. It is not pertinent to your case.

AENEAS CUSTER: I'll try to contain it, your Honor.

THE JOURNAL OF GEORGE CUSTER PART III—

"Okay, so much for Eros. What about that Nirvana instinct?"

Joelle regained her thread. "Ah yes," Joelle answered. "I had some education about that too. This time my professor was my old dealer. My earlier life as a drug abuser wasn't entirely wasted. I understand clearly that even at best, life is hard. If we can't escape the self, sometimes we get frustrated, angry, and dangerous. Some people are fortunate enough to lose the self in work or art. Most of us need more heavy-handed medication. In the commune we have mushrooms, psychedelics, opiates, and narcotics of all kinds, except alcohol. That stuff will kill you.

"More conventional spirituality comes into play too. We have a soothing religion, a sort of Wiccan variation with a lot of seasonal holidays that the people seem to like. Also we have a very direct way of channeling the death instinct when it emerges as aggression, but you will see that for yourself."

Joelle looked at Le Clerc. "You seem impatient, Captain."

"Yes, Madame. Your psychobabble excuses for this den of perverts and drug addicts offend me. Your people will never achieve anything unless you sober them up and straighten them out. You have no sense of decency. These people are bums, tramps, and dope-heads and proud of it. What is right is right, and this isn't right."

Le Clerc held up a dismissive hand. "However, your degradation is not my responsibility."

"How open-minded of you," replied Joelle with amusement.

"What matters to me are those Minuteman missiles.

You've killed civilians with them three times."

"Twice. What you call the Firecracker landed in the ocean."

"Three times. Fishing boats were destroyed by the Firecracker.

Your explanation for that is still missing something. You never felt the need to threaten your husband's life before. Why now?"

"Well actually…" I recollected.

"All right! You haven't felt the need to threaten him lately. Why now? And who is next on your hit list?"

Joelle changed the subject. "First we talk about birth. Then we celebrate life. Then, Captain, we can talk about death."

Joelle clapped her hands. One of her gorgeous guards peered into the chamber. Joelle motioned with her finger and the guard disappeared. A few moments later she returned escorting a pretty young woman with light brown hair and hazel eyes. She was dressed in white, but not like a love priestess. Her robe was like that of Joelle. She stood by Joelle's side and faced us.

"I want you to meet someone, George. You obviously know Aeneas is the child of Ulysses."

Aeneas looked thunderstruck.

"Here is someone we made together, George. This is your daughter Selena."

Aeneas looked thunderstruck.

INTERRUPTION OF JOURNAL:

AENEAS: George looked thunderstruck. I think this was the moment he went native, Your Honors.

THE JOURNAL OF GEORGE CUSTER PART III—

Aeneas managed to speak before I did.

"My sister?"

"Half-sister," answered Joelle.

Selena smiled coyly at Aeneas. He flushed.

"One of my guards will show you and George where you can rest and clean up. We're going to have a party tonight."

"But…"

"Not now, Aeneas. You can get acquainted with Selena later this evening. Hold off your questions until then."

We were led away to a side chamber with beds, a bathtub filled with deliciously cool water, and bedpans. I suppose these were some of my "more equal than others" perquisites. I claimed the tub first. After all, I was "the Custer." Everyone said so.

Le Clerc used the tub after. Aeneas didn't bother.

INTERRUPTION OF JOURNAL:
AENEAS CUSTER: Of course not! After two grimy old men?

THE JOURNAL OF GEORGE CUSTER PART III—
Aeneas was sullen. Sometimes he looked at me with murder in his eyes. He was angry with me for concealing his origins from him, but I did not do that out of malice. My attempts to talk to him foundered in his anger.

"I don't want to talk about it," he responded tersely.

After a time I gave up. Le Clerc observed us without comment. I then dozed for what felt like hours, but which may have been much less.

INTERRUPTION OF JOURNAL:
AENEAS CUSTER: It was much less.

JOURNAL OF GEORGE CUSTER PART III—
At length a warrior awoke me and led us outside. The party already was in full swing outside the cave entrance. The sun was sliced in two by the horizon. The sky was cloudless. In the east it was just beginning to shade to black. Le Clerc, Aeneas, and myself took our places next to Joelle and Selena under an open sided tent. We sat on oversize pillows. We were very much on display. Two new guards flanked us. They were not as attractive as the first ones. I don't know if this variation in pulchritude was happenstance or if there was a first string and a second string.

At least twenty tables were laden with food and drugs laid out in a buffet style. Everything was casually self-service. Joelle led me to one of the tables. The guards did not follow us. There were no plates for the food. Thick hard slices of bread, which Joelle called trenchers, served the purpose; edible tableware saved labor. Clay goblets were available for liquids. Some of the drinks were not identifiable and I was disinclined to experiment with them. Joelle picked out one for me. It tasted like carrot juice. Perhaps it was.

Sitar music and the sickly sweet smell of marijuana filled the air. As always, the locals wore bright clashing colors when they wore anything at all. Lighthearted sexuality pervaded the event. Couples — and triples and quadruples — did as they wished openly.

"Reminds me of those old Grateful Dead documentaries," I commented.

"Animals," muttered Le Clerc.

"What are you complaining about now, Maurice?" asked Joelle.

Le Clerc, as usual, winced at hearing his first name.

"This is awful. You and your people have no morals, no decency. There are children here watching while grownups fornicate right in front of them."

"So what are you saying?"

"This is shocking child abuse. This is a perverted atmosphere for children."

Joelle was offended.

"It is a healthy atmosphere for children, unlike the repressed society in which you were raised. Besides, we keep adults' hands off kids (one of our very few rules) because it is better for young people to develop sensuality on their own. But they are free to develop it on their own and with each other at their own pace."

"Horrible!"

"Beautiful!"

I shifted the conversation away from a topic that was growing too heated. "What is that area next to the cliff? It looks like a stage. Are we going to have a play?"

"We do have plays there sometimes, but tonight we have a sporting event. This is how we channel surplus aggressive energy. Not all of those instincts are defused by a tender touch." She tickled me under the chin as she said this. "On major holidays and special occasions we have a battle of Champions. There always are enough volunteers. Champions are honored, feasted, and pampered right up until the contest. They then fight to the death. It weeds out the thugs and the violently insane. Sometimes one of the fighters is a criminal in which case his participation is not voluntary. That is rare but it happens to be the case tonight. He is treated the same as a volunteer Champion and he is redeemed if he wins."

"What did the criminal do?"

"He was jealous of a woman. He acted as though she had no right to make love to some one else. That was bad enough, but he was sentenced to this contest when he lost his temper and hit her. We don't tolerate that."

"So we are about to witness a murder?" asked Le Clerc.

"No, we are about to witness justice. The Champion who plans to mete it out is a volunteer and takes his own chances. Do executioners in Quebec give the condemned a sporting chance?"

"There are no executioners in Quebec. We do not have capital punishment anymore except in special cases in wartime."

"You see my point though."

"What happens if no one volunteers to fight a criminal?" I asked.

"That doesn't happen."

"Suppose it did."

"We would let the criminal go."

"Where?"

Joelle smiled. "In the middle of the desert somewhere."

The game began as the sky turned a blood red, a fitting color for the upcoming display. A steel mesh fence was unrolled and erected in a semicircle in front of the stage. A small cliff formed a back wall. Two warriors with bows and arrows stood atop the cliff from which they could pick off a contestant should one of them attempt to escape.

The Champions entered the stage and faced the crowd.

They were bare to the waist. Joelle pointed out the criminal to me. He was blond, muscular, and slightly shorter than average. He had a smile that was very close to a sneer. His darker opponent was taller but less athletic. His expression was stoic. Each contestant drank from a bowl of mushroom soup that likely had intoxicating properties.

The two faced each other and began to circle. At first their barehanded strikes were cautious and tentative, but they grew in strength and violence as each began to discover the other's weaknesses. Despite trading some solid blows, for at least a quarter hour neither could get the best of the other. Tired of the standoff, the blond suddenly charged and caught the challenger in the waist with his shoulder. The two fell to the ground and wrestled desperately. This continued for a few minutes.

My eardrums were hurt by a shrill noise. Joelle had blown a police whistle. The extent to which I had been absorbed by the fight surprised and embarrassed me.

In response to Joelle's signal, one of the guards on the cliff picked up two long wooden poles measuring approximately two meters each and tossed them into the arena. At soon as they clattered on the ground the opponents released each other and dove for the weapons. Each quickly got his hands on one. They circled each other again. Both were sweaty, dusty, and bruised but neither looked seriously hurt. This changed rapidly. The darker Champion caught the blond on the side of his head with a loud crack. Blood flowed from his ear and nose as he dropped to his knees. A pole jabbed toward him end first and caught him in the chest. He fell back as his ribs splintered.

The dark man moved in to finish off the man who had been charged with domestic abuse. Overconfidence slowed his attack. The delay allowed the injured fighter to roll and avoid the blow. Seeing he was about to lose the match, the blond fighter tried a desperate maneuver of the type that usually fails. He staggered to his feet, ran to the cliff and jammed his pole into a cleft. He used leverage to snap the end. He spun as his opponent rushed him. He dodged the darker man's swing and stabbed. The broken end of his pole was as sharp as a spear point. It penetrated into the Champion's heart. With open arms as a gesture of victory, the survivor stood tall and faced the onlookers. They shrieked and applauded.

"Why are they so happy the criminal won?"

"By defeating the other Champion he takes on his opponent's virtues and passes off his own offenses. He is redeemed. He is once again at peace with the Earth Mother. Unburdened of his crimes, he can be reincarnated as a better person. He is now worthy of sacrifice."

"Sacrifice?"

The warriors on the cliff aimed their bows and shot the winner through the back. The arrowheads protruded through the Champion's chest. He fell.

"Barbaric! Grotesque!" shouted Le Clerc who had watched the contest as transfixed as anyone.

"What would be more civilized, Maurice? Hanging him? Or keeping him caged like an animal? There always will be people who cannot live in ordinary society — people against whom we must protect ourselves. Every society removes these people in one way or another. This is never a pleasant business, but at least our way even the criminal feels good about it."

"Your sophistry only makes it all the more horrible! That man didn't want to die."

"Well, perhaps not, but he died a Champion instead of a petty lowlife and he knew it. What would you rather see us do with criminals?"

"I don't know! But not this!"

"Thank you for your recommendation," she answered ironically.

The contest had been a real crowd pleaser, and the party resumed in earnest. The sweet smell of marijuana intensified. Mushroom soup passed about. Pills and powders circulated freely. People made love in bewildering combinations of number and gender. Aeneas gaped at this in the way of a shy backward teenager.

INTERRUPTION OF JOURNAL:

AENEAS: Umm.

HIRISAWA: If you plan to deny this admittedly cruel observation you are likely to damage your credibility.

AENEAS CUSTER: Ah.

THE JOURNAL OF GEORGE CUSTER PART III—

Joelle took no part in the excesses except as an observer. I thought at first that she was distracted by the need to explain things to me.

"What about you?" I asked. "Are you normally a head love priestess at these parties?"

"No. Don't be jealous," she laughed. "Strangely enough, I

have been quite virtuous, even by Mr. Le Clerc's standards since I arrived. From the beginning my instincts told me that having sex and getting high would damage the family's sense of awe toward me, and I rely on that. As I'm afraid you know, I'm not pleasant when I'm drunk or on drugs. As for sex, I'm just a woman, George. Sometimes I smell or have bad breath and I'm not as young as I used to be either. Someone sticking his tongue in my mouth is likely to notice such things.

Temperance and abstinence, on the other hand, enhanced my status in a profound and unexpected way. I realized that people really do have a sense of guilt about enjoying themselves, so I became a sort of scapegoat for repression. I behave chastely and soberly on the family's behalf, and so free our people from guilt about what they do.

"There is something sad about that."

"I'm glad you feel that way because you can change it."

"I can? How?"

"We two can have fun, George, so long as we do it together faithfully. We can be a couple and take all those ugly desires for monogamy upon ourselves. We can free the family from them. That is why you have an important role here."

Thinking about my newly assigned role made me forget the next question. I remembered it when Aeneas sneezed.

"Oh, what are your plans for Aeneas? I gather you have something in mind."

"You can see the obvious occasionally."

"You flatter me."

"Probably. Aeneas is what this is all about."

"Aeneas?"

"Yes. He is why I called you home to the Black Hills. We won't live forever. Aeneas and Selena are our logical successors. I mean to preserve this culture."

Joelle leaned toward our logical successors and said, "Have fun children."

I wasn't sure I understood her correctly. I did. Selena kissed Aeneas on the lips and began to disrobe. Aeneas actually backed away from her.

"Don't be self-conscious Aeneas," she said. "We are beyond that here." He stopped backing away.

Le Clerc was more outraged at this than he was at the contest. "Custer! You can't allow this! They are about to commit incest — and the girl is only 15!"

I must admit to being shocked myself, but my reflex to argue with Le Clerc forced me to rethink the matter.

"It is incest by our rules," I said to him, "but in old Egypt brother sister marriages were the rule. Fifteen is old enough in many places. Even in the old USA some states allowed girls of 13 to marry if they had their parents' permission. These folks have the right to set their own standards. Try to be amenable."

"How can you say that? Your own daughter! You are not really buying into this snake pit, are you?"

"These people do seem a lot happier than you, Maurice."

"Maurice?"

This came from a young woman who tittered behind Le Clerc. She began to massage his neck. He shrugged her off more gruffly than roughly. She laughed. So did a score of onlookers.

"See everyone?" pointed Joelle. "Civilized men don't even know how to have fun. Learn from this man. Don't be like him." She questioned Le Clerc teasingly, "You weren't always this way, were you sailor boy?"

"No. I used to be younger. Now I'm old enough to know better. So are you."

"Your gallantry knows no bounds."

"Don't tease him too much, Joelle," I urged. "He is a good man. He can have fun too. He just prefers to do it anonymously. While maintaining a public image he is just a little stiff."

"That's not such a bad thing," chirped Le Clerc's masseuse.

Joelle responded with only the tolerant smile the joke deserved. She leaned over to me.

"Don't disagree with me in public, George," Joelle whispered in my ear. "Not even good-naturedly. We always back each other up."

What she really meant was I always must back her up. However, such one-way streets are far from uncommon in marriages. "OK. I'll play."

In truth I understood what troubled Le Clerc better than I let on. Sexual mores are arguably matters of fashion and taste.

Joelle's casual bloodiness was something else again. Her ruthlessness had unnerved me when we lived together back in Morrisbourg. The desert hadn't mellowed her any in the years since then.

When it isn't painful to be in the path of Joelle's ambition, it is lethal. The woman is not evil in a conventional sense. She is not a sadist. She often is generous. She doesn't inflict pain for the sensual pleasure of it. Rather, she inflicts it coldly. Her pleasures are rather gentle. This duality of her nature permeated the culture she shaped in South Dakota. Part of the primordial appeal of South Dakota, like the appeal of Joelle herself, was the co-existence of a light and dark side.

Joelle has started something promising here, and she is offering me a chance to help shape it further. Perhaps my intervention can trade away some nirvana for a little more eros.

Aeneas, however, has had as much eros tonight as he can handle. He rapidly has gained worldly experience with

Selena, though I have tried hard to avoid watching their activities.

INTERRUPTION OF JOURNAL:

AENEAS CUSTER: Not hard enough.

THE JOURNAL OF GEORGE CUSTER PART III—

One can adjust to foreign customs with surprising ease when one is away from home. Back in Morrisbourg it would appall me to have a teenage daughter display such aptitude, but here it seems natural enough. Looking away from them, I locked eyes with Joelle.

"You'll play, you say? Good, because playing is just what I had in mind. It has been a long time, George."

Joelle smiled at me.

It had indeed been a long time. It is embarrassing to admit it, but I had avoided sex for many years. However maudlin this may seem, Joelle was my true one and only. Other women simply didn't rate with me. To be fully honest, a West Virginian lass once tempted me, but a little war came between us before anything came of it.

INTERRUPTION OF JOURNAL:

AENEAS CUSTER: Your honor, I question this. He may have expected that Joelle would read his journal one day. That is a motive for bending the truth. The fact that Miss Weston…

HIRISAWA: Mr. Custer, your adoptive father's sex life is not relevant.

AENEAS CUSTER: But it reflects on…

HIRISAWA: No it doesn't. Move on.

JUDGE JEANIE: Nor are his remarks as incredible as all that, young man. Some spouses are faithful. One should allow for the benefit of a doubt.

AENEAS CUSTER: Yes ma'am. I ask for no more than that for myself.

JUDGE JEANIE: I have many doubts about you, Mr. Custer.

THE JOURNAL OF GEORGE CUSTER PART III—

The conservative Mr. Le Clerc led a far more promiscuous life than I. I wonder if Joelle is right about him. Does his bad conscience about having fun really do him harm? Does mine do me harm?

Joelle pushed me back on the pillows and drove any such conscience into hiding. She began to pull at my garments.

"Don't move, George."

Joelle began to work on as I lay there quietly. She did not trust to my skills. This was wise. I lost consciousness of everything but her featherlight touch as she explored my body from my neck to my thighs. She gently brushed aside my hands when I reached out to return the favor. I took the hint and lay still. Her touch grew firmer. She slid her arms under me and gripped my shoulders. Our lips met and we were one. The process was slow. It was luscious. When we were done, I was startled by applause. We had collected an audience. For a moment I turned beet-red, but as they laughed at that too, I joined them. Joelle gave my life renewed meaning. I don't know if I have the courage to die for her but most certainly I would kill for her.

INTERRUPTION OF JOURNAL:

AENEAS CUSTER: I need to draw the judges' attention to this scary statement.

HIRISAWA: Attention drawn.

PROUDFOOT: Surely the defendant is not trying to blame his parents for his crimes.

AENEAS CUSTER: No, Mr. Prosecutor. I deny they were crimes. I am merely trying to establish the milieu in which actions were taken.

PROUDFOOT: Using a passive verb doesn't diminish your responsibility for those events; they are crimes whether you deny it or not.

HIRISAWA: Both of you address the court, not each other. Go on, Custer.

THE JOURNAL OF GEORGE CUSTER PART III—

Just when the festival threatened to wind down it was reinvigorated by the arrival of food. The aroma of succulent meat and vegetable platters filled the air. The platters looked wonderful. We hurried to the tables to fill our plates.

Even Le Clerc sampled the fare.

"Pork?" he asked.

"Champions."

It took a moment for the meaning of this to sink in.

He then spat out a mouthful. I was taken aback myself, but

Refrained from spitting. Customs vary and I don't like to be rude.

"We have a protein shortage," Joelle explained. "There is not enough crop surplus to use as animal feed. Not yet, anyway. Recycling, so to speak, helps. We only eat

Champions though and it is always a respectful feast." Le Clerc gagged again. He washed his mouth with a swig of water. It plainly wasn't enough to wash away the taste.

"Couldn't you at least brew some beer?" he complained.

"Yes, but we won't."

Le Clerc sat on his pillows and retreated into himself.

The phantasmogorical orgy continued. A group of four men and two women without a stitch of clothes among them danced in front of us while they shared a bottle of blue fluid. I don't know what their unfocused eyes saw, but it wasn't anything in this world.

"So George," cajoled Joelle, "tell me what you did to the missiles. I know you did something. Your airship was seen at one of the control centers. Some boys who were on a snake hunt spotted you. They observed you enter the center and tamper with it. I actually considered launching a preemptive strike before you did any more damage."

"A strike on whom?"

"Well, that was the problem. Holding all of Quebec accountable for your actions seemed, as Maurice would say, excessive. Besides, I wasn't sure which control rooms were still safe. So tell me, what did you do?"

"We bugged the targeting programs…"

"George! Shut your mouth!" cried Le Clerc.

"…and the warheads too."

"I see. Very naughty. Is the damage reversible?"

"Yes. The weapons aren't really damaged. We just installed some funky software."

"How do you undo that, honey?"

"Enter code name 'Luggage.'"

"How nostalgic."

"You've murdered thousands of people," said Le Clerc in a near whisper.

"Don't be melodramatic. Joelle isn't going to shoot at Quebec. She has no reason to. She's not a mindless killer. The missiles are just a deterrent."

"Tell that to Rapid City."

"I'm sure she had a good reason for what she did. The survival of this place must have been at stake."

Joelle graced Le Clerc with a grin.

END OF JOURNAL

AENEAS CUSTER: Your Honors, George's journal ends here. I surmise that he scribbled these last entries after the party wound down. This happened slowly. One by one the participants passed out. Even Joelle was sleeping soundly within an hour after dinner. George reclined on an elbow next to a gas lantern. He had a self-satisfied smile on his face. Due to excitement over recent events in my own life, I couldn't sleep either. About this time Maurice Le Clerc sat down next to me. Joelle's guards watched him but didn't interfere. Selena lay asleep on the pillows on the other side of me.

"Aeneas, may I speak with you?"

"Sure."

"Let's take a walk."

He stood up and gestured me to follow. My upbringing caused me to don my pants first. I doubt a local would have bothered. He led me away from Selena.

"Aeneas, I'm sure that you find Selena fascinating, but you know the world is full of women."

"So I hear. What is your point?"

"Back home you are a very wealthy young man. You live in a mansion. You can be anything you want. You can have a political career. You can experience life. You are quite a catch. Girls will flock to you, if you only let them. This place is a cave, a gaudy cave perhaps, but a cave. You are only 16. Yet Joelle plans to lock you into a life with Selena, and only with Selena, in a cave. Forever. George is prepared to let her do it to you too."

"Is that so bad? I like Selena."

"Of course you do. But you want to keep your options open, don't you? You won't have any when Joelle obliterates Quebec."

"Dad says...I mean George says Joelle won't do that."

"He's wrong. George is a pragmatist when he isn't being mindlessly sentimental. He never did understand people with real ideals. Idealists are willing to be ruthless in service to a greater good. George doesn't comprehend the concept. I understand Joelle all too well."

"Because you are an idealist?"

"Yes," Le Clerc answered quite seriously. "The difference is I know what the greater good really is, while Joelle whipped up this warped philosophy that is just an excuse for aggrandizing herself. That doesn't mean she doesn't believe in it though, because she does. Believe me, she will launch another strike: preemptive in her opinion. Do you want to be responsible for the death of thousands of people? You can stop it."

"Assume for the moment you are right…"

"I am right."

"Maybe. How possibly can I stop it?"

"With the Z16."

"You want me to steal it? Why?"

"Actually I want you to help me steal it. There is only one guard by the airship. Go talk to her. Divert her attention. I'll climb in and cut the ropes. Once I get away Joelle won't dare launch missiles."

"Why not? We may provoke her to do just that."

"No, she is not suicidal. Quebec would strike back with whatever they had left. Once I am away neither of us will dare to strike first. Don't you see? We will have mutual deterrence and all of us can go on living."

"Back on the airship you argued for a first strike against this place. Why should I believe you have changed your mind?"

He spoke in a hurt voice. "You and George are my friends!"

I must have looked skeptical.

"OK, a more hard-nosed reason is that then I was proposing a surprise attack. That option is gone. I can't risk attacking her now because I can't be sure she won't get a crew into a control room before I have a chance to launch. Look, Aeneas, I'm not some mad bomber out to kill for no reason. I just want to preserve my own homeland — *our* homeland. Think of your friends and all the people you know."

The people I knew back home aroused a mild sympathy at best. The moral issue carried some weight with me though. Maurice was right that Joelle had indeed bombed Rapid City when it suited her. Also, he had a point about money and all the girls back East. There were worse lives to lead than that of a rich young man in Morrisbourg. It wouldn't do to shut out that option for myself by letting Joelle blow up the place.

The notion of mutual deterrence was at least speciously logical. This was why the missiles were built in the first place. The fact that they were still in their silos demonstrated that the concept was valid.

Truth be told, however, my decision to help Le Clerc ultimately was based on none of this. My primary motivation was the enjoyment I felt at being taken seriously as an adult. For the first time I was committing myself to a weighty purpose of my own free will. It was a heady rush.

"You'll be noticed by someone other than the guard if you just walk over to the Z16," I advised. "You are pretty high profile."

"Yes, that occurred to me. I think the answer is to go with a girl. If they think I'm fornicating these deviants will leave me alone."

"Some may decide to watch just for fun."

"Let's hope not. I think it is worth a try."

"All right, let's do it."

I waited while Le Clerc approached the young lady who had tried to massage him earlier. He tapped her shoulder and muttered. The girl teased him with a gesture of mock disdain. Then she smiled and nodded. As he took her arm and helped her to her feet I walked as nonchalantly as I could to the airship which still was tied down tightly in the old Visitors Parking Lot. The night was dark. The moon was a sliver. The stars were bright, but they didn't light up the ground much.

I approached the single warrior on duty by the airship. There must have been a height requirement for the job. The tall young woman wore lighter armor than the two guards by Joelle's tent. Leather chaps protected her legs. She had wrist guards as well. A leather halter and shorts completed the uniform that was bare at the midriff.

JUDGE JEANIE: Enough of the fashion report, Mr. Custer.

AENEAS CUSTER: Yes, ma'am.

PROUDFOOT: Your Honors, while I am conscious of the latitude you have chosen to give the defendant in presenting his case, I wish to point out that these recounts of speeches are highly suspect. Surely the defendant does not remember every conversation word for word.

JUDGE JEANIE: That very point has occurred to me as well. Any comments, Mr. Custer?

AENEAS CUSTER: The conversations are as I remember them. They are accurate in essence, ma'am.

MAGGIO: [Inaudible whispers to colleagues.] The defendant may complete his story in his own way. We shall take into account the 'in essence' qualification.

AENEAS CUSTER: Thank You.

Anyway, I kept the guard's attention away from the blimp. "Hi, I'm Aeneas."

"Yes, I know. Welcome home."

"Thanks. You haven't had much fun tonight."

She smiled. "I'll get my chance. We rotate duty." The young woman was quite voluble. She spoke of scheduling and the responsibilities of being a guard. She even was kind enough to flirt. "Maybe Selena can spare you one night, cutie."

"You know about us?"

"We all know about you two. We have known about you for years."

"Wow. For years I've been famous and spoken for and never knew it."

"I'm sure the Custer had a reason for keeping some things secret from you."

"Yes. He is such a good secret keeper that he kept things secret from himself."

The guard looked at me quizzically.

"But," I lowered my voice conspiratorially, "isn't it against the rules for us to, um, rendezvous? I took it for granted that the free love thing didn't apply to me. Joelle said something about sticking with George and I sort of figured the same restriction applied to me and Selena."

"Do you always do what you're supposed to do, Aeneas?" The woman was a rebel in her own fashion.

"Not always. What's your name?"

"Jennifer."

As we spoke Le Clerc and his young girlfriend slipped into the far side of the gondola. I asked Jennifer if she liked her job.

"It has its perks," she answered. "I have the respect of the community."

"Or the fear?"

"The respect. I have my own private quarters. If I miss a few parties because of duty, hey, I always can party the next day." Ropes slid to the ground from the gondola. The dark airship rose silently into the air. I do not know how Le Clerc kept the girl silent. Maybe she considered taking the airship for a ride a lark. Perhaps he knocked her out. Then again, maybe he really made love to her.

"Were you one of the warriors who shot the Champion?"

"No," Jennifer sighed. "I didn't even get to do that."

Air movement on Jennifer's back caused her to glance over her shoulder. The airship was missing. She looked up. It was rising above us.

"Hey!"

She spun and threw her spear. It passed through a gondola window but apparently missed Le Clerc. The engines roared to life. Two other guards with bows came running. The dark shape passed beyond a hillside as the warriors aimed and shot. The arrows fell far short.

Jennifer stared at me with dismay as she comprehended the scale of my betrayal. Feeling guilty about the position in which I had put her, I turned away and found myself facing Joelle. Even in the dark I could see the cold fury in her face.

"What have you done?" she demanded.

I had no answer.

"When we catch him we will have another feast," stated Joelle flatly.

George arrived on the scene in time to hear that.

"We won't catch him now."

"We have another airship and we will catch him. Bring it here!" she ordered the warriors. "And you!" she shouted to one, "Go get my accessories!" One woman ran up the hill above the cave entrance. Soon she was flashing a light signal in the direction of Mount Rushmore. Another warrior disappeared into the cave.

"But we don't know where he is going," George complained. Generally east, for sure, but who knows at what exact heading? He has a big head start too. Maybe it is for the best."

"I know exactly where he is going. He is going to the nearest Minuteman control room. You told him how to undo your sabotage at the same time you told me. That is best only for him."

"I don't think he will attack us."

"I don't either," I added. "He said he just wanted mutual deterrence."

"Ass! Look, little boy, mutual deterrence is based on a *second* strike capability. If one side can obliterate the other totally, there is no deterrence. There is a big advantage to striking first. Don't play around with what you don't understand. Le Clerc thinks he can take us out at a single blow."

"You need two people to launch a missile," George reminded her.

"There are two people. He has a hostage. He can make her do whatever he wants."

"But he needs the access codes."

"I stole the access codes from you, George! What makes you think he didn't? You are so naive! Man, you have killed when you thought it best. Why do you think he won't?"

"I killed only in war."

"He thinks this is a war! And he is right! You just don't understand us."

The parking lot began to fill with confused onlookers. A sputtering sound grew louder. The huge paisley airship from Mount

Rushmore already loomed above us. Ropes were thrown over the side. Commune members held the ship in place in adequate, if inelegant, fashion.

Joelle ordered George and me up the rope ladder to the gondola. She quickly followed. She ordered the pilot out. Her "accessories" soon arrived below. They were an AR15 and, of all things, a hand held antiaircraft missile she called a Stinger.

Joelle waved to ground crew. The ropes were released. Joelle revved the engine as we ascended. This ship had directional thrust like the Z16, but the two encased rotating side props were geared off a single turbine engine mounted in the gondola. Four smaller propellers, mounted on aluminum frames extending halfway up the airbag, provided additional directional control. Each of these were powered an individual electric motor and could swivel separately. The large ship responded more slowly to the controls than the Z16, but it could land or hover just as precisely. Straight ahead at full throttle she was even a tad faster.

We proceeded southeast at full power for twenty minutes. The turbine was an unusual multifuel design that ran on almost anything flammable. At the moment, our fuel was high-octane gasoline. I was impressed. The big old paisley beast may have had lesser fuel economy than the newer craft, but in many ways it was the more ingenious design. The Le Pens built good aircraft.

I assumed our odds of catching Le Clerc were remote. If he was fleeing to Quebec as he had promised, we had virtually no chance at all. Even our marginal edge in speed was useless without knowing his precise heading.

My assumption was wrong. My chest constricted when something caught my eye in the night sky ahead. A dark shape in the distance occulted stars. Joelle had been right. Le Clerc had made a beeline for the nearest Minuteman control room. It was time to salvage what I could of my status with her.

"Over there!" I pointed. "Le Clerc is over there."

"Yes, of course he is. If you were anyone else, Aeneas, I'd send you to the arena for what you did. I don't believe in third chances, so don't ever cross me again."

"Yes, ma'am."

We closed slowly on the Z16. The silhouette grew more discernible. Le Clerc surely saw us too.

"Take the controls!" Joelle ordered George.

She picked up the Stinger and leaned out the window. She aimed carefully and fired. A whoosh from the rocket launcher was followed by moments of silence. The Stinger missile locked on to the heat from the Z16's engines. A flash of light appeared on Le Clerc's port engine. Flames licked up to the airbag. It quickly erupted. A soft rumble from the explosion reached us as Le Clerc's blazing airship descended to the ground at a leisurely pace.

Within minutes we skimmed over the wreckage. Le Clerc and a young woman in a sarong had been thrown from the gondola when it hit the ground. They lay face up in the sand.

"Keep the blimp steady," Joelle directed.

George lowered the airship carefully to within a few feet of the ground. The lightest of the three of us, Joelle leapt out. The airship lurched upwards but settled again as George adjusted the gas pressure and the directional motors.

"Stay on board," George ordered me, "and hold her steady."

Then he went over the side with the AR15. The ship lurched again. I struggled at first to hold my position. It became easier when I identified the wind direction and turned the nose of the ship into it. The electric motors then were enough to hold the base of the gondola on the ground. I could hear most of what George and Joelle had to say.

Le Clerc was burned and bleeding badly from shrapnel wounds, but his eyes opened when Joelle kicked him in the side.

"Cover him," she ordered George. Joelle walked to the young woman. She knelt over her.

"Sue Ann. Sue Ann!"

She felt for a pulse and didn't find one. She turned her eyes to Le Clerc.

"I am going to enjoy every morsel after the next contest!"

George spoke to the injured man more soothingly, "Don't take her too seriously, old boy. But, you know, this is your third crash in one of these things. With a record like that you'll never get insurance."

Le Clerc managed a pained smile.

"Come on, George!" demanded Joelle. "Throw his worthless

carcass into the gondola. Then let's go to Control Room 2. It is only a couple miles away."

"That can wait. We need to get Le Clerc back to the cave. He is hurt pretty bad."

"He'll live, for a while anyway. The control room comes first. We have work to do."

She strode determinedly back toward the paisley airship.

"No!" gasped Le Clerc. "Stop her George! Don't let her get to the missiles. She'll launch them! She is going to attack Quebec!"

"No, she isn't. She just wants to undo my programming. Besides, she needs my help to launch a Minuteman."

"No, she just needs a second person. Even if you or Aeneas don't help her now, she will go back and get someone who will!" Le Clerc coughed, wheezed, and sputtered, "Don't you understand what is going on? She is going to slaughter our countrymen."

"Her people are my countrymen, Maurice, and she is my wife."

Joelle, whose hands were on the rail smiled at this answer from George.

None of us had considered that Le Clerc might have an accessory of his own. Le Clerc rolled painfully on his side, pulled out his handgun from behind his back and aimed it at Joelle. A burst of fire erupted from George's AR15.

"I'm sorry, Maurice," said George. "I can't let you hurt her."

Le Clerc didn't answer. He would never answer anyone again.

"Come on, George," said Joelle in an even voice.

George stared at Le Clerc's body for some moments and then walked back to the ship. He and Joelle climbed aboard. Joelle resumed the controls.

We completed to trip to the Minuteman control room in silence. Once again we touched ground.

"Aeneas," said Joelle softly but authoritatively, "keep this ship steady for the next half hour."

"Yes, ma'am."

She swung her legs over the side and lowered herself to the ground.George adjusted the craft for the change in weight. Then he turned the controls over to me. He patted the rail.

"This is a good ship Aeneas," he said in an oddly distant voice. He smiled and added, "We should name it *Nearer.*"

I was too numb to ask way.

He suddenly became more commanding. "Do not hold her steady. Listen to me. This is an order and it is a plea. Lift off. Full throttle this thing. Go in a straight line. Get as far away as you can. If nothing unusual happens in half an hour you can turn back and get us. Don't be early."

George looked at me for a long moment. He detached his little leather bound journal from a belt loop and tossed it to me. He went over the side.

I faced a dilemma. I didn't fancy becoming a Champion for defying Joelle. George on the other seemed pretty definite too. I felt I owed him something. I made a fateful decision; I dropped ballast and shoved the throttle wide open. My airspeed climbed to 100 kilometers per hour.

I was not more than twenty miles away when, for the second time in my life, I experienced an artificial dawn. A fireball in the east turned the sky bright blue. The shock wave reached me in seconds. Even at this distance it knocked the airship on its side and nearly flung me out of the gondola. The windshield shattered. The radio sparked and went dead. I could smell oil.

George had not been altogether honest with Joelle. The code word "Luggage" removed only the block against missile launch. It left intact the target lock on the control room itself.

George had answered his own question. He was willing to kill for Joelle and he was willing to die for her too. As usual, George added a mind-bending complication. He did both in the same night and took Joelle with him.

Nearer limped back to Beautiful Rushmore Cave. I wanted desperately to return to Quebec. I had had enough adventure and, quite frankly, wanted to resume my pampered life in Morrisbourg.

A crowd waited for me at the cave. They had noticed the fireworks in the east. I landed. As soon as a few people secured the aircraft to the mooring rings, I alit and walked to the arena. The commune gathered around me. Jennifer, replacement spear in hand, stood in the front rank and treated me to a murderous stare.

It seemed unwise to reveal to them that George and Joelle were dead. In a rare burst of inspired prevarication, I concocted a story intended to pacify the Dakotans and to hurry my departure. Joelle and George, I said, had defeated Le Clerc with his own evil. He had been allowed to escape as a test of his decency and humanity — a test, which he failed. George and Joelle, I lied, deliberately had let him hear false information about how to aim the Minuteman missiles. Le Clerc immediately escaped, reached a control room, and had attempted to destroy the Rushmore commune. Thanks to Joelle and George, the missile he launched simply destroyed himself. That was the explosion that had lit up the sky. Sue Ann had been in on it too, I said. She helped Le Clerc with the launch sequence and then escaped from the control room.

Before the missile landed and while Le Clerc was inside the control room, my lie continued, George and Joelle recaptured the Z16. Sue Ann joined me in the paisley airship. We high tailed it away. My one regret, I explained, was an unfortunate accident. Before I could reach a safe distance my airship had been struck by the shock wave from the explosion. Sue Ann had been killed.

"Where is her body?" asked Jennifer.

"I dedicated it to flames that burned below. It seemed appropriate," I quickly answered

This experience proved to us that the outside world was desperately in need of enlightenment. George and Joelle communicated to me that the time had come to provide it. The Rushmore commune now was advanced enough to continue on its path without them. The two flew off in the Z16 on their mission. At first they would travel north.

I told them Joelle had ordered Selena to assume her place as Mother. Selena was to be treated by the family with the same respect due to Joelle herself. My own task was to return to Quebec where I was to sow the seeds of enlightenment as best I could. In time, I should return to South Dakota to be at Selena's side.

They bought it. Selena, I think, was more skeptical than most of the Dakotans, but since my story put her in charge she chose not to question it. You may notice I recreated the same situation for Selena that had existed for Joelle. I was the new Custer whose arrival would be awaited.

The airship *Nearer* was repaired and resupplied. In only three days I was on my way.

The Le Pens did not benefit from my return. I came back with the wrong airship, two missing crew, and a garbled story.

I explained that we three had found this airship deflated near Chicago. There were no signs of its crew in the area. I had no explanation for the paint job. I told them that we had managed to repair it well enough to be flightworthy. We re-inflated it using our on-board electrolysis equipment.

Meanwhile, unfortunately, the Z16 had been destroyed on the ground in bad weather. George and Maurice, I said, had disappeared in the city ruins. My searches for them were in vain though I did catch glimpses of a few savages hiding in the shadows in the city. I feared Maurice and George had met a bad end at their hands.

This story did not make good advertising. Whatever PR benefit there was to the Le Pens from the recovery of the older ship was negated by the loss of the newer one.

I, of course, did not benefit from my return either. My inheritance soon was stolen. Thanks to the generosity of Pierre Roulant, however, I was able to purchase a used airship of my own several years later. It was very same one and it was still paisley.

This brings us back to the reporter Boris Fontaine and my supposed threat to civilization. It was an addendum to the journals I sold to Boris. Here is the full text.

"The submission of this last and uncompleted journal clears my debt to you, Boris, and to *Pierre Roulant.* By the time you receive this I will be in South Dakota. I have used the money from this sale to finance my trip. It may interest you to know that I intend to place crews on continuous alert inside the Minuteman missile control rooms. The movement of any outside military force of any size across any border of North or South Dakota will be considered cause to launch those missiles against targets in Quebec.

I have not yet decided whether George or Joelle had the correct philosophy. If I tip toward George I will trust in this deterrent. If I decide Joelle was right, the warheads are already in flight."

CHAPTER 4

SNOW

INTERRUPTION OF TRANSCRIPT BY AGENT 4:

The courtroom was quiet. Aeneas remained on his feet but was lost in his own thoughts. The Prosecutor took the opportunity to rise slowly. All eyes turned towards him.

TRIAL TRANSCRIPT:

PROUDFOOT: Your Honors, the defendant has described himself as an inspired liar. I will grant him that. His testimony is also an admission to the charges against him. I ask that his plea be changed to guilty.

AENEAS CUSTER: Mr. Prosecutor, I admit to nothing! My supposed threat, for example, obviously contained a mighty big "if" as you just have heard.

HIRISAWA [consults colleagues]: That is not at all obvious, Mr. Custer. However, there is a slight wiggle room in its interpretation. The prosecution's motion to change the defendant's plea is denied.

PROSECUTOR: Your honor, do we need to produce radioactive rubble as evidence to prove his threat was real?

HIRISAWA: You are flirting with contempt.

AENEAS CUSTER: Your Honors, the point is I never had any real authority over the Minuteman force. When I wrote my note, any such idea was wishful thinking on my part. I was then and am now an unarmed man.

HIRISAWA: Mr. Custer, you promised to sit down and be quiet once you were done with your story. Are you done?

AENEAS CUSTER: No, sir. I'm just now getting to the heart of my defense.

HIRISAWA: Please get on with it then.

AENEAS CUSTER: Yes, your Honor. Heraclitus said that you cannot step into the same river twice.

HIRISAWA: You had better make that pertinent immediately.

AENEAS CUSTER: Yes, sir. You can't walk in the same desert twice either. The South Dakota I knew as a teenager was gone long before I had a chance to return. I should have expected that, but somehow I didn't. More wishful thinking, I suppose. Whatever Joelle's character flaws, she had created something special in the Black Hills. With a slightly softer touch it would have been as close to a paradise as human beings are likely to create anywhere.

JUDGE JEANIE: That is highly debatable, Mr. Custer. It also is irrelevant.

AENEAS CUSTER: Yes, ma'am. I request forgiveness for my nostalgia. George told me that in his youth he was driven to distraction by old men and women who recounted endlessly tales about some Golden Age of Love that existed some decades before the climatic disaster. All these people were born at someplace called Woodstock. Perhaps I and my fellow Dakotans are similarly annoying.

JUDGE JEANIE: No perhaps about it.

AENEAS CUSTER: Yes, ma'am. I'm sure you are right.

As for my "crimes against humanity" which took place in that desert, there is no doubt that if crimes they are, they are quite awful ones. Yet I pulled no triggers. I pushed no buttons. If there is some way in which I am culpable, all I can say in mitigation is that I didn't mean it. Intent should count for something. At the time none of my actions seemed the slightest bit hostile, unreasonable, irresponsible, or reckless. It is easy to be wrong about such things.

I admit to being stupid. Writing that minatory note to Boris may not have been criminal, but it was certainly a mistake. It was provocative to the Quebecois to a degree that I failed to predict. Never doubt the power of words.

To be sure, I was smart enough to realize I had put myself in some danger, but it simply did not occur to me that I might have endangered others. I was not accustomed to being taken so seriously. Boris, I expected, would call the police. I assumed they would consider my threat just barely credible enough to justify a warrant for my arrest. My plan, therefore, was to flee Quebec's jurisdiction before Boris could make his call.

In order to give myself enough time, I arranged for a courier to deliver the journals and my note to Boris after a five-day delay. I had determined that this interval would allow me to reach Montreal. There I would take possession of an airship I already had contracted to purchase. By my calculations there was a 72-hour margin of safety for me.

Never trust your life to such armchair reckoning. There was no margin of safety. I missed a morning boat connection on the St. Lawrence. The next boat was behind schedule. When I reached Montreal I barely had time to find the offices of *Selon Lui*, the advertising company that owned the blimp, before they closed for the day. The receptionist referred me to the Resources Manager, whatever that job title means in any language, who refused to hand over the title to the airship even though I had pre-paid for it. More precisely, her administrative assistant refused. The manager herself was too busy to see me at all.

The assistant informed me there was a new transfer tax on motor vehicles. Quebec had determined airships were covered by it. I would have to pay the tax and return with the receipt before I formally could take ownership. There was no point in seeing the manager before then.

I spent that night at the Montreal *Chateau Champlain*, a 36-story structure that had held up rather well to the passage of years. Keeping a building of this size in operation in the modern world is a labor of love. There is far too small a customer base to make the enterprise economically sensible. Modest motels make better profits. Maintenance is far more manageable. However, I was pleased that some business owners were motivated more by panache than by the bottom line.

The desk clerk looked at me suspiciously when I told him my backpack was my only luggage, but when I paid him in advance in gold he started to speak in a halting but serviceable English and he called me "sir." The rooms and the other hotel facilities were lovely.

For a time that evening I sat at the bar at the hotel's *Le Gauchetiere* restaurant and watched a table full of pretty girls have an animated conversation. I am clumsy with women and clumsier yet with French, so the prospect of dealing with a French woman deterred me from making any advances. Yet, I began to wonder if I had made a mistake about leaving the country. With money in one's pocket Quebec wasn't so bad. Then too, maybe Selena was no longer the sweet young thing I remembered. Maybe South Dakota wasn't so grand.

I put my doubts aside. They didn't matter. I was committed. My arrest was near certain if I stayed. I also felt obligated to warn the Dakotans that the Quebecois knew of their existence. I returned to my room and sunk my head into the down-filled pillow. The fresh linen smelled wonderful. Sleep arrived quickly.

I spent all of the next day waiting in line at an understaffed motor vehicles office in order to pay my tax. Why there were lines when motor vehicles all but had disappeared from the roads was a mystery. Near the end of the workday my payment was processed.

Receipt in hand, I rushed back to the advertising firm a few minutes before 5 o'clock. The Resources Manager had gone home early and she had left no instructions with her assistant who refused to act on her own authority. Another night of good food, unrequited lust, and sound sleep followed.

I was waiting in the Resource Manager's office again when she arrived at work the next morning at 9:10. The woman did not make any eye contact with me. She entered her office and closed the door behind her. Half an hour later a buzzer sounded on the assistant's desk. The assistant stood up and entered the manager's office. In one-quarter hour she re-emerged and asked me for my receipt. I gave it to her. The assistant went to her own desk and retrieved a paper, already signed and sealed, from the top drawer. She proffered it. The blimp was mine.

Back out on the street, I hailed a horse-drawn taxi. The ride to the airfield was bumpy and long. The suburbs around Montreal had deteriorated but still felt somehow comfortable. Most of the streets were overgrown and most of the houses were in ruins. Yet here and there were cul-de-sacs where the houses were freshly painted, the lawns were mowed, the streetlights worked and the asphalt pavement was in perfect repair. One almost expected the Beaver to walk down the sidewalk and twirl around a lamppost.

At long last we approached the airfield. I fought back a sudden and embarrassing urge to cry as the faded paisley airship came into view. The taxi driver drove out onto the field and pulled up alongside the gondola. I over-tipped him.

An inspection of the craft revealed a sticker on the windshield indicating the engine was 800 operational hours overdue for service. This seemed rather a lot. I buttonholed a voluble mechanic in a nearby hanger and he agreed. I never did catch the fellow's name. He probably included it in the suffusion of French, but I understood only one word in three.

Taking advantage of a pause while he caught his breath, I begged him and bribed him to work overtime on my engine. A handful of gold coins persuaded him. Nevertheless, he insisted the work couldn't be done until the next day. He needed some parts from the Le Pen factory.

I was surprised the Le Pens were still in business and said so. The mechanic said they had landed a new government contract.

At my urging he called the factory and left an order for the parts with the answering service. I told him to offer 50% over standard price for rush delivery. He frowned, but did as I asked. After hanging up he talked about engine repair, his wife, his financial problems, and his dog. Then he left for the day.

There was little more I could do that night. I wished I was as mechanically adept as George had been. He would have taken apart the engine himself. Our parents sometimes cripple us by giving us an academic education at the expense of more practical skills. I slept in the gondola that night and dreamed of Selena.

To my pleasant surprise, a diesel powered delivery truck with *Dirigeable Fabrique Nordique* emblazoned on the side rumbled onto the airfield early the next morning. I paid the driver on the spot for the parts. I hoped the gold would reach the Le Pens. I had been trouble enough to them in the past and didn't want to cause them further outrage. The mechanic showed up for work an hour after the delivery. I'm sure he wondered what my rush was as I paced restlessly.

The mechanic was happy to have someone listen to his troubles as his tools squeaked and his liquids glugged. He chattered incomprehensibly over his shoulder at me the entire time. I was growing nervous. In only a few hours my courier would be knocking on Boris' door. The sun was low in the sky before the mechanic wiped the oil off his hands with a rag and totaled his hours for me. When I paid him he finally went quiet. He seemed sorry to have our relationship end. Minutes later he helped me untie the ship and I was airborne.

The engine started smoothly and the big propeller blade delivered a powerful thrust. I had no wish to re-experience the brutal weather George, Maurice and I had encountered over Lake Ontario and Lake Erie on our last trip, so I steered southwest toward the Finger Lakes district of New York State. I planned to fly over Pennsylvania. This proved an auspicious choice. The weather was magnificent the entire way.

There was a reason besides weather to prefer an overland route. West of the Poconos, Pennsylvania was wild and virtually unpopulated country. Although nominally part of Greater

Quebec, it was beyond the rule of law. The Pennsylvania route therefore denied the Quebecois any realistic chance to locate or intercept me. On Lake Ontario there would be fishing boats equipped with radios.

The airship felt like home. The very scratches on the control panel were familiar. The gondola's aroma, rich with hydrocarbons, evoked memories of George and Joelle. I carved the name *Nearer* on the rail. George would have liked that. The name suited the vehicle somehow.

My southerly route was pleasantly uneventful. The only being to express an interest in me was a hawk. For a minute or two he glided with motionless wings less than a meter off my port window. Then he veered to the left and was gone.

The succession of hills and valleys below was soporific. I nodded off at the wheel. Eventually, some minor turbulence shook me awake, but a quick look around showed the autopilot had done its job without my supervision. Ahead the downtown towers of Pittsburgh soared out of the green jungle looking for all the world like Oz. Tall factory smokestacks also poked out of the canopy. I couldn't help picturing a workforce of munchkins.

The jungle gave way to savanna in Ohio. The grass shifted from green to brown as we continued west. By the Indiana line, I saw barren desert below. Feeling safe, I intentionally settled down for a long nap and allowed the autopilot to guide the ship over the Midwest.

I awoke feeling refreshed. Below was a landscape of magnificent sand dunes. Rudolf Valentino on a white stallion would have finished the scene to perfection. It occurs to me, and probably to the learned judges, that I watched too many movies in my youth.

Guesstimating my position to be west of the Mississippi, I swung the ship northwest. Sunsets in the desert are fast and colorful. Sand turns blood red and then fades to gray. Stars brighten overhead like electric lights on a dimmer switch.

As the winter constellation of Orion fought a losing battle with the moon for dominion overhead, the land below grew ragged. Buttes and spires glowed in the reflected light and seemed as unreal in the bright moonlight. The range of hues reminded me of some Loony Tunes artist's conception of Mars.

These were the Badlands of South Dakota below me and that meant home was near.

Memories swept me up once more. I eagerly awaited my reunion with Selena and I hoped she remembered me fondly. If only in deference to the last wishes of Joelle she surely would welcome me back. Hours dragged as Nearer was slowed by a head wind. Not too soon for me, red reappeared in the sky, this time in the east.

A view of the Black Hills filled the windshield. Flying above them felt as familiar as a walk on a hometown street. The four faces of Mount Rushmore peeked over a far hill. They grew slowly as I flew closer. Abe Lincoln's beard had acquired some gray. Whether this was deliberate aging by the local artists, or simply weathering of the paint, I couldn't tell. All the faces looked a bit pale, but the quality of the morning light made this uncertain too. The entrance to Beautiful Rushmore Cave came into view.

It was a gorgeous new day. I needed a shave and a bath but I felt strong, healthy and enthusiastic. My life, which had been interrupted for the past five years, was about to resume.

I made a low pass over the site as an announcement of my arrival. The grounds outside the cave were neater than I remembered. A handful of farmers in clothes of muted hues were tending to the sheeted gardens, while two other workers adjusted photoelectric panels. These few had started work early, but the commune members always worked and played when it suited them. So long as people completed their chores, Joelle had not been a stickler for schedules. The farmers stopped work to watch me but did not leave the gardens. The panel workers disappeared inside the cave. I circled while news of my presence spread.

Nearly fifteen minutes passed. The farmers resumed their work, though they looked up at me frequently. No colorful merry throngs rushed out to greet me. It was still early, I reminded myself; most of the commune might still be sleeping off the effects of a party.

At last a response came from the cave, and it was not comforting. Two men dressed in desert beige uniforms scurried out. They carried deadly accurate M40A1 rifles. These weapons had been hand-made specifically for the US Marine Corps back around the turn of the millennium. I wondered who had found them and where. They took sniper positions by the rocks near the cave entrance. They aimed at me.

As soon as they were in position, a third young man, also dressed in a beige uniform, walked out of the cave. He strode to the large flat sand-covered area that once had been the visitor's parking lot for this former national park. He motioned for my line. I tossed it over the side.

The directional maneuvering thrusters allowed me to steady the craft while he secured the rope to a steel ring mounted on one of four concrete posts. The ring was rusty. Using the winch I lowered the craft to the ground. I tossed him three more ropes in order to secure the craft firmly. As soon as they were tied I shut down the engine.

I was shocked by the military response to my arrival. I was disturbed not only by the sniper rifles, but by the fact they were fielded by men. Something was horribly wrong. It was too late to retreat, however. So, I put my misgivings aside, swung myself out of the gondola, and dropped to the ground.

"Come," said the beige man laconically.

We walked up the path. Two 7.62 muzzles followed my movement until we entered the cave. The familiar coolness of the cave air washed over me. The smell, however, had altered. The underlying odor of the rocks remained the same and evoked old memories, but the anticipated overlay of incense and perfume was gone. Gone also were the wall-coverings and murals of orgiastic scenes. The latter had been painted over with off-white paint. White florescent lights shone overhead in place of the party lights that once had marked the way.

The Big Room was as impressive as ever, due to its size and natural formations. The human aspects of the place had changed radically. Gaudy tribal chaos had been replaced by understated compartmentalized order. The space was subdivided into distinctly defined areas. Carpets hung on wooden frames formed walls of private units. In front of many of them were tables stacked with trade goods. The very existence of these divisions suggested that the family had broken up into families.

From the quiet I guessed that most of the residents were still asleep. The handful of people who were awake busied themselves at productive tasks. They stacked clothes, sorted items at the tables, swept up, and performed household chores. In place of the former outrageous and suggestive fashions were practical work garments. Blue jeans and tee shirts were typical.

The early risers present in the cave seemed only mildly interested in my appearance. They glanced my way occasionally but none called out or approached me. My attention was so diverted by this unexpected environment that I didn't notice my guide had stopped. I walked into him and he elbowed me back gruffly. We stood before the entrance to Joelle's old throne room. The beads, which once separated it from the Big Room, had been replaced by a six panel steel door set in a mortared stone wall. My guide knocked.

"Enter!" a muffled female voice commanded.

The guard opened the door for me. He remained outside when I entered.

The interior furnishings had been rearranged but still were conservative and homey. Couches, a dining table, and a four-poster bed occupied most of the available floor space. A red runner carpet ran straight from the entry door to the niche in the wall that had been Joelle's throne. There on the throne sat a trim Selena. The trace of baby fat she had as a teenager was replaced by muscle. She casually leaned back holding one knee with two hands as her heel rested on the seat edge. Instead of a white robe she wore blue jeans, a crisp blue denim blouse, a wide brown leather belt, and brown cowboy boots. A white Western-style hat lay by her side. Joelle's spear-wielding Amazons were nowhere in sight. She was not without protection, however. Selena was flanked by two handsome young men in beige uniforms. They carried classic Colt .45 automatic sidearms and stood in an "at ease" posture.

"Hello, Custer. Or do you call yourself Johnston these days?"

"Just call me Aeneas. I've wandered enough to earn the name."

"You only have begun to earn it, I'm afraid. You'll forgive me if I don't play Dido."

I don't know why I expected Selena to be illiterate.

"You are forgiven. My namesake needed help from his mom to manipulate Dido anyway. Venus doesn't love me that much."

"She used to, kid. She used to. Lot of good it did her. I've seen the blast site where Control Center 2 used to be. You killed Joelle, didn't you? George too."

"No. Actually, George targeted the warheads himself."

"Really? Hmm. Well, that makes you much less interesting."

"Sorry to disappoint."

"Don't fret about it, but please don't tell me why an older chick named Jennifer is gunning for you. She says you ruined her life. That impressed me when I heard it. Now I'm worried your offense will turn out to be something trivial."

"I betrayed her trust."

"That doesn't sound terribly villainous, but it is something I suppose. So, why are you here, Aeneas? Why aren't you back in Morrisbourg spending all your money? Or have you already spent it?"

"No, some other folks were kind enough to spend it for me. I'm here because I hate the East. I miss this place. I miss you. My fondest memories are of here and of you. This is where I belong. Joelle made something very special out of these Hills. She was a visionary and a genius."

"Joelle was an idiot. That whole commune scene was unsustainable. We followed her orders because she was a big cult heroine and because she would have thrown us in the arena if we didn't. But even if she had lived, the next generation wouldn't have taken her seriously. Teenagers already were snickering at all her hokum."

"Teenagers always do that. They prefer their own hokum."

"You know, Aeneas, Le Clerc was the most admirable fellow of the bunch of you. He stood up to Joelle and argued with her face-to-face. I never saw anyone do that before. He helped me to start thinking for myself. A few of the things he said were even true. He was right to criticize all the drugs around here for example."

"Maybe. Everyone here seemed pretty happy though. Joelle was just trying to get people to expand their minds."

"All she did was fry their brains. That woman had a screw

loose and so do you for trying to justify her. Damn! My own mother gave me opium and LSD and who knows what else? How sick is that? How can you think that was good for me? None of that stuff expanded my mind. It just made me stupidly euphoric at the cost of whopping hangovers.

"All that poison nearly killed me, especially the uppers, which I started abusing seriously after you left. They made me crazy at night and useless all day. I can't count the number of times I was on all fours heaving into a bucket. I had the complexion of a corpse. Whenever I forced myself to look in a mirror I knew it had to stop. I did one day when I actually spoke the words, 'OK, Maurice. You win this one.'"

"You know what Paracelsus said about that kind of thing."

"No, I don't."

"He was..."

"I know who he was. Make your point."

"He said everything is poison and everything is medicine. It is all a matter of dose. Moderation..."

"The proper dose of some things is zero. Look, I don't stop the folks here from killing themselves with drugs if that is what they want to do, but I sure don't encourage it or waste precious resources making the stuff. Anyway, rampant drug abuse was just the beginning of what was wrong around here. Economically and socially Joelle made this place a lunatic asylum.

"Hey, I'll give credit where it is due. Joelle did invest in enough basic industry to make civilized life here possible; but she had no interest in productivity beyond the barest minimum. In fact, she set up huge disincentives. She made personal achievement a crime. There was no way for anyone to get ahead. Joelle talked about freedom, but locked up everybody in her communalist prison."

"There is more to life than material gain," I suggested tritely.

"Oh, please. Don't try to act all spiritual with me. I grew up with people who were experts at that. You aren't even an amateur. You just told me that other folks spent all your money. Would you have come back here if you still had it?"

"Perhaps not."

"Definitely not. We all want more for ourselves, my dear brother. Life is about getting it. I hope you noticed Joelle knew that well enough to enrich herself. She also knew that the point of rules is to make the getting easier for the rulemakers. Joelle made herself a queen and the rest of us her serfs. Glorified, doped up, oversexed serfs, because that was how she wanted us, but we were serfs all the same."

"And now you are the rulemaker."

"Right, and I'm not ashamed to use that position to benefit myself and my buddies."

Selena tickled the posterior of the guard to her right as she said this. He did not alter his stance or change his stony countenance.

"But I'm not a monomaniac about it," she continued. "I've made it possible for other people to benefit themselves too. Hard work can get you somewhere for yourself and your own family now. Some of our more successful farmers even own their own caves. If you can't see that my way is kinder than Joelle's, you are as blind as the cultists."

"From that remark I gather there are some cultists who object to your new methods."

"There always is a lunatic fringe, Aeneas, but the better classes support me and my reforms 100%. I'll do you the favor of assuming you are not a total fool. Despite your sentimental tripe, you really have come to me because you are broke and you know it. Well, I'm sorry, but you do not have a home here. Your presence is very destabilizing."

"For you."

"Of course for me. Who else?"

"Why am I destabilizing?"

"Because of the fringe. I read once that the world is divided between the have-nots who want something and the haves who want everything."

"That's Gore Vidal, I think."

"Was it? Anyway, while basically true, there is a more sinister side to those basically healthy desires. If the have-nots can't or won't get more, they will settle for seeing their neighbors get less. Envy is powerful, popular, and self-destructive. For their own good the lower orders need to stop demanding and start producing."

"I didn't think the population was large enough here for class to be so important."

"Class starts to be important when the population reaches two, Aeneas. You encourage social discontent."

"How? I haven't roused a single rabble."

"Because of our peculiar history, our malcontents have their political goals all mixed-up with mysticism. They want a revival of Joelle's quasi-religious egalitarianism. As 'The Custer' you are the cultists' obvious hero."

"I see. So now I'm a working-class hero. All I wanted was to be king."

Selena laughed, "I suppose that's the dialectic of history. Quite honestly, I'm tempted to kill you, but you are as dangerous as a martyr as you are living among us. It is much better for me if you run away. So, you can be king of the road. Get out."

"You mean get out of South Dakota?"

"Yes, I mean get out of South Dakota! I'll tell everyone you approve of my social and market reforms and you saw no need to stay. Even the ones who don't believe me will at least believe you are a coward. Go!"

"Go where?"

"Don't tempt me to be crude. I don't care. Your airship is being fitted and supplied as we speak. Be grateful I'm letting you keep it instead of making you walk. You will do me the return favor of taking three passengers with you."

"Who?"

"Subversives. Mystics who pine for the old ways. You should be pleased. Two of them are pretty women. You communalists can burn incense to the memory of Joelle, fog your minds with whatever dope you please, and have a love fest in the sky. Enjoy yourselves. But do it someplace else."

"You are missing one option, Selena. I could back you up in your policies without leaving. I'm not opposed to plutocracy if I get to be a plutocrat. We could rule together..."

"Please! One, I don't trust you; two, a relationship between us would be perverse and I'm old enough now to know it; and three, you weren't that good."

She turned to the guard she had tickled, and gently ordered "Escort Mr. Custer to the holding room, Brown Eyes."

He returned a crisp salute.

"Catherine the Great," I muttered to myself while being escorted to the door.

"I heard that!"

I was led to the same side chamber where George, Maurice and I once had rested before Joelle's big party. The décor was more utilitarian, but it once again contained a full bathtub and grooming tools. A touch with my left index finger proved the tub water was hot. I stripped and relaxed in the tub for more than an hour. Selena's efficiency had some advantages. I'm sure that if there had been any trains in her domain, she would have made them run on time.

I was still soaking when a soldier entered and ordered, "Come."

"I come," I answered in my best Tarzan mode.

The soldier didn't find this amusing. He waited impatiently as I dried off and donned my clothes. We walked back to the cave entrance. Once again I attracted subdued attention from people we passed on the way, but none spoke to me.

The sudden rise in temperature as we exited the cave made me dizzy. The bright sun was painful. Only by squinting could I see my fellow subversives. Flanked by uniformed men with M16s they stood by Nearer. One of my passengers was a strapping young blond man who would have been at home in an old surfer movie. Next to him were two young, dark-haired women. Selena was right. They were pretty. All three social undesirables wore bright colors and unruly hair that clashed with the current clean-cut fashions at Rushmore.

The soldiers wasted no time. They helped us into the gondola with more force than was necessary, and unceremoniously released the mooring lines. The ship rose gently and a light wind carried us away from the cave. The faces of Mount Rushmore looked on. The unattended paint would fade to white in only a few more years. This thought made me sad.

As I fussed with the controls, I felt myself being evaluated. I looked over my shoulder into the blue eyes of the fair-skinned brunette.

"You're really the Custer?" she asked.

"Yes. Disappointed?"

"Yes," she answered with simple, brutal honesty.

"And your name is?"

"Charlene. That's Chester and Maggie. Where are we going?"

"I don't know yet. We can't go back East. I burned a few bridges there. I am open to suggestion."

"Greenland is supposed to be nice," Charlene offered.

"Yes, but Quebec is in between. I don't want to over-fly it and I definitely don't want to go around the long way."

"How about California?" asked Chester.

"It's pretty stormy there I understand."

"BC? Alaska?" he asked.

"Maybe. Russian pirates are wreaking havoc along the coasts, but the inland areas should be fine. There is a good chance the Canadians would be hostile simply because I'm from Quebec, so Alaska might be the better choice. Fairbanks is nice I hear."

"This is all about you, isn't it? I want to go to Greenland," complained Charlene.

My response was equally childish. "It's my airship."

"Let's go anyplace with a coast. I'd rather be on the beach regardless," said Chester.

"How would you know? You've never seen a beach," I reminded him.

"Dakota is a beach. I've never seen an ocean. I would like to."

"The Canadians won't shoot at us if we fly over them to Alaska, will they?" asked Charlene.

"I don't know. They might."

"That's not good."

"South." It was the first word spoken by the woman with a rusty complexion and distinctly Native American features. The name Maggie didn't fit her.

"What?" I wasn't sure I heard her right.

"Go South."

"You are aware that the sun lives down there."

"Yes, but what you said about going around the long way made me think. Why not make it a long trip? Suppose we go beyond the equator? Argentina. Maybe Chile. Let's get out of North America. Can we make it that far in this contraption?"

"Possibly, if we loot along the way."

"Abandoned property is not loot. It is salvage. That's what Selena says, anyway, and she is the law." There was undisguised bitterness in Maggie's voice.

"You don't think very highly of her."

"Do you?"

"Yes, as a matter of fact I do. But we have no choice but to leave. Hmmm... South. Well, that would be an adventure and it's not as though I have something better to do. Okay, I am up for it. All agreed?"

Maggie nodded. Charlene was silent. Chester waved a hand non-committally.

"South it is."

The engine responded to the throttle. There is something enjoyable about the feel of acceleration against the back of the seat. We flew toward the sun as it rose toward noon.

My passengers looked back toward Beautiful Rushmore Cave with unvoiced regret. I knew how they felt. There is no patriot like an expatriate. Chester picked up my binoculars and looked back every three or four minutes. Over the next two hours Mount Rushmore shrank to an unrecognizable bump on the Horizon. It was about that time that Chester leaned over the rail. He seemed to strain his eyes into the glasses. He grew agitated. He tapped my shoulder.

"What is that?" Chester pointed to the distant sky.

I looked, but saw nothing but blue. I grabbed the binoculars from him and looked again. Just barely I could see little dark cigar shaped objects.

"Airships! The French must be attacking Rushmore Cave."

As I watched, thin vapor trails leaped from the
ground. My stomach turned.

"Missile tracks. Shit. Shit!"

I couldn't help feeling responsible. I hoped Selena survived the next half-hour. Boris too.

It is unrewarding to brood over what is past, or at least it is unpleasant. The future is enough to consider. We tried to ignore what we had seen. That night we took up Selena's suggestion and had an orgy in the sky to celebrate the resurrection of Joelle's

Utopia. We told each other we would bring our commune in pure form to wherever we were going and spread enlightenment to whomever we found there.

As a recently designated working-class, hero I recalled the dictum of Marx that history repeats itself, the first time as tragedy and the second time as comedy. We reversed that order. Our sexual groping and panting had none of the spontaneity, joy, or sense of play that I had recalled from my last visit to South Dakota. Our sweaty task was depressingly like work.

Perhaps I am projecting too much. Perhaps my joy alone was curtailed because the two ladies gave Surfer Boy much more attention than they gave me, despite my being the Custer. Afterwards we were oddly quiet, except for Chester who cheerfully muttered the occasional inanity.

In order to get my mind on something else I explained the controls to Maggie who seemed the most competent of the three passengers. She seemed to understand the controls instantly, so I let her navigate. She chose a course of SSW. We throttled down to our most economical setting and slowly churned south.

The landscape below stayed persistently Saharan. Wherever we could identify old settlements we located fuel and topped up our tanks. Water was the scarcer resource. We tried to identify old food stores. Usually some water was to be found inside. Our biggest score was at a Shop Rite in Littleton, Colorado. Oddly, the ancients sold water in plastic bottles. The prices on the bottles were higher than the prices on nearby fuel pumps. I thought water was too abundant in those days to sell for so much.

The foothills of the Rockies were nearby. The upper slopes of the mountains might have been habitable and inhabited, but I didn't question Maggie's determination to continue south keeping the mountains on our right. I enjoyed surrendering responsibility to someone else. Near the New Mexican border she checked our maps, looked thoughtful, and made a sharp turn west. The mountainous terrain remained arid and uninviting. Eventually I grew curious.

"You have something in mind closer than Argentina, don't you?"

"Yes. Or rather I had something in mind. It doesn't look promising now. You took long enough to ask."

"We trust you."

"You do? Why?"

"You've got me there. So where is this unpromising place of yours?

"We're here."

"Where is here?"

Low canyon walls opened up on each side of us. The canyon walls held giant caves with extensive whitened ruins.

"What an odd place to build."

"We're at Mesa Verde. Anasazi settlements. I heard about them as a girl."

"They look rather light on the modern conveniences, like roads and drainage."

"No doubt. They were abandoned 800 years ago. Perched on cliffs the way they are, I figured they were very defensible. I hoped with the climate all topsy-turvy maybe the area was getting some rainfall these days. I hoped we could start another Rushmore here."

"It doesn't look as though it has rained here in years. You can fry your dinner on those rocks."

"Yes, so I see. Never mind. It doesn't matter. This

place is unlivable. I'm glad we came here though because it gives me another idea."

"A better one I hope."

"Me too. How high can this thing fly?" Maggie asked.

"I don't know. My dad took one over the Appalachians

once without a problem — until he was shot down."

"Our present elevation above sea level is higher than the Appalachians. Maybe we can do a lot better. Let's take her up and get out of this heat. Let's see what Nearer can do. I like that name by the way."

"Why?"

"You don't know?"

"No. It was George's idea."

"I'll tell you one day if you are good. Take her up."

"Roger."

"Who?"

Uncertain if Maggie was teasing me, I retreated behind dignity and stated, "We are going up."

The ground fell away beneath us.

"Nice machine."

"The Le Pens would be gratified to hear your opinion. Maybe I can short wave them a message one day ... if they are still alive... if there is still a Montreal."

"Selena is a bitch."

My instinct was to argue this point, but evidence was on Maggie's side. There was no excuse for firing those missiles. I hoped they weren't aimed at civilians. If they were, unless the Quebecois soldiers were almost inhumanly civilized, Selena likely wouldn't survive her capture. This thought was depressing.

I spoke to Maggie. "George, Maurice and I sabotaged those missiles. Did Selena undo that somehow? I guess you wouldn't know about it."

"I know about it. I was part of a control room crew until I opened my mouth and got labeled a subversive. Now she has only her soldier boys on alert status. Those anal retentive robots will obey any order she gives them."

"So how did she undo the sabotage?"

"She didn't. She suspected that you guys didn't get around to all the control rooms, so she just looked for ones with no sign of tampering. The ones with targeting computers that responded to the Custer's code word 'luggage' obviously were ones to avoid. She didn't trust the Custer."

I ignored her reference to George as the Custer instead of as the former Custer. Wasn't I the Custer now?

"The lady has a suspicious nature. She was right though."

"It would have been a little hard on the control crews if she had guessed wrong, wouldn't it? Why did you and George lie to us?"

I stole from Mark Twain, "Truth is a precious resource. One should be economical with it."

Charlene and Chester violated their free love principles by becoming a couple. They made love that night and didn't invite us. I doubt they even gave it a thought. Maggie ignored them. Maggie didn't invite me either. The commune was already in trouble.

Our southward flight continued with a slight western detour. The Grand Canyon was spectacular. We probably were the first tourists in a generation to see it. The jungle returned somewhere near the Mexican border. Then we were forced into strict rationing. No trace of old cities could be seen through the steam and growth.

We got a break at Acapulco where the foliage began to thin. Several seaside resort hotels looked almost as though they were open for business. We landed under a brilliant full moon. Even at night the hotel interiors were like ovens, but we were able to replenish our supplies of water, canned goods, and fuel without incident. I joked with Maggie about taking a room for half an hour but she ignored me in the way that a genteel host ignores a guest's flatulence. I avoided suggestive humor with her after that.

We grew accustomed to the blazing sun. In the rarefied air of higher altitudes the heat was surprisingly tolerable. We proceeded southeast. The foliage below us continued to thin out until it disappeared altogether. The barren desert beneath us was not the windswept sandy sort. The ground looked hard and solid. Heat waves seemed to make the rocky surface ripple.

My desire to sightsee was outweighed by our need to make time. Make time we did. We kept our distance from a volcanic eruption in progress in Nicaragua but couldn't avoid some of the airborne soot. I worried about the turbine clogging. It proved to be a very forgiving engine, however, and delivered its power without interruption. I thought I detected a slight increase in its noise, but I couldn't be sure. I vowed silently to clean and lubricate the engine at the earliest opportunity. Even though the engine could not appreciate my thoughts, I felt more confident after making the promise. An opportunity to top our tanks appeared near the Isthmus.

"Let's pause here," I recommended.

"Are you nuts?" Maggie asked.

"Possibly, but we should top our tanks."

"Where? I don't see anything down there but dirt. Keep going."

"See that big ditch and those chunks of concrete? I think it's the Panama Canal. There must be loads of stored fuel around there."

"So what? I don't see any buildings. They must be burned to the ground."

"Probably."

"What if even buried oil tanks boiled over or exploded?"

"Then we're out of luck. I think anything buried in the ground should stay cool enough though. Up North the earth is a constant 15 degrees C year round once you dig down a meter. I doubt it is much different here."

"I'll bet that top meter is mighty warm though."

"No doubt. In fact, we had better wait until night to land. The daytime heat down there is a killer."

"Land where?"

"There. See that?"

"What?"

"A broken up concrete strip. It looks like an airport runway. I'll bet those big rectangles are hanger foundations. That smaller one is what we need. I think that was a garage for trucks. They must have had their own tanks on site."

"All right let's circle until night and then take a look around."

Charlene and Chester made love again while we circled and waited. They seldom talked to Maggie or me any longer.

They were getting on my nerves. Maggie took no notice of them. As the sun set, a thick fog formed at our altitude and descended to the ground. We followed it to the surface.

"Chester, Charlene, make yourselves useful and try to keep this ship on the ground while Aeneas and I look for fuel."

"OK." Charlene took the wheel. Chester put his arms around her from behind. She giggled. Somehow these two naked people fondling each other at the controls were not reassuring.

The fog was a sauna. I kept dancing to make the ground bearable through my thick leather soles. By one foundation wall a pipe stuck out of the ground. I tapped it with my foot and smiled at Maggie. She shrugged and walked back to the gondola to retrieve the hose. I burned my fingers on the pipe cap. I returned to the gondola and asked for the toolbox while Maggie stood with the hose.

"The black tool box?" asked Chester.

"The only tool box. Yes it is black."

A few moments later the judicious use of a hammer removed the cap. A musty petroleum smell exuded from the pipe.

"What do you think it is?" Maggie asked.

"I don't know. It doesn't matter." Our multifuel turbine had a wonderfully varied appetite. It would run on almost anything, maybe even tar though I never tried it. The pump hummed as it sucked the mystery fuel into our tank. As I shifted my weight from foot to foot I grew aware of a susurration like the shifting of sand in the wind. There was no wind. I spotted the source.

"Look at those." I pointed out to Maggie.

A mat of mushrooms pushed up through the soil. Their heads expanded as we watched. These fungi already had adapted to the brutal environment, perhaps by forming hardened spores for the day and absorbing moisture from the night fog.

"Do you think they are edible?"

"You are welcome to try them," she offered.

"Maybe next time."

The fungi rose around our feet. I kicked at them, and they fell over easily.

"Look at the size of them. That one is a foot high and still growing."

"They get through their lives in a hurry though. The ones that first sprouted are rotting away already."

The mushrooms where she pointed trembled and toppled.

"I don't think they're rotting." A rustling and crunching sound grew in intensity all around us. "Something is eating them. Bugs."

"I hate bugs."

Maggie had a lot to hate. Beetles emerged from the ground everywhere. The oversized mushrooms all around us turned black with them. The mushrooms were eaten as fast as they could grow.

"Yuck. Are we done here, Aeneas?"

"Near enough."

I called to Chester to kill the pump. Then I rolled the hose and lifted it up into the gondola. Behind me Maggie shrieked.

"What's the matter?"

Then I knew.

"Ouch! Damn it!"

My legs were covered with beetles and blood. "Into the gondola now!" I lifted Maggie by the waist over the rim. I was right behind her.

"Lift out of here!"

Charlene fumbled at the controls until I pushed her aside. I dropped ballast, adjusted ballonets, started the engine, vectored our thrust, and pushed the throttle.

The only time I ever saw Maggie cry was when she was picking off beetles. I joined her. So did Chester and Charlene because some of the bugs crawled off us and onto them. They gave their lovemaking a rest for the remainder of the night.

We were able to remove all the beetles. Wherever one was present was a painful certainty. There must have been some toxin in the insect bites. I don't remember passing out, but all of us were unconscious within the hour.

Once again, we owed our survival over the next few hours to the simple but solid engineering of the Le Pens; for when I awoke the unattended engine was purring steadily. We were over open ocean and heading south. I felt ill.

I nudged Maggie. She groaned and lifted her head. I never have seen her look worse.

"Where do you think we are?"

She groggily took in the situation. "I don't know.

Pacific probably. Go east. Southeast."

"We may not have been going south all this time. We didn't engage auto-pilot."

"You mean you didn't. Why not?"

"I just didn't. Look, if this is the Atlantic, going east will take us further out to sea."

"True. But if it is not the Pacific, it is probably the Caribbean and east will take us over islands. Would you rather go west?"

Odds favored Maggie's bet. "No."

"Well?"

I nodded and turned our machine to the southeast. After several hours a shoreline came into view. Maggie smiled.

"We're still in the equatorial zone," Maggie stated. "In fact I think that's Ecuador. There could be more of those beetles down there. Let's follow the coast. Think we can make it to Lima without refueling?"

I was embarrassed that Maggie's sense of geography was better than mine.

"Sure, but I like to keep the tanks as full as possible. If we had run out of fuel over the we would have been in serious trouble."

"If we hadn't stopped for fuel we wouldn't have gotten lost over the ocean. We should go as far as we can if that will get us past the bugs. I'm not tangling with overachieving cockroaches again."

"Do you really think they live this far south?"

"How would I know? They probably need that awful environment at the Isthmus, but then again maybe they don't. You know, there must be another element to the ecosystem we didn't see. The mushrooms need to grow on something. Maybe there are heat-resistant bacteria in the soil or something."

"Do you want to go back and research the question?"

"Pass for now. But someday, yes. The next time I'm wearing a beetle-proof suit though."

We reached the Peruvian border and continued south. Lima appeared oddly tidy. To be sure, there was some fire damage and many roofs were gone, but most walls were standing and the streets were clean. We saw no evidence of living people. They would have kept the place messier.

There also was no evidence either of the type of erosion caused by nightly fungal blooms like those in Panama. The chances were good we were outside the mushroom beetle ecosystem. The surface temperatures in this part of Peru were similar to Panama, but perhaps, I reasoned, some element in the environment might be different. A more frightening thought was that local mutations might be even worse. We accordingly were cautious. We passed the time until well after nightfall watching from overhead for anything peculiar. Maggie and I did this anyway. Charlene and Chester once again entertained each other.

The sightseeing was good. The Rio Rimac was a dry gully. We floated over the curiously named Avenida Roosevelt. I don't know for which Roosevelt it was named or why. Steel hulks of former automobiles lined the curbs. We swung around toward the

Plaza de Armas. The 400 year old bronze fountain still stood but it long since had run dry. We waited for more than an hour after dark for any sign of disturbance below. In the moonlight all remained peaceful.

"It's the fog," said Maggie.

"What fog? It's clear as can be."

"Precisely. The fog in Panama makes the mushrooms grow. There is no fog here so there should be no mushrooms and no bugs."

It sounded reasonable to me. Everything below looked peaceful so we decided to chance a landing in the Miraflores south of Centro. This was formerly the wealthy resort district where we hoped our pickings would be easy. For once we had made a good choice. Resupply went smoothly. Maggie stayed aboard this time. I quickly found a heating oil tank. While I topped the tanks, Charlene and Chester picked up some tourist knickknacks in a hotel gift shop and gave them to each other. Before midnight we were aloft again.

"We can be in Chile tomorrow. I'm sure there are some people living in the southern regions," I commented.

"Are we looking for people?" Maggie asked.

"I am. No reflection on present company intended."

"Hmph. I doubt that. The Chileans weren't at the UN were they? I mean since the climate change."

"No, but that doesn't mean anything. The US wasn't there either. There are still people within its old boundaries. They just aren't organized in a national way. The UN is a lost cause now anyway. Only the Russians and Scandinavians bother to show up anymore. Except for Quebec and Tibet, the world is still decaying rapidly."

I thought of those missile tracks again and hoped Quebec remained an exception to global decline. Had my nasty little note really destroyed a nation by triggering an attack on South Dakota? I dearly hoped Selena was not so bloody-minded as to target cities. Maybe the warheads were aimed only at military or demonstration targets.

Quebec was not really such a terrible place. I should have stayed. The cash from the sale of those journals would have put me back on my feet again.

I tried to get my mind off the calamity in back of us by considering what lay ahead. "I don't suppose any of you speak Spanish."

"I do a little," answered Maggie. "Joelle used to encourage language classes in case we ever expanded out of

Rushmore or had to flee for some reason. The Southern Hemisphere must have intrigued her. She even talked about teaching some kids Afrikaans but she couldn't find any textbooks."

"Interesting woman."

"Yes, she was. But I'm beginning now to think I idolized her just because I didn't like Selena."

"Honest appraisal. You're an interesting woman too."

"I don't want to have sex right now, Aeneas."

"Who said anything about that?"

"I know when I'm being buttered up and why a man spreads the butter. I don't think we should go to Chile. There is someplace closer. Let's go inland."

It took me a moment to adjust to the change of subject.

"Take *Nearer* into the Andes? Why? To put it mildly that is very dangerous, especially at night. Even in daylight we would have to pick our way through the peaks very carefully. That is if we even can maintain the altitude to do it. What are you looking for? Living space on the cooler upper slopes? We could have done that in the Rockies."

"Maybe we should have. But right now I'm playing a hunch. Trust me."

For no good reason I decided to trust her.

Even by starlight the landscape was breathtaking. We passed above gorges and flew by sheer cliffs. There were valleys, hills, and mountains of every shape possible. The upper slopes were rich in vegetation. The view and the occasional need to dodge a mountain kept me awake during the next several hours. My eyes complained at the lack of sleep.

A gentle glow over the mountains ahead presaged a new dawn. Just at the edge of my perception below was a frantic scurrying on the mountainside. I grabbed the binoculars in hopes of seeing people. There were no people. There were lizards. A cloudbank up ahead worried me enough to throttle back.

"Go on through it," Maggie ordered.

"We could fly into a mountain. I'd rather go
around it. South looks pretty clear."

"This is the way!" Maggie insisted as she studied her
Atlas.

"Maggie, we don't have good charts except for North America, and even those are hopelessly out of date. That Rand McNally you are looking at was never intended for this purpose. I wouldn't trust our navigation skills that much even if it were. We don't have GPS anymore. This is verging on suicide."

"Go straight through the cloud. Do it!" When this elicited no response she added, "Please."

Do most men have a hard time arguing with women about directions?

JUDGE JUDY: No.

HIRISAWA: Yes.

AENEAS CUSTER: I apologize to the court for failing to make that question sound rhetorical.

Anyhow, against all common sense we entered the cloud. For the next hour we were blind and flew only by compass. I expected to smash on something at any moment. At one point a darkness loomed on our right. It looked suspiciously like a rock outcrop. At another point I heard a scrape very much like that of a tree brushing the bottom of the gondola. Then the cloud abruptly ended and we emerged into morning sunlight. We floated high over a valley. In contrast to the desiccated region behind us, below us was a jungle oasis. Straight ahead was a steep acclivity. An overgrown but still discernible road switched back and forth across the face of it.

"Go for altitude! Head toward that cone-shaped peak." Maggie commanded.

Nearer once more made me proud as she ascended gracefully. For vision's sake, we circled so as to approach Maggie's proposed destination from the direction of the rising sun. To my amazement, next to the conical peak was a mountaintop city. Even from this distance one could see the masonry buildings were sizable. Stone retaining walls formed terraces on the surrounding slopes. Spring water flowed through an aqueduct. Smoke from fires arose from the city.

"Incredible. An active, living town this close to theequator. You knew it was here. Where are we?" I asked.

"Machu Picchu."

"*Gesundheit.*"

"Not funny. This is a very old and very special place."

Maggie gave me a brief run down. Machu Picchu was a major ceremonial Inca city that the Spanish invaders never found. It was abandoned for unclear reasons at about the time of the conquest. There is some dispute as to whether it was abandoned before or after. The city was not rediscovered until 1911. A Connecticut archeologist followed up on old legends and local gossip. Usually such sources are about as reliable as eyewitness accounts of Nessie. No doubt to his own surprise, on this occasion they had some substance. His climb up this isolated mountain was rewarded by one of the greatest archeological finds of the 20th century.

At that time the city was extraordinarily well preserved. Little was missing except for the thatched roofs. The site had many oddities, not least of which was the startling inconvenience of the location. Also, digs of the graves revealed a ten-to-one female to male ratio. This suggests priestesses in some sun or moon cult.

In an arena in the midst of the city stood a large rock called the Intihuatana stone. This means "hitching post of the sun." Similar stones at other Inca centers were used ritually to "hitch" the sun at the winter solstice to stop its slide north and to pull it back to the south. The stone and the area surrounding it are arranged so they can be used as a very accurate astronomical calculator.

It was clear upon our arrival that Machu Picchu was no longer an archeological curiosity. It breathed again.

"How did you know?" I asked Maggie.

"I just asked myself where I would go if I lived in Peru when everything fell apart."

Thatch roofs were back in place. The terraces below the city were actively cultivated agricultural plots irrigated by spring water. Peasants could be seen working with hand tools. We later learned the denizens relied primarily on root crops: yams, potatoes, onions, and such. The existence of a social hierarchy was visible even from the air. One section of the city had the grimy crowded look of worker housing. The opposite end was neat and included a large decorated structure.

"The castle," pointed out Maggie. "That's where we'll find the head honchos."

We definitely caught the attention of the citizenry as we approached from the direction of the sun. They stood at attention and stared.

"Hover over the hitching stone," Maggie ordered.

"There are a lot of flowers around the stone, aren't there?" I observed.

"So there are. What is the date?"

"I don't know. Early December sometime."

"So in the Southern Hemisphere we are near the summer solstice. Maybe they celebrate that too."

"Does it matter?"

"Yes."

"We may as well talk to them. You can ask all the questions you like."

"That's my plan. Let me do the talking."

"Easy. I don't speak Spanish."

"I hope they do."

I worked the tilt rotors and the maneuvering thrusters to hold our position over the Intihuatana stone. Chester threw lines over the side but none of the Machu Picchuans made any move to take them. "Take the controls and try to hold her steady," I told Maggie. "I'll slide down the rope and tie us down."

We had drawn a crowd and it was growing larger. Workers from the agricultural terraces ran into the city. None came closer to us than five meters or so. In fact, the front rank edged backwards as I moved toward them. Most of the locals were women. They wore simple brown clothing woven from some broad fiber.

Jewelry of colorful stones and crystals added the only individual fashion statements. The people looked much like pictures I had seen of Peruvian mountain dwellers: a mixture of local Native American and Spanish stock with the former predominant.

The hitching stone made a convenient anchor for the primary rope. I tied three other ropes and secured the ship more firmly. The rest of the crew then slid to the ground. The crowd parted as four men in capes of wildly colored plumage marched toward us. They must have been excruciatingly hot in their heavy garments, but they looked impressive. They were followed by six women carrying a single litter. Maggie greeted the men. I have no idea what she said, but Maggie stepped into the litter as though it were her proper due. She motioned Charlene, Chester, and I to follow on foot behind her.

The caped men led the way toward the castle. Maggie was carried behind them. The rest of the *Nearer* crew followed at the litter carriers' heels. The crowd watched our procession and avoided all physical contact with us.

The walls of the castle were freshly and brightly painted with rather scary looking squarish faces. A painting of the sun, which also had a face, graced over the main entrance. The walls themselves were beautifully crafted. They were made of huge mortarless granite blocks fitted expertly together. Each block must have weighed tons. According to Maggie, the Inca had neither iron tools nor the wheel. It is hard to imagine how they did it. More impressively still, they did it on top of a mountain.

Every door and window in the castle had a trapezoidal shape with a massive lintel forming the small base at the top. While not as effective at transferring weight as a true arch, it is nonetheless superior to the simple vertical pillar and horizontal lintel that characterized Egyptian and Greek architecture in the ancient Mediterranean world. Plainly this design has stood the test of time.

Maggie stepped off the litter at the entrance to the castle. We followed the caped men into a sizable room furnished with a set of four raised large chairs against the far wall. On the wall was a sun symbol about a meter in diameter that appeared to be molded gold. My eyes were not yet adjusted to the light, however. It might have been just painted wood. We passed through a dining hall with a table of intricately carved mahogany. It was large enough to seat ten or twelve.

A hallway led to a room comfortably outfitted with carpets and pillows stuffed with feathers. The window in the room was too narrow for escape. It barely admitted enough light by which to see. This apparently was to be our guestroom and our holding cell. Maggie examined the room, and nodded at the men. She looked sternly at us. "Stay put and keep your mouths shut," Maggie warned.

Maggie then exited with the men. A few minutes later a young local woman brought us a platter with sliced yams, potatoes, and a pitcher of water. The woman nodded and left.

Hours passed. The lack of toilet facilities engendered a growing unpleasantness. I used the narrow window opening and hoped no one was below. A grateful Chester copied me. Even in the scanty illumination provided by the shreds of moonlight that infiltrated the room, Charlene's resentful looks were withering. They inspired me to remove a feather arrangement from a pot in the corner and hand the vessel to her. I hoped the pot had no ceremonial significance.

My ingenuity must have made Charlene happy. After some relieved sighs on the pot, she made love to Chester. She squatted over him as he leaned back on a pillow. They were at it for what seemed an exceptionally long time. I began to resent Joelle.

Some time around midnight Maggie returned to us. She carried a lamp with a candle but it scarcely illuminated more than her hand. Maggie shushed us as we all began to ask questions at once. We all shut up. Maggie started to talk, but then stopped. She stood there pensively.

I broke the silence again. "Well, I'm glad you can talk to them."

She sighed and then responded, "Actually, that worked out well. They speak Quechua..."

"What?"

"Quechua. As an everyday language, that is. It's a Native American tongue. They remember Spanish as a language of power and government. The bigwigs use it among themselves so they thought it was appropriate that I use it."

She paused again and then continued to me rather than the others.

"Look, some things are going to happen in a couple of weeks that you won't like. But we're not in a position to stop them so there is no sense raising a fuss. Maybe next year I will be able to do more about it. Just don't try to interfere with anything."

"You're advising me to do nothing. Okay, that's easy."

"Not as easy as you may think."

"You underestimate my capacity for lassitude. What worries me is your 'next year'? Are we staying that long?"

"I am. This is my home — or as close a place to it as I am going to find. Besides, you might say I have an opportunity for a lucrative career path. I am a 'Messenger from the Sun,' you see."

"You are? Hmm. Fancy that. Are we?"

"No, you three are my servants."

"Ah. So how did you swing your celestial status?"

"Politics. I didn't give them much choice really. This is a theocracy, but the priests rely on a secular aristocracy that owns the houses and farmland. They also lend money."

"Business leaders and bankers."

"Something like that. They run the economy and pay the taxes. Only superstition prevents them from dispensing with the priestly rulers altogether."

"So keeping that superstition alive is important to the current rulers."

"Essential. That is why some of the priests didn't like being upstaged by us. They obviously were planning something nasty in order to express publicly their dominance over these visitors from the sky. I headed them off by announcing in front of them and the leading aristocracy that I was the Messenger from the Sun. A lot of servants heard me too."

"Why the would the priests buy that on your say-so?"

"Oh, most of them didn't. It is hard to find more dedicated atheists than in a theocracy, but that makes them open to negotiation. The minority who take their religion seriously, who believe that they themselves understand what the gods want, are far more dangerous. They will kill you in order to save your soul."

"That sounds a bit harsh. I'm sure there are kind priests."

"True, but they do harm by giving the other sort a good name."

"I'm glad you aren't cynical. You know Selena called you a cultist."

"That is why I understand."

"But if the majority of the priests didn't believe you, why did they allow you to act the part of Messenger From the Sun? What gave them no choice?"

"As I said, the secular aristocracy. True, the priests could have denounced me as a liar, but that surely would raise a question about the veracity of the priests themselves. That is just the sort of doubt they can't afford to encourage. It was easier for them to go along with me so long as I didn't seem to be undermining their rule. Also, a few of them were superstitious enough to wonder if maybe, just maybe, I was telling the truth."

"Why do I get the feeling they may live to regret backing you up?"

Because they will. The adult priesthood rotates authority in a somewhat disorderly fashion. Four of them sit on the Council, one for each season. The current season's representative has primacy; he is chief for three months. The four representatives are chosen by lot from the priestly order at the time of the summer solstice."

"That's in a couple of weeks."

"Right. I intend to bully them unto making a fifth chair that is permanent. The chair will be occupied by…"

"…the sun's personal messenger?"

"Yes."

"Is it a problem for them that you are a woman?"

"Yes and no. Yes, they don't like it. No, in a way it suits their mythology."

"Is that why there are so many women in this town?"

"Yes. This is a very religious city and women perform almost all the rites, except at the highest level. Somehow the male priests set things up so they are in overall charge." Maggie paused, shook her head and continued, "They use sacrifice, dangerous rituals, and, I suspect, simple male infanticide to maintain a ratio of about twelve Maidens to each priest. I'm not sure, but that ratio probably has to do with the lunar calendar. About a third of the women in the city are 'Maidens of the Sun.' They don't have children. They're virgins."

"Really?" asked Chester with interest.

"Don't even think about it!"

"I don't mind," chirped Charlene, true to her religion. "He can make love to whomever he pleases."

"I don't care if you mind or not. These people would mind and would kill the girl and Chester both. Maybe everyone who laid eyes on him too. There are women here who are not off limits, Chester. Two thirds of them are assigned the job to breed. You can play with them if you get the chance. They are not as socially honorable a caste, however."

"Will I get the chance?"

"No. In fact all of you have to be isolated for now. It's for your own good. We can't have you walking around fumbling and belching and smelling like ordinary people after the priests accepted my quasi-divine status. Even though you are only my servants, it just won't do. Sorry. It won't be for long."

"Uh-huh. Let me guess. A couple of weeks. So what exactly is happening on the solstice?"

"Well, our timing was propitious that way. They perform a sort of reverse hitching ceremony to stop the sun's scorching southward movement and send it away back north. They offer sacrifices of course."

"Of course. Let me make another guess. Does this have something to do with what I'm not going to like?"

"You are just full of insight today. Four male babies will be sacrificed to begin with, one for each solstice and equinox."

"Uh-huh. Is that a traditional Inca thing?"

"No, Inca society was destroyed hundreds of years ago. Even though there plainly was a intention to resurrect a large part of it by the settlers of this place, the founding fathers or mothers weren't university archaeologists — or if they were they still didn't just ape the old customs. These guys made a lot of stuff up themselves as they went along. The customs differ a lot from what the textbooks say about pre-Columbians."

"The phrase 'to begin with' when you mentioned those four babies did not escape my attention. Who or what gets sacrificed next?"

"You and Chester."

"I thought so. You're right. I don't like it."

"Me neither," said Chester.

"As a Messenger of the Sun, couldn't you tell them no?"

"I'm afraid not. I guess they didn't like the way I bullied them into accepting the Messenger line, so the Autumn priest bullied me back. He announced to everyone that I had been sent by the sun for the precise reason of enhancing the sacrifices. He let on that the sun had spoken to him about it already so my arrival was no surprise to him. In truth, I'm sure he just wanted to deprive me of my servants. I don't want to stretch my credibility by arguing too much with the priestly class about this sort of thing."

"Stretch it. I am not 'a sort of thing.'"

"No, but don't worry. I think I figured out a way to satisfy them and you too. We even can save those four kids. Remember them?"

"What have you got in mind?"

"The traditional way they perform sacrifices is by cutting the victim's heart out on the hitching stone."

"I never have been a slave to tradition."

"Good, because I think I can convince them to send the lot of you directly back to the sun in Nearer."

"With my heart in place?"

"Assuming you really have one, yes."

"Okay. I can live with that."

"This is very important. If I can do this for you, when we cut you loose, you must fly directly into the sun. I'm trusting you to obey me on this. I don't want to explain why you are going in some other direction."

"Okay, it's a deal.

"Cool."

"Why do they want to sacrifice Chester and me anyway? Why not Charlene? Whatever happened to sacrificing virgins?"

"She would hardly qualify," remarked Chester.

"Don't try to be witty, Chester. You'll sprain something,"

Maggie admonished.

"But really," I persisted. "What have they got against males? The guys in charge are men after all."

She smiled sourly. "Funny how they managed to work that, isn't it?"

"Well, I must say this is all very far removed from the dream of egalitarian free love that got you banished from Dakota."

"I didn't make the rules here, Aeneas. Maybe I can change them somewhat, though."

"If not, you'll still be Messenger of the Sun."

"Precisely."

"What about me?" asked Charlene who suddenly realized that Maggie's rescue plan made no mention of her.

"They want you for a breeder."

"Hey!"

"Of course I'd have to perform some ceremonial mumbo-jumbo in order to make you fully mortal. That would explain your human imperfections."

"Hey!"

"Don't worry. I'm hoping it doesn't come to that. Just play along with me. There is a chance I can get you sent along with Chester and Aeneas as a custodian or something."

"A chance?"

"I'll work on it."

"Okay, I'll trust you. Slightly more than I trust the jungle around this mountain anyway. I don't think I would survive long if I fled here on foot."

The room was a boring place for the next two weeks. Our hosts fed us well enough, but I don't ever want to see another yam. They provided only enough water for drinking, which made Charlene and Chester rather ripe. I didn't notice any aroma of my own but it is within the realm of possibility that that my roommates did. My beard filled in nicely. Chester grew a scraggily one. I noticed Charlene sprouted a wispy mustache too. Their wrestling matches grew tiresome to me, if not to themselves. We didn't see Maggie again until December 21 at noon.

On the day of the solstice we were brought hot water, soaps, a very dull razor, and perfumes. We got the idea and cleaned up.

Shortly thereafter Sun Maidens armed with lances escorted us outside. I do not know if the warrior women were traditional or if Maggie already had introduced them as a reform.

We were led along a path strewn with wildly colored plants and flowers. Revelers lined the walkway. On a newly constructed timber platform next to the hitching stone stood Maggie wearing a dress made entirely of feathers. It looked somehow familiar. I remembered a woman on a burlesque stage in New York who had had worn something similar. This probably wasn't Maggie's intended association, but it didn't make me like the dress any less. The Machu Picchuans seemed impressed by her too. Maggie spoke something incomprehensible to me and then outstretched her hands toward the sun. Nearer was at her back. Drums rumbled and flutes played a haunting tune.

Wooden steps led to the gondola of Nearer. Sun Maidens carried four wailing babies up the steps and placed them in the craft. They descended back down the stairs slowly. Our armed Maiden escorts prodded us with lance tips. Chester and I understood the point and climbed the steps. Once aboard the ship I immediately scrambled into the pilot's seat and grabbed the controls. I heard the ropes being hacked through. The airship lurched as the last rope was cut and I fired up the engine. The people below cheered and waved. The ship swung around with its usual slow but sure responsiveness. If one can love a machine, I loved Nearer. True to my promise, Nearer soared sunward.

I turned in my seat to smile at Chester and Charlene, but Charlene was not on board. I hope she likes kids. I felt rather guilty for leaving without her, but not so guilty as to turn back and argue the issue.

As soon as I felt it safe for Maggie, I turned Nearer east toward the Amazon basin. This was the easiest path out of the mountains. I planned to make for Argentina. Tierra Del Fuego probably was lovely.

"What are we supposed to do with these bawling brats?" asked Chester. His irritable phrasing poorly masked abject fear.

"I don't know. What do we have to feed them?"

"They loaded us with sweet potatoes. I think the white stuff in the clay pots is goat's milk.

"Better use that first before it goes bad."

"Use it how? I don't think they can drink out of clay jars."

"I don't know. Oh, there is an eyedropper in the med kit. Use that."

"An eyedropper? These are kids, not pet mice."

"It will be tedious, but at least you'll get some in their mouths. If you try just pouring the milk out of the jar you will probably drown them. Then mash some sweet potatoes and see if you can get them to eat."

"What about you, Aeneas? Are you going to help?"

"I'm driving," I shamelessly excused myself.

"Want to trade jobs?"

"No."

I was pleased when the Andes were behind us. As so often on this trip, my pleasure was premature. Buffeting winds kicked up over the Amazon watershed. The environment below looked quite arid, but the sheer size of the drainage area was enough to create real rivers. Despite climbing to the maximum altitude consistent with easy breathing, we were battered harder by the wind with every kilometer we advanced. Severe gusts raised dust that obscured the ground. We shook and rattled onward. Keeping the ship on course and in one piece through the afternoon, evening and night was an arduous task. Often the ship's fabric deformed and threatened to tear. High blown dust particles stung my eyes.

At daybreak the winds at last began to ease and I fell asleep at the wheel. Chester must have been successful with the babies. They were remarkably quiet. Then again, I may have been too soundly asleep to hear them scream. When I awoke we were over blue ocean. The light shimmered off the waves below. Chester must have fallen asleep too — or he trusted me to pilot us even when I was unconscious. If the latter is true I am flattered. I don't trust myself even when I'm awake.

"Where are we going now?" Chester asked when he noticed me stretching.

"That depends on where we are."

"Don't you know?"

"No. Well, sort of. This time we must be over the Atlantic. We can't be too far out even if we had a big tail wind. We'll go southwest, I guess. I hope we spot some land before our fuel runs out."

Arguably, this heading was foolish. It might have been more sensible to fly due west for the nearest land and sources of supply, but I didn't want to face those winds again. We flew through another night over water. We had a good tail wind, so as the gauge descended near empty I throttled back to a minimum and let the ship be carried southwest.

I saw no need to communicate my concern to Chester but I had already accepted the high probability that we would be helplessly adrift by mid-morning. Landfall was a necessity for us, but, with all due respect to the *Rolling Stones*, sometimes try as you might you don't get what you need.

I was reflecting on life and death just after sunrise when a hint of a form manifested on the southern horizon. It might have been a cloud or it might have been land. I gambled and throttled the engine. The form got larger and began to solidify. Ahead of us most definitely was land. It was an island or peninsula by the looks of it.

Chester, who continued to display an unjustified faith in my competence, was not excited. He had assumed I would bring us to safety somewhere. I, however, was suffused with the mellow joy of a survivor.

The land was an island, a big one. Our craft glided over dry ground. Rugged rocks outcropped from white quartz beaches. A hilly terrain followed. Subtropical flora flourished. We passed over grassland filled with moving sheep. A black and white dog herded them energetically. I was ecstatic. The island was occupied and civilized enough to support sheep farming!

After a time, the opposing shoreline came into view. A small village was situated by an inlet. The houses were well kept and whitewashed. A banner fluttered on a flagpole in front of one of them. It was the Union Jack, something of an anachronism, even before the heat. We were in the Falklands. A quick look at my map told me that the village must be Port Howard. Much as I was tempted to land immediately, I had grander plans.

I expended our last fuel reserves by accelerating across the channel between West and East Falkland Islands. We were going to the capital city of Stanley. Nearer cleared the channel rapidly.

We passed Mount Usborne and the hills beyond until the capital came into view.

Stanley is a picturesque port and fishing town with low-rise wood frame buildings. It does not look at all like a capital. We picked out the building that looked the most official as the most likely candidate for the primary government building. We lowered our craft down to the street in front of it. I jumped to the ground and Chester tossed me the ropes while he worked the directional motors. As I secured the craft to a fire hydrant, a stern looking man approached. He wore a white shirt, pith helmet, shorts, white socks, sneakers and a badge. A whistle hung on a silver chain on his neck.

"Good afternoon gentlemen. You really can't park that machine here."

"Where should we park it?"

Something about my accent gave him pause. He looked at us carefully. Our clean-up back in Machu Picchu had not lasted. We were ragged, unshaven and dirty.

"Not in town," he answered slowly. "Shouldn't you be at the army barracks at Goose Green?"

"Should we? Okay, I'll be happy to go there. We don't mean to be any trouble. We're a little low on fuel. If we could buy some we can go somewhere less obtrusive. Almost any petroleum product will do. Alcohol will work too."

The officer's suspicions were deepening. I supposed our arrest was imminent, but we hadn't done anything seriously wrong so this did not concern me greatly. How bad could a parking violation be? After that was cleared up I was willing to bet I would be a minor celebrity on the islands. There surely wasn't another airship there. I could open a charter passenger service between islands or even to the mainland.

"Aren't you from the west island?" the policeman asked. "I've heard rumors about a secret project there. If you have compromised it you may be in serious trouble. The paint job is in pretty bad taste, isn't it?"

This last observation struck me as an odd and somewhat snippy irrelevancy. I had grown fond of *Nearer.*

"The paint job? That was the work of previous owners, but I

wouldn't change it for the world. And no, we are not from West Falkland Island. I don't know anything about a secret project there or anywhere else."

"I see." Then came the expected and overdue statement, "I'm afraid it would be best to take you and your machine into custody until we straighten this all out. It will be returned to you if it is your rightful property, or if you are the rightful operators."

"It is and we are, and we certainly want to cooperate with you."

One of the babies chose this moment to fuss. The others joined him.

"Are those babies?"

"Yes. We picked them up in Machu Picchu."

"Machu Picchu! Is that where you are from?"

"Well, South Dakota actually. Quebec before that."

"South Dakota! You mean the paint job isn't a sick adolescent joke? This is the real one?"

"The real one?"

"The real paisley airship! Not a tarted up copy? Stay right there! We know who you are!"

He blew a piercing whistle that set the babies screaming louder.

"I'll inform the Royal Palace!"

I had been right about my celebrity status. I was wrong about the rest of it.

The police officer ran up the steps of the building in front of us. We had chosen correctly. An old plaque on the building said "Government House." Apparently it had been elevated to the status of a royal palace.

I already liked this place. It had an easy-going feel to it. Despite having placed us in custody, our arresting officer had just left us alone with an obvious means of escape. Clearly, he had little experience with true lawbreakers. This bespoke a civilized citizenry. Fortunately for the man's career, we were nearly out of fuel and I had no wish to leave anyway.

A number of townspeople began to gather on the sidewalk next to us. The officer emerged from the Palace and started shouting orders to the bystanders. He knew most of them personally.

"Freddie! You, Bob and Alice take those babies over to Mae's place. Jack, call the army base. Tell them to send some men to take away this thing." He waved at Nearer as though Jack might think he meant some other thing.

Chester handed off the babies over the railing to the three townspeople.

Several minutes later, two more men exited the Royal Palace. They were dressed much the same as the first officer except that their shirts were red. Their demeanor was much calmer than that of the policeman.

The one with lieutenant's bars spoke up.

"Gentlemen, I understand you are short on fuel. Can this device make it as far as Goose Green?"

"I don't know. Where is that?"

"At the isthmus. About 100 miles."

"Maybe. Maybe not. I would feel safer with a few liters of something. Almost any flammable liquid will do."

The other red shirt had white sergeant's stripes. He also suggested, "Ethyl alcohol, sir?"

"Perfect."

Within minutes we had twenty liters of alcohol. I don't know what proof it was, but it burned. The red shirts accompanied Chester and me in Nearer to Goose Green. Once there, I gave an army mechanic in green fatigues an introduction to the airship. The red shirts returned us to Stanley in a horse drawn carriage. It was after dark when we arrived back at the palace.

"Please come with me, gentlemen," said the lieutenant politely to Chester and me. We stepped out of the carriage and followed him. The sergeant remained with the horses.

My first impression of the palace was that it was pleasantly homey. The interior smelled of old wood. We climbed stairs to the second floor. The handrail rattled on its hardware. In an odd replay of our arrival at Machu Picchu we were led to a waiting room. In about ten minutes we were served tea by a woman in a white apron. She wore the stern expression of a woman confronting a neighborhood boy who had just thrown a ball through a plate glass window. My attempts to engage her in conversation fell flat. She instructed us to be patient.

"You will be sent for soon. You may wish to clean up, gentlemen."

She put an ironic emphasis on the "gentlemen" and nodded toward a side door. Then she left. Behind the side door I found a bathroom with hot and cold running water. The electric lights worked. This was true luxury. I tried to tidy up as much as possible, but our long adventure had taken a toll on me and my clothes. Even when scrubbed, shaved, and combed the image in the mirror was neither handsome nor dapper. Chester's subsequent efforts were less thorough than mine, but somehow he looked better. It was after dark before the guards returned.

"Her Royal Majesty will see you now."

"Her Royal Majesty?"

"Queen Anne."

The Queen held court in a simply decorated room sizable enough for a poorly attended town meeting. Queen Anne, wearing a tan business suit, sat behind an executive desk. She was in her forties and had red hair. Her smile indicated a sense of humor, but there was a hard edge to it too. She reminded me of my sixth grade English teacher. To her right, wearing shirtsleeves and seated at a folding table, were two middle-aged men. I guessed they were her advisers. I also guessed she ignored their advice more often than she accepted it. The elaborate rituals of Royal protocol obviously had not followed the monarchy from Britain to these islands. If anything, the atmosphere of Anne's Court was less deferential than Joelle's, or Selena's for that matter. I instantly liked Anne.

"Wait outside," the Queen ordered the red shirts. They nodded and left.

She briefly assessed Chester and then stared at me sternly before speaking.

"Aeneas Custer, I presume."

"Yes, ma'am... um... Your Majesty. I wasn't aware I was famous."

"Infamous. So sorry about your homeland."

"Which one? How bad is the damage?"

"Both homelands. The damage is horrific. In case you really don't know, your attack was quite successful. You vaporized

Montreal, Boston, New York, St. John, and Morrisbourg. The City of Quebec survived only because the warhead failed to detonate. The surviving Quebecois are very angry with you, as you might imagine.

"Mr. Custer, you are a war criminal convicted *in absentia* of treason, terrorist acts, and crimes against humanity. There is a very big price on your head. Quebec brought back capital punishment just for you and your cohorts. Is there any reason I shouldn't ship you back to Quebec tonight?"

"They would kill me."

"That is not a reason. Executing you may be appropriate."

"It is not appropriate because I did not launch those missiles. I had no authority in South Dakota whatsoever. In fact I was thrown out of the place. I have no cohorts. The fault lies with the Quebec government. They knew about the missiles and yet they attacked Selena."

"And where is she? There is a price on her head too. Did you drop her off someplace? Machu Picchu, perhaps?"

"Uh, no. That was Maggie."

"Maggie?"

"A subversive. Messenger from the Sun."

"Try to be coherent, Mr. Custer."

"Sorry. Maggie was just a passenger. We left Selena back at Beautiful Rushmore Cave. I gather the French didn't catch her. It doesn't surprise me to hear she escaped. She is a resourceful woman. But I don't know where she is now. Honestly. I had nothing to do with any of it."

"Mr. Custer, I suggest you come up with another line of defense. Clearly you had something to do with it. There was a nuclear threat to Quebec written in your own hand. Then the bombs actually fell. What should we think?"

"All right. Writing that note was rude of me. I admit it. It was a petulant thing to do. But I was just posturing. I never seriously intended to cause any harm. In fact, I meant to deter a war by what I wrote."

"Didn't work out, did it? You launched the missiles, Mr. Custer."

"No ma'am. I mean yes, I know they were launched. I saw

them in back of us. But I didn't launch them. I never killed anyone, Your Majesty, and I never helped Selena kill anyone. I am an innocent man and I throw myself on the mercy of the Court. I ask for asylum."

"Ah. Well, that puts us in a very awkward position, young man. I'm not convinced our public would approve. The trials have been broadcast over short wave for the past few weeks, you know."

"Trials?"

"Yes. Dakotan prisoners brought back to Quebec have been tried for participation in a criminal regime. The broadcasts are quite a hit. Go into any pub and the radio is likely to be tuned to them. None of the prisoners admits to being a member of a control room crew but all of them have opinions about you. Those journals you gave to the *Pierre Roulant* reporter have been read over the air too.

"The statements of the prisoners about you conflicted wildly. Some said you were a nobody and that Selena gave all the orders. Others thought you were Selena's lover and she at least consulted you about the war. They surmised she saved you by sending you away. This story has a romantic appeal, but for that very reason it is not convincing. Still others said that you ordered the launch and then saved yourself by fleeing the scene. Then there are the cultists. They describe you as a mythic avenger of the prophet Joelle. The cultists sound chillingly satisfied about the destruction both in Dakota and Quebec. A handful of Dakotan soldiers had an even more interesting interpretation. They said you were a Quebecois secret agent and that you called in the attack on Dakota. They say you mistakenly believed the missiles were sabotaged so the attack would be safe."

"I am not a secret agent."

"Quebec officials deny that you are too, but then they would. I suspect both you and they are telling the truth, however. There really are conspiracies in the world, but conspiracy theorists almost always miss the real ones. This idea sounds like a chimera to me.

"There is one element of agreement in all the testimony. You knew Selena very very personally, and you met with her the actual day the war happened. Either you or she ordered the launches. Those facts were enough to convict you *in absentia* in Quebec. They are pretty damning here too."

"Your Majesty, Selena despised me and threw me out of South Dakota. As for knowing her very personally, that was when we were younger. It is not a crime to have slept with a pretty girl in one's youth."

"Well, actually it is if she is underage and a close relation, but it is not a war crime."

"Nevertheless I'm relieved you believe me."

"Don't be too relieved. I believe you are not a Quebecois agent, Mr. Custer. I said nothing about the rest of it. However, I have an open mind. I am not about to risk the safety of my people for one refugee whether he is guilty or not.

"Quebec is a terrible disaster. Politically the country is falling apart. There are rumors the Canadians are going to finish the place off, but for now Quebec still can throw a few punches. I am not inclined to provoke what is left of her military. The *La Salle* alone could do us real damage were she to turn up off shore.

"Then there are those damned missiles of yours. Who controls them now? Quebecois? Dakotans? Canadians? Anybody? We have no way to know. We surely don't want to offend anybody who commands them. Protecting you would be very offensive in many quarters.

"One more thing troubles me, Custer, and it should trouble you if you have any conscience at all. Even if you are not guilty precisely as charged, you are far from innocent in a broader sense. You are deeply involved in this whole sorry affair. Simply setting you free does not strike me as right, even if you have been truthful in every word you have spoken to me tonight."

"I don't know what to say, Your Majesty."

"Too bad words didn't fail you with Boris Fontaine. So, the question remains. What are we to do with you? We have little time to make a decision. Your airship was not a very discreet means of arrival. By now news about your arrival is all over the islands. The story will get back to North America soon enough."

"I apologize for my indiscretion."

"I'm afraid that doesn't help. Perhaps we can buy ourselves a little more time, though. We can't stop rumors, but we don't need to confirm your identity publicly quite yet. Your airship is unmistakable, but your personal appearance is not especially striking. The public does not have a clear idea of what you look like. Aeneas Custer could have gotten off at an earlier stop; you could be someone else. So, for now, reveal your name to no one."

"Yes, ma'am. Who should I be?"

"Well now. Let us think about this. Your vowels are about as gratingly North American as can be imagined. There is no sense trying to hide that, so we might as well confuse matters instead. Why don't you be Chester?"

"I can be Chester."

"What about me?" asked Chester.

"No one cares about you. But let's give you something appropriate anyway. Ah, how about John Hancock?"

"You are joking."

"No, that is much too unlikely a name to seem fake."

"If you say so."

"I do." She smiled at the two of us. "Don't leave town."

We exited. A guard outside the door of the audience room pointed the way down the hall that led back to our room. He did not escort us. At the door to the room we were met by a lovely aroma. I opened the door with high hopes and was not disappointed. Inside on a small table was the most wonderful sight we had seen in the last 15,000 kilometers: a hot meal of mutton and potatoes and fish. It was beyond delicious.

After the feast I lingered in a long shower. No one bothered us for the rest of the night. A bookshelf contained the complete works of Dickens. I actually began *A Tale of Two Cities*, which I had escaped reading in school by buying summary notes. Once I peeked into the hall and found it was empty. Palace security was relaxed. Of course, escape was not a real option. There was nowhere to go. I went back to my book. I nodded off by page 40 and slept deeply on the couch.

The next day after morning tea, a red shirt arrived.

"Her Majesty will see you."

We returned to the Queen's reception room.

"Good morning Mr. Custer," she greeted me pleasantly. "We

believe we have solved our problem. You will be shot trying to escape."

"I'm not happy with that solution, ma'am."

"I think you will be. Chester!" the Queen called to Chester whose attention had drifted to the window.

"Yes, ma'am."

"You have two choices. You can be sent to Quebec where you will be executed, or you can live under your false identity on South Georgia Island where you never will reveal to anyone that you are from South Dakota or that you ever knew Mr. Custer."

"South Georgia sounds nice."

"Fine. We are done with you now."

It took Chester a few moments to realize he had been dismissed. He looked uncomfortably around him and then walked to the door. The guard outside pointed the way back to the waiting room.

"Now you. That fellow is someone you must never contact again. You do not know him."

"I never met the man."

"Good. Many people saw a dark-haired, bearded man and a blond man arrive in that airship, so I'm going to ask you to shave your beard and dye your hair."

"So I'm Chester permanently?"

"Correct."

"Do I surmise correctly that you plan to shoot an imaginary person and say it was me? I mean I. I mean Aeneas Custer."

"Inelegantly stated, but you have the idea. The real Chester, now Mr. Hancock, will be secreted to South Georgia. We need some of your clothing and some of your blood."

"Blood, Your Majesty?"

"We need to identify the late Mr. Aeneas Custer convincingly to Quebec."

"Thank you very much. I can't begin to express my gratitude. But..."

"Yes, Mr. Custer?"

"Well, foolish though it may be to question such a good thing, why are doing this for me?"

"Might it not be a simple display of generosity on my part?"

"Yes, I suppose it might be. But is it?"

"No, actually. We have a job for you."

This made me feel more comfortable as self-interest was a motive I understood better.

"I am at your service, ma'am."

"Yes, you are. As that police officer carelessly told you when you arrived, there is a project on the western island. It is of national, perhaps of global, significance.

"We have a very comfortable life in these islands, Mr. Custer. We have not been affected much by the world's crises. Climate change arguably has benefited us. Due to a policy of strict isolation at a crucial time, we were spared the worst of the world's plagues. Our population declined only modestly. Stanley alone numbers more than a thousand people.

"All of this good fortune burdens us with responsibility. We need to re-engage the world beyond our beaches if humanity ever is to recover. This is especially true now that you and your Dakotan friends have set everything back so enormously. It is our duty to spread civilization and the rule of law once again."

"A noble goal, Your Majesty."

"Please do not be so nauseatingly obsequious. We both know you couldn't care less about civilization, or about our plans to build an empire. However, you are going to help, and thus repair a small part of the damage you have done."

"How can I help?"

"Let me first state the problem. As sparse as the world population is, there are very few places we can colonize without a fight from the natives. This is definitely true of Argentina, which otherwise would be the geographically logical place to start. In Argentina no government extends beyond village level, but so far every village has resisted any offer of aid."

"The aid, I presume, involves military presence."

"Yes, Mr. Custer. While we could force the issue in at least a few places, I have no wish to wage an endless low level war against guerrillas."

"Understandable. It sounds as though you found someplace more congenial to plant the flag."

"Quite right. Several months ago we launched a secret expedition from Fox Bay East to the Southern Continent."

"Australia?"

"Antarctica. Already we have a secret base on Adelaide Island just off the Antarctic Peninsula. The old Rothera Point research station proved quite salvageable. As soon as the colony is more firmly established and properly defended we shall go public with the information."

"Why would you want to occupy that desolate place?"

"Except for our colonists it is deserted, but it is not desolate. In fact it is quite pleasant much of the year. Grasses have spread down there. Sheep and goats are doing well. Fisheries should do spectacularly well. Our colony will soon not only sustain itself but will build an export trade. It is through settlements such as this that a global economy and civilization slowly will re-emerge."

"This has something to do with my job."

"We mean to secure the continent further by establishing a second colony on Ross Island at the old American McMurdo Station. This is a much more inhospitable place I should warn you."

"I'm not going there, am I?"

"You are to join the first expedition. Your airship will be useful for transport and exploration. Your experience with the craft is valuable to us. I trust I can count on your loyalty."

"Because I always can be exposed as a war criminal."

"There is no need to state the obvious."

"My apologies. If I may ask, what are the conditions that far south in the Antarctic? Has the ice retreated?"

"The conditions are cold. The sea ice at the periphery has diminished substantially, but the interior ice pack seems stable. You can talk to our geologists about all that."

"The airship will need a hanger down there if the weather is still very harsh. I'm amazed it has survived what I put it through. We have been very lucky."

"You must make do with what you find. We will supply you with what materials and manpower your airship can carry. The rest is up to you. Our interview is over."

HIRISAWA: Mr. Custer, I must ask you. Did not your cover

identity strike you as exceedingly thin? Dozens of people knew precisely who you were. She sent you back to the helm of the most identifiable craft on earth.

AENEAS CUSTER: Yes, sir. It also struck me that the thinness was intentional. The Queen is not a stupid woman. I guessed she wanted to delay my interception by my enemies rather than prevent it. That my cover identity was maintained so successfully for so long no doubt was perturbing to her. Had my disguise held out for much longer, it is likely Anne's own red shirts would have arrested me as part of some diplomatic maneuver. But what could I do? There was no alternative but to go along with the Falkies.

HIRISAWA — I see. Are you nearing the end of your testimony?

AENEAS — Yes, sir.

After my makeover as a blond, I was sent back to Goose Green. The airship was still there. Nearer had been fitted with hinged plexiglass windows, but otherwise looked the same. There was no time to worry about my future. That very day two soldiers accompanied me on a flight to an outpost on the west island. The soldiers disembarked and three civilians got on board. After topping of the tanks, the four of us lifted off from West Falkland Island.

The civilians, a man and two women, were scientists. I learned their names (Bob, Laura, and Abigail) but adopted a gruff style towards them that discouraged personal questions. They talked among themselves and discussed nothing remotely political. I found them refreshing. I hoped nothing would go wrong with the engines because, despite my cover as an airship specialist, a mechanical genius I was not.

The flight over the Drake Passage started out pleasantly enough. Sea gulls took an unusual interest in us. One was almost tame. It repeatedly landed on the steering wheel, and it took cover behind some baggage when the trip turned harrowing. A front moved up from the South. What we hit was not a storm. It was just the Antarctic puffing in our direction. It was an unnerving omen of what lay ahead. We fought winds the rest of the way. For the first time in my life I experienced bone-chilling cold. Ice formed on the aluminum struts and on my eyebrows. My companions seemed unconcerned.

The Antarctic Peninsula, much of which is north of the Antarctic Circle, is a spectacularly beautiful place. The mountains, an extension of the Andes, are majestic in height. They are mostly white with gray granite outcrops. We floated over deep fjords that lacked only fishing villages to be carbon copies of those in Norway. Queen Anne planned to add those villages in the coming years. We floated over a huge form that looked like an abstract ice sculpture of a bear. I began looking for more natural ice sculptures and found them everywhere. The snow looked pure. The cold soon stopped bothering me so much. Already I loved this place.

A medley of colors bordered the beaches. There are no trees on this continent, but in the summer flowering plants cover flourish in the lower elevations. As Queen Anne had mentioned, grasses have a firmer hold than they did a century ago. On the beaches seals played and sunned themselves. Penguins bodysurfed ashore and then swam back out to catch another wave. Large dark shapes could be seen beneath the surface further out at sea. The occasional spout identified them as whales. Marine life was rich beyond imagination. The new colonies would not starve. Fish, krill, and kelp abounded in quantities beyond any possible demand.

We arrived over Adelaide Island. Rothera Station is located on a promontory on the southeast of the island. There is a runway of crushed rock and a sizable aircraft hanger. A trawler was tied up at the wharf. Several buildings containing laboratories and living quarters were arranged tidily near the foot of a hill. Grasses and flowers covered the lower elevations around Rothera. Sheep and goats grazed in the unfenced pasture. There were scattered patches of snow. The hills had substantial quantities of the stuff.

Two dozen people assembled by the runway building to watch *Nearer* as we drew closer. The winds were blustery, so even with all our thrusters working we needed their help to land. Not without difficulty, several Rotherans caught our ropes and helped guide us to a mooring mast that evidently had been erected just for us. The airship's nose locked onto the mast.

I opened a plexiglass window, swung over the side, and dropped several feet to the ground. There was a mound of snow on the ground next to where I fell. I removed a glove, reached out, and touch snow for the first time in my life.

"There is more where that came from," said a man wearing an unfastened parka and sunglasses. "My name is Professor Watersby and I am the Chief Administrator here."

"Pleasure."

"You are the optimist."

Abbie had unrolled a rope ladder and was descending to the surface. Bob and Laura prepared to follow.

"Let us go inside and plan your flight to the south," Watersby continued. "I need to tell you that I don't approve. It is a foolish dispersion of resources that we can ill afford. The Peninsula is more than enough to colonize and it is infinitely better suited to habitation. This is where we should be investing manpower and money. Besides, your blimp probably will not even make it to McMurdo."

"I don't make those decisions."

"Nor do I. However, consider yourself warned."

"So considered."

"Right. So, come along then. We shall determine how to send you on your way, while disrupting our station here as little as possible."

This greeting, including as it did a prognostication of our imminent demise, struck me as rude. My first snowball ever struck the Rothera Administrator on the back of the neck. He turned and stared in disbelief. Laura, the meteorologist member of the Nearer crew, unleashed supporting fire with a snowball that struck Watersby square on the forehead.

With enormous dignity the Administrator said, "Get them."

The islanders scrambled for the nearest snow patches. The four of us newcomers did the same. The barrage and counter-barrage lasted the better part of an hour. The exchange ended when someone of high intelligence and good will shouted "Tea!"

The battle had been good for all of us. We entered a large

structure. It was ramshackle on the outside, but quite homey on the inside. A few of the station personnel began clinking and clattering in the kitchen, while the rest of us settled down in the adjacent dining room. I hung my heavy jacket on back of the chair. The refreshments were not long in coming. We chattered, drank tea, ate muffins, drank wine, and then drank more tea. I let my guard down and joined in the conviviality.

It was all very enjoyable until Laura suddenly pointed her finger at me. My lapse in gruffness now had consequences. Laura took a verbal crowbar to my cover. "Are you who you say you are, Chester?" she asked with the knowing smile one so often sees on guests at cocktail parties who are intent on generating an effect by means of some indiscretion.

"Are any of us?"

"I shan't be offput by that nonsense either. You are from South Dakota."

"We all have to be from somewhere."

"South Dakota is not just somewhere. You piloted this ship all the way from South Dakota to the Falklands. Nor were you just some aerial chauffeur, were you? You were the right hand man of that Aeneas Custer fellow — sort of his Martin Bormann."

The tea party had turned extremely dangerous for me, even though Laura had an essential fact wrong.

"That is a disagreeable comparison if I ever heard one," I objected. "It's not fair either. I'm not a Nazi or even a common criminal."

"I never used the word common."

"Look… We all know the terrible things that happened up north. I wish I could change them, but I can't. I didn't make those things happen. I didn't hurt anyone. I'm not giving you an 'I was only following orders' excuse. I didn't follow any orders. I didn't give any either. I'm sorry for the people in Quebec. I'm sorry for the people in the Black Hills."

"Yes, I suppose you lost friends and family."

"Probably. I honestly don't know. I don't want to know either. I take it you had suspicions about me from the start. Why are you bringing this matter up now?"

"Because I'm tired of tip-toeing around the subject. Don't

worry, Chester, you got away with it."

"There was no 'it' with which to get away."

"Yes, there was, but I believe you were not a key player. Maybe the Bormann jab was harsh. No one will go to the trouble to arrest you. The authorities back in Stanley didn't. In fact, they hired you for this trip on account of your expertise.

"That makes him von Braun," interjected Abigail mischievously.

Laura smiled.

"You are not a big enough fish, Chester, for anyone to bother to chase. You don't need to look over your shoulder for Quebecois assassins or any such thing."

"I'm not so sure."

Laura swiftly aimed her index finger and mock shot me. She giggled when I jumped.

"Relax. Now if you were that horrible Aeneas it would be different. There was a man who deserved to die. You spent a lot of time with him. What was he like?"

"Over-rated. But, you know, he wasn't as evil-minded as everyone seems to think. I'm sure he didn't mean for things to turn out the way they did."

"True. He meant to destroy Quebec City too."

"I really don't think so."

"Then you are wrong. He fooled you. Pathological liars are good at that."

"Pathological? That doesn't sound right to me. I'll admit he did fool me more than once though."

Laura twirled my recently dyed blond curls with a finger. Everyone in the room was listening carefully. Laura had achieved her desired effect.

"See? No judgment of that man could be too harsh. Now you worry me, Chester, for defending him. Maybe we should radio Quebec about you after all. Maybe there is a price on your head. A small one."

"Is that what you want to do?"

Laura laughed. "Oh, no! Don't take my teasing to heart. If we are going to make it down here, Chester… do you have a last name by the way?"

"No. Joelle didn't believe in them for anyone except herself."

"My, you must tell us about Joelle one day too. Anyway, if we are to make it down here, we all have to hang together."

"'Or we shall hang separately.' Yes, I've read my Ben Franklin."

"Actually, only you are at any risk of hanging, my dear boy."

"How reassuring."

"But we might all freeze to death or something equally dreadful. My point is that none of us here want to hurt you. We need you. That is all I'm trying to say. This place can be a fresh start for you. You can count on us." Laura asked the room at large, "Can't he?"

No one wanted to sound churlish so all murmured assent.

"All of us will keep your big secret," Laura added with a wink. "Someday, when tempers cool enough for you to go public safely, you should write about all that sex in South Dakota and about your flight here with the fiend Aeneas Custer. Call it *They Hied with Their Boots On.* Subtitle it *And Nothing Else.* Errol Flynn would approve."

"An ancient movie buff! A woman after my own heart. About all that sex though … love really wasn't so free after Selena took charge."

"Love is never free at any time. Anyone who thinks so simply hasn't received the bill yet. Anyhow, my intention simply is to say you can count on us. Can we count on you?"

"Absolutely. I made a promise to the Queen."

"Really? Personally?"

"Yes. Besides, I had better do right by the Falklands. I have no place else safe to go."

Watersby raised a wineglass. "That sounds like a declaration of loyalty to me."

"Here, here!" chimed in the others.

"Here, here," I answered. No doubt the alcohol assisted the general mood of camaraderie. From that moment on Adelaide Island I felt secure among the Falkies. No secret is better than an open one. No one attaches to it enough significance to take any action on its account. I had no intention of ever publishing a book, of course. In fact, I was a little worried that the real Chester might do so one day, but the odds were that he would just settle into an obscure life on South Georgia.

In preparation for our flight to McMurdo, the geologists and climatologists at Rothera filled me in on the polar conditions. As the Queen had said, the continent's interior ice cap appeared stable. There had been a retreat of the ice shelves, but little additional melting. This is why the ocean rise in the past century has been modest. Sea ice displaces the same volume as liquid water. Only ice resting on land adds to the ocean when it melts.

There does not seem much risk of a sudden polar disaster despite fears voiced at the turn of the century that the West Antarctic ice sheet might one-day slide into the ocean. As best we can tell, it is firmly held in place by the shape of the crustal base which forms an enormous bowl. This shape is created by the weight of the ice itself. Our scientists say it will take hundreds if not thousands of years for higher global temperatures to affect the land ice substantially. However, the continental fringes, in particular the Peninsula, are far more livable than they once were.

All too soon it was time for *Nearer* to go. The flight to McMurdo was cold. Very cold. Three hours out from Rothera our fuel line froze. At Adelaide Island we had filled up on kerosene. Some water must have been mixed in with it. The wind blew us off our course. Below us were the desolate, white Transantarctic Mountains. My companions discussed what our prospects might be if we made landfall and marched back. The prospects, they agreed, were not good. On the other hand, we had no chance at all if we drifted much farther.

At the best of times I am a mediocre mechanic. At 15 degrees below zero C with thick gloves (without which I would have lost my hands) I didn't rise to the level of mediocrity. My companions were no better. The first settlers sent to McMurdo should have been electricians, plumbers, and practical mechanics instead of three theoretical scientists and a political refugee.

For once I had grounds to criticize the Le Pens; they had too much confidence in the reliability of their machine. It was not well configured for repairs, especially by novices. There was no obvious way to get at the line without causing additional damage that we couldn't repair with the tools and parts at hand.

After persistent and fruitless fumbling, at last I had an inspiration. I snipped a length of bare #12 ground wire from a spool in *Nearer's* inadequate repair kit. I removed a glove and my coat, rolled up my sleeve, and reached into the fuel tank. My hand and arm went numb in the cold kerosene but I managed to snake the wire into the fuel line. After poking and twisting the wire repeatedly in an attempt to clear the blockage, I withdrew my arm from the tank. My fingers no longer obeyed my commands but they gripped onto the wire by themselves. With high hopes, but little confidence, I cranked the turbine again. It roared to life.

Bob took the controls as I covered myself with blankets and stuck my hand between my thighs. Life returned to my hand slowly. It tingled painfully.

The engine gave us no further trouble on the trip but we were far from safe. The Antarctic is not a forgiving environment. We had failed to take the simple precaution of properly insulating the gondola. Our new plexiglass windows proved extremely leaky, and the leaks nearly killed us. Wind chill factors are to be taken seriously in those latitudes. We hung blankets over the windows, but these helped only a little. Wind whistled around the edges and through the fabric itself. We reached Ross Island before hypothermia had taken any of us, but had our flight lasted only a few hours longer a tragedy might well have happened.

We approached our destination.

"That's it?" Bob asked.

"It has to be."

"How depressing."

From the air, McMurdo Station had all the charm of some late 19th century coal town. Uninteresting industrial buildings sprawled at odd angles over gray dirt and gravel.

"Well, it's large enough," he added.

"They told me about 1,200 people used to live here in the summer. About 250 stayed the winter."

"It won't always be so bleak," chirped our botanist Abigail optimistically. "Our hybrid grasses should take hold here. They may even survive in some of the inland dry valleys."

"It is dark here a very long time each year," I objected.

"That isn't the problem. Moisture is the problem. Don't let

the ice fool you. This is a very dry place. I think there will be just enough water, though."

"If you say so."

We descended slowly. We passed over Hut Point Peninsula where Scott's hut still stands. The shelves carry his original supplies from nearly two centuries ago. Beyond the Peninsula were the blue waters of McMurdo Sound. The port is usually ice-free during the summer months.

"Where do we set down?" Bob asked.

"I don't know. Any chance of getting *Nearer* under cover?"

"Not unless we deflate the airbag. There are some helicopter hangers to the south, but they are not big enough for this thing."

"Okay, let's try landing in the open area with all the big containers below that hill."

"Observation Hill?"

"Whatever. Maybe we can secure the ship to one of the containers."

Bob went over the side and down a rope ladder while I tried to hold the ship steady. He tied us down. I wasn't happy with these arrangements but they would have to do. The rest of us disembarked.

Once we were on the ground the town didn't seem so bad. Only the absence of other people made it strange. All abandoned towns are unsettling, but the well-preserved ones are the spookiest. The sounds are wrong. A living community is dominated by clanks, rumbles, and background voices. McMurdo was filled with rustles, creaks, and whistles of wind.

We explored methodically. Most of the buildings needed little in the way of repair. In one building a bar named *Southern Exposure* was still well stocked with excellent ancient brands of wine, beer, and whiskey. A much larger building nearby sported the number 155. It contained a cafeteria with a working kitchen and recreational areas. We found a firehouse with equipment that, flat tires aside, looked almost new. In a multi-bay garage we found trucks and snow cats in excellent condition.

We decided to occupy an administrative building called the Chalet. There we laid out plans to bring life back to McMurdo. In addition, we each claimed homestead rights to one structure.

I claimed the building containing Southern Exposure. It was a business with a future.

Our work was cut out for us. The last occupants of the station had done a very responsible job of winterizing everything before they left, so remarkably little of the mechanical systems needed replacing. Naturally, they needed servicing. Every switch and valve needed to be tested. Every door, window and shingle needed to be checked. It was slow, tedious, but satisfying work. My proudest moment came after servicing a snow cat. Bob had bet me that we couldn't get it started. I took the bet but secretly agreed with him. Yet, after lubrication, refueling, and recharging, the machine roared healthily.

The big fuel tanks outside of town were full, but we didn't want to squander the contents. They would be hard to replace. Fortunately, a source of power was readily available. Strong winds, called katabatic winds for some reason probably known by the meteorologist on our team, blow constantly from the interior. Wind turbine generators, with their attendant batteries and control equipment, had been shipped to the station toward the end of its previous occupation. We found several stored in crates in a warehouse near the helicopter hanger. We assembled two and were rewarded with electric power. We soon learned why they had been left in storage. The winds often blow so hard that they tear the windmills apart. We used them anyway even though we had to fix them repeatedly. They helped conserve our fuel.

The environment on Ross Island, as the Queen had warned, was far less hospitable than along the Peninsula; but the resources were as abundant as on Adelaide Island. We mounted two expeditions using *Nearer* to scout out the surrounding territory. The airship then was deflated and housed, lest it be destroyed by winds. We would use electrolysis to manufacture hydrogen when the time came to use the airship again. We spent the remaining summer months preparing for the long winter ahead. Laura had some success planting her grasses. We hoped they would survive. Seals and penguins supplied us with meat, but our goal was to make the land suitable for goats and sheep.

A sail-powered wooden ship arrived in April bringing supplies and more settlers. Among these were practical artisans of the sort we desperately needed. Our first dog teams arrived at this time as well. *Southern Exposure* turned a profit for me that month and for every month thereafter.

When it came, the winter came hard. Snowfall was relatively modest, but the temperature plummeted. The winds blew so fiercely that dustings of snow built up on interior carpets. Weather-tight as we tried to make the doors and windows, the particles found their way through. Sometimes air movement could be felt at the surface of apparently solid walls. The sea froze over and locked us out of any outside relief. It was dark. In June there was no sun at all. If you could stand the cold, however, the frequent *aurora australis* displays were breathtaking.

During the dark months, we still needed to hunt, work, and maintain our machinery. It was easy to make a painful error. After re-bolting a damaged wind turbine on a fairly balmy — 20 degree Celsius night, Bob lost a finger to frostbite. He was lucky. On the same repair job I touched steel with an exposed bit of wrist. A patch of skin was torn off. It never did heal properly.

Despite all our difficulties, I was truly happy. Our adversary, the weather, was ruthless but not malicious. More satisfying still, we prevailed. Our colony hung on. In the Spring a ship arrived carrying more supplies and more settlers including fishermen, butchers and furriers. McMurdo rapidly became self-sustaining. Before the end of the summer we were exporting, and I ordered imports of wine and liquor.

Within a remarkably few years, hundreds came to live in our improbable place. They found their way here from the Falklands, from South America, from Australia, and from Africa. Antarctica never will be a crowded continent. However, our settlements contribute to the world economy. Trading vessels from as far away as Alaska and Greenland turn up in our port.

We were a small part of a worldwide recrudescence. Nothing could undo the tragedy of Quebec, but at least it was not fatal to the rest of civilization. On the Peninsula, Adelaide Island thrives. Up North, Canada, though still under-populated, is no longer threatened. In an ironic role reversal the Canadians made a protectorate of Quebec. They are not popular there, but they have prevented a further slide into lawlessness and barbarism. The

Russians slowly have evolved a less piratical way of life. Ships flying the white, blue, and red more often are traders than buccaneers. The Tibetans occupy parts of the jungles of the old Celestial Empire. Functioning governments have appeared in Tasmania and Capetown.

Much of this improvement was owed at least indirectly to the Falklands and her colonies. Her stable currency, stable government, free trade, global presence, and good example have helped enormously. Part of that presence was provided by the state airship *Ark Royal*, which duplicated *Nearer's* specs. She appeared only a year after the McMurdo resettlement and has shown the flag around the world ever since.

HIRISAWA: Are you arguing that the destruction of Quebec was for the best?

AENEAS CUSTER: No, your Honor. I merely wish to declare that I am not hostile to civilization in Quebec or anywhere else. On the contrary, I am enthusiastic about it.

My happy life in Antarctica ended with the arrival of a trading boat from Alaska. I spotted the flag as soon as the ship arrived. I looked forward to meeting the crew and passing gossip with fellow Americans. There was no doubt that they would show up at *Southern Exposure.*

Sure enough, that evening six sailors entered and took a table. All were dressed in parkas. One left as I approached the table. The others placed orders. Although I made an effort to chat with them, they were disappointingly laconic. The five men had some questions about McMurdo, about its export goods, and about the local prostitutes, but they had little to say about their travels or about Alaska. As soon as I gave them directions to the brothel they left. They tipped poorly. Just prior to closing, the sixth sailor reentered the bar. She pulled back the hood of her parka.

"Hello, Aeneas."

"Hello, Selena."

"Close up so we can talk business."

I agreed. This was yet another faulty life decision.

"You seem to have survived your death rather nicely," she

observed.

"I work out."

"Ah. Miss me?"

"Not as much as the French do. How did you get out of South Dakota?"

"By ultralight airplane. I had one hidden in an escape tunnel in case of emergency. It was a fast little thing. Even if the French had seen me fly away, they probably couldn't have caught me."

"You made it to Alaska in one of those?"

"Not quite. Saskatchewan. Then I worked my way under a false identity to BC. I didn't have any cash, but I brought bags of weed with me. I had enough left when I reached the coast to open a head shop in Vancouver."

"A what?"

"Head shop. You know, pot and bongs and such. If you really need to make a living, it is best to supply people's vices. As you should well know," she added with a wave at the liquor bottles on the shelf behind the bar.

"If you were making a living, why did you leave?"

"Things change. Some stupid provincial law was passed about pot. They made it illegal, if you can imagine that. All the publicity about it made me rather more high profile than I wanted. Reporters asked me my opinion about the new law after I closed up shop. What did they think my opinion was? Anyway a couple of them whom I had blown off started following me. I think somehow they guessed who I was and were working up a big exposé. It was time to go. I packed a few bags, gave my shadows the slip, and checked out the docks. There was an Alaskan boat down there. One of the sailors said they were going to McMurdo. I bought a ride. Here I am."

"Here you are."

"Nice bar."

"Thanks."

"Make a good profit?"

"Yes."

"I thought as much. That is why I took the liberty of writing up a bill of sale. You are going to sell me *Southern Exposure* for one pound."

"Of flesh?"

"Falkland currency."

"I think not."

"Then I'll expose you."

"You show them mine and I'll show them yours."

"Haven't you learned not to play chicken with me? The French tried that once."

She had a point.

"Assuming just for the moment that I were to cave in to your blackmail, where do you suggest I go with my one pound?"

"New Zealand. You'll like there."

"I hope the exchange rate is favorable. That's 3,000 kilometers away, you know. Should I swim?"

"I advise against it."

"Would you help me steal *Nearer*?" I asked more seriously.

"Don't be so dramatic. Take the boat I came in. Don't steal it either. It is stopping in New Zealand on the way back to Alaska. In fact, I'll give you my return ticket."

"Very generous. They actually wrote you a ticket? And you bought round trip?"

"It was cheaper. Don't ask me why."

Selena had cornered me. Murder was an option and I considered it, but somehow I didn't have the heart for it. I also could have gone to the authorities and hoped for the best. My expectation, though, was that the Queen would express dismay that she had been taken in by my clever disguise. She would express remorse that her guards evidently had shot the wrong man. She then would arrest me and ship me off to Quebec City, or, possibly, I would be shot trying to escape again, this time for real.

If I had chosen to accept personal disaster I could have dragged Selena down with me, but my instinct for self-preservation was stronger than my instinct for revenge. Selena had judged me correctly. I sold her the bar. She paid me the pound out of my own cash register. I packed my bags and headed for the dock.

HIRISAWA: Excuse me, Mr. Custer. You have sworn that you didn't know Selena's current whereabouts. Are you telling us now that she is tending bar in McMurdo?

PROUDFOOT: If I may interrupt, your Honor, I was told by the ABI that this information about Selena was given to them on the first day of Mr. Custer's arrest.

HIRISAWA: By Mr. Custer?

PROUDFOOT: Yes. The information wasn't made public because the agency didn't want to tip off Selena. Instead, the State Department informed the Canadians, and the Canadians immediately shipped out their own agents to arrest her. She was gone from Antarctica when they arrived. She had sold the bar for considerably more than one pound. The best guess is that she bought a ride on a fishing boat to New Zealand or Australia.

My understanding is that Canadian agents followed up in both places, but didn't get very far. Those are big countries and there isn't much central authority in either one of them. The few denizens interviewed were unhelpful. In fact they were profoundly disinterested in the whole affair.

HIRISAWA: So no one knows for sure that where she is?

PROSECUTOR: Yes, sir. For all we know she could be in South Africa or Tierra Del Fuego. On this one occasion the defendant was telling the truth.

HIRISAWA: I understand. Go on, Mr. Custer.

AENEAS CUSTER: Well, your Honors, you know the rest. As soon as the Alaskan boat was at sea the crew attacked me and tied me up. Selena must have told them who I was, and they were after the reward. They stuck me in a dark hold. The trip was terrible. It didn't help that the seas were rough. The only reason I didn't throw up the entire trip is that the crew didn't feed me. I suppose I'm lucky they gave me water.

The next time I was saw light was in Alaska. I was dragged out onto the deck and handed over to the police. The crew collected the money for me and I have been in jail ever since.

HIRISAWA: Why didn't you tell the crew about Selena?

AENEAS CUSTER: I did, but for some reason they didn't go back to get her too. I guess they figured I was a bird-in-hand. If they had gone back, McMurdoans might have gotten involved and claimed the rewards for both of us. Maybe they were worried I was under official Falkie protection and they themselves would be in danger if they went back. You'll have to ask them, your Honors.

HIRISAWA: Is that the whole of your defense?

AENEAS CUSTER: Yes, sir. That is what happened.

HIRISAWA: Mr. Prosecutor?

PROUDFOOT: Your Honors, I wish to submit into evidence photographs of the ruins of the Eastern cities. Also, several survivors are on hand to give a first hand testimony regarding the attacks.

HIRISAWA [consults with colleagues]: We don't believe that is necessary at this time.

PROUDFOOT: Your Honors, the prosecution wishes to detail the scale of the crime. The suffering caused by this man is immense.

HIRISAWA: We understand, Mr. Prosecutor. That will be taken into account in the event there is sentencing. Please present the rest of your case as to the defendant's guilt.

PROUDFOOT: I believe the defendant has presented it for us. Even if one accepts the whitewashed version of events we just have heard, he is an accessory to the crimes with which he is charged. Since accessories are as guilty as the perpetrators we will not quibble with his story. The prosecution rests.

REPORT BY AGENT 4:

The remainder of the transcript adds little to an understanding of subsequent events. Regional intelligence sources helped supply some of the following details.

It didn't take the Court long to come back with a verdict of guilty. Each judge made a brief statement. Judge Judy chided Aeneas as she would have chided a juvenile delinquent. Hirisawa made clever jokes. Maggio expressed disapproval of the prosecution's presentation and briefly reviewed the law regarding accessories.

The prosecution was given a chance to present some of its evidence for the sentencing part of the hearing. The panel, however, rushed and generally curtailed the victim testimonies. The defense made no further plea for mercy.

An element of Alaskan jurisprudence that alternately fascinates and appalls outsiders is its open recognition and embrace of retribution as the essence of punishment. Although prisons exist, they typically are passed over in favor of a punishment more satisfying to the convict's victims.

For example, a reckless driver who has caused death or injury is likely to be released in the middle of a nearby racetrack. There his victims, or the families of his victims, are free to attempt to run him over before he reaches the safety of the viewing stands. Those convicted of theft legally may be robbed for a period of time chosen by the court. Those guilty of domestic violence may be beaten. Murderers may be killed. Some of the more detestable convicted criminals are lucky to make it down the courthouse steps unscathed.

Alaskans by and large were happy with this brand of justice. Foreigners typically decry it as barbaric. Barbaric or not, it works. The crime rate is low.

Aeneas Custer was sentenced to be released on a tiny rocky islet outside the Sitka Sound. The Republic of Alaska then offered use of the islet to the warship *La Salle*, now with the Canadian Royal Navy, for gunnery practice. The CRN accepted the offer.

Aeneas was held in the largely empty jail while the *La Salle* made the arduous journey around the Horn. Aeneas didn't mind the wait. He read extensively and agreed to several interviews with reporters. Eventually the day came when he was escorted to the docks.

The hold of the wooden hulled boat was dark. At least this time he wasn't tied. The air was still. Aeneas felt neither cold nor hot. He once had read about sensory deprivation tanks. The smell of fish and the pain in his buttocks on the hard bench prevented a full parallel experience, but Aeneas did lose all sense of time. That was fine with him. He was in no hurry. He felt no relief when the hatch above opened and bright white light surged in. Two burly men entered the hold.

Four large hands grabbed both his arms and pushed him roughly out of the hatch. He babbled to them about sensory deprivation. His eyes had not yet adjusted to the light before he bodily was lifted over the side and dropped. Aeneas stumbled as he landed. His right foot splashed in a few inches of salt water. His left foot twisted painfully on a rock. He fell forward. Sharp edged rocks bit into his hands but he avoided hitting the ground with his face.

"You wanted to rule, Aeneas! You are sole ruler of this land! Enjoy the role while you can!" called out one of the large men on the boat.

The deck hand placed the end of a long pole at the water's edge and pushed. The boat slowly backed away from the shore.

Aeneas could see well again. The rocky outcrop on which he knelt was no more than 5 meters wide by 10 long. In the far distance he could see an irregularity in the horizon that might possibly be land. It just as easily could be a cloud. Swimming that distance surely was out of the question.

Aeneas climbed to the top of the highest rock and sat down. He watched the puttering boat depart. The sea breeze was mild and pleasant. Aeneas smiled.

On the deck of the *La Salle* a full admiral handed the binoculars to the female ensign standing next to him.

"That's it there."

She tweaked the focus. "I see it." It was a tiny islet with an oddly shaped rock near the southern end. "After this can we discuss my rank?" she asked.

"No, that would draw too much attention to you. Be satisfied you are an officer. Be satisfied with your very large bonus too. I still say you just should have come to us at the beginning."

"No, it all was too fresh then. Emotions ran too high. Your people would have locked me up, or worse. I made a better deal by staying free and waiting."

"You are sure you still remember the control room locations and all of the codes?"

"I'll never forget them," replied the officer formerly known as Selena.

"Do you want the honors?" asked the admiral.

"It's not an honor, but I suppose it really is my job." The ensign turned to the gun crew and without hesitation shouted, "Fire!"